1932

Karen M. Cox

Meryton Press

Oysterville, WA

1932

ISBN: 978-1-936009-05-3

Graphic design by Ellen Pickels

Acknowledgments

My first and foremost thanks are for the incredible Jane Austen. Her genius reaches across time, making her characters as real and fascinating today as they were two-hundred years ago and inspiring us to revisit them time and again.

I also wish to express my heartfelt gratitude to the readers at *A Happy Assembly* for their interest, comments and encouragement on an earlier version of this story. This book was written as a token of my affection for you all. Special thanks go to Karen Adams, Jane Vivash, M. K. Baxley and Matt Duffy for their input and advice. Thanks also go to my editor Mary Anne Hinz, to Ellen Pickels for her graphic design work, and to Michele Reed at Meryton Press for making this book a reality.

I also want to thank my husband and my children for their patience with my little writing obsession and for their unfailing love. In all areas of my life, they make every challenge worthwhile and every accomplishment sweeter.

Chapter One

A crack opens in the Earth

July 13, 1932

Lizzy, my dear, will you come into my library for a moment?"

Elizabeth Bennet looked up from her reading and rose from her velvet chaise lounge, laying the book aside. A knot of anxiety formed in the pit of her stomach. Her father rarely asked her into his inner sanctum, although she had been in there more often than any one of her four sisters or her mother. He had been sequestering himself almost nonstop over the last month or so. No one ever thought to ask him why; if he was working on a paper for publication or editing a journal article, it was his usual behavior. During those times, he only left the library for meals or teaching his literature classes at the university. But something about his demeanor when he appeared in the doorway worried her. He looked as though he had not slept well for days, and he looked subdued — dejected, even. His shoulders slumped as he turned and headed down the hall.

Elizabeth entered the study and closed the door quietly behind her. She was not sure why, but it seemed that a quiet, almost reverent approach seemed appropriate to her father's disposition.

"What is it, Papa? Is something the matter?" she asked tentatively.

Dr. Bennet stood at the window, looking out into the small garden below. The sounds of his wife giving shrill gardening instructions to the two youngest girls could be heard through the open window. The garden plants

— tomatoes, squash, cucumbers and beans — were growing in place of daisies and morning glories this year. But it was all too little too late to make even the smallest dent in the family's financial woes. He closed the window sash, shutting out the cacophony outside. Dr. Bennet took a deep breath to fortify himself, squared his shoulders and turned to face his brightest and most practical daughter.

He gave her a kind smile. "Have a seat, Lizzy; I need to discuss something with you."

Elizabeth came around the chair facing his desk and sat down, poised on the edge of her seat. "You sound worried. Please, tell me what is going on."

He sat heavily in his high-backed leather chair. "I have been let go from the university."

"Let go?" She blinked several times, an uncomprehending look on her face.

"Yes, let go... fired."

"What?!" Elizabeth's eyes were round with shock. "Why?"

"It seems the enrollment is down for next year, and with the financial situation the way it is, the university senate has decided to cut costs. One of those costs is 'extra' faculty."

"But, Papa, you've been there for nine years!"

"Well, it would seem that nine years is a relatively short term of employment for a professor. Everyone else has been there longer, and I was the last hired."

"How long have you known about this?"

"Since May."

Elizabeth put her elbow on the arm of the chair and her hand over her eyes. "Papa, why didn't you tell us sooner?"

"Ah, well... I suppose I was hoping to find another position before I said anything—give you good news with the bad."

Elizabeth sat in glum silence, not knowing what to say, or how to console her father. She knew this was a serious matter for all of them. Several of her classmates had been required to relocate because their fathers had lost their jobs. Many of the students had to leave college to work and help out their families. Sometimes, a student would just disappear from class one day, never to be heard from again.

College! Elizabeth had not even considered that yet. In May, she had finished her second year at the university where her father taught. Without the reduction in tuition for professors' children, and without his income, there would be no money to pay for college. Her dream of being a teacher was quickly being devoured by the need to focus on the necessities of life: food, shelter, and clothing for seven people. No wonder her father looked so hopeless.

"Surely, there has to be something you could do — something we could do," she began.

Dr. Bennet stared at the desk in front of him. "No, I've tried for two months to find work somewhere else, anywhere else, in my field, or even outside of it. There's nothing, not even a nibble."

"I'm so sorry, Papa."

"There's more," he grimaced. "I'm not sure if you were aware, but there is a mortgage on this house, which means there is a payment to be made every month."

The color drained from Elizabeth's face; even her lips turned white.

"Of course, without my income ..." he continued.

"The payment can't be made, and the bank will take the house," she finished in a whisper. She looked at her father's face. "Does Mama know?"

"Not yet."

"She loves this house."

Dr. Bennet nodded. "Yes, I know."

"Is there no savings? I thought you had other investments." Elizabeth desperately grasped at any sliver of information she could remember hearing about her father's finances.

"I did, but because I started saving so late in my career, I thought I needed to catch up. To make money quickly, I invested most of my savings in the stock market."

Acid churned in her stomach.

"And of course, you know what happened there. When I was finally able to sell the portfolio last year, it was one third of its original value. It is my own fault; I should have saved more, should have taken better care of you all."

"Where will we go?" she whispered, almost to herself. "What will become of us?"

"That is the other part of what I need to tell you. I received a letter from your Uncle Ed Gardiner in Kentucky." He reached into the top drawer and drew out a piece of paper, covered with slanted, firm handwriting. He handed it to her.

Elizabeth looked up and raised her eyebrows questioningly, asking for confirmation. Her father nodded. "Go ahead, Princess, read it."

He said nothing else, so she bent her head and began reading:

Longbourn Farm
Meryton, Kentucky
July 6, 1932

Dear Thomas,

I received your letter on Thursday last. I am most profoundly sorry about the loss of your university position. I well remember how happy you were to finally be settled and working with your books, as you always loved to do. I have several colleagues in academia struggling as you are right now. The times are very bad indeed. I'm not quite sure how we will extricate ourselves from this Depression mess; perhaps a new leader will have a different approach. Hoover's laissez-faire policy obviously did not work, and I fear his recent proposals are too little too late. Ironic, isn't it, as he was the poor man's friend a few short years ago, head of the American Relief Administration and such.

You should not blame yourself for the situation in which you have landed, Thomas. You are certainly not alone. No one could have foreseen the widespread panic and devastation our markets and banks have suffered since '29. I, myself, lost a considerable sum in the months following the stock market crash. Such is the price of our individual and societal avarice, I'm afraid, and a pity all our children must suffer because of it.

I regret that I cannot help you in the manner that you wrote to me. To be honest, I have no money to lend you. Cash flow is almost at a standstill in our little corner of the South. Do not worry for us though; we are getting by. My veterinary practice is not overflowing with cash money, but my services are still valuable to the farmers around the area and, therefore, worth bartering for. I have been paid in various types of materials, foods and supplies: eggs, cloth, cornmeal and such, and even a mama goat last month! (Madeline was not so pleased with that payment, especially when she found the little fiend gorging herself on the carrot patch in back of the barn!)

I do think I might have a solution for you, though, or at least a safety net for the time being. As you may remember, I ceased planting crops after our father died a few years back — too much for me to handle in addition to the vet office, and there was little help to be found at that time. Besides, as my agriculture colleagues and some of the older folk around here informed me, the soil was becoming increasingly depleted by planting the same crops year after year. Prices were also coming down, making it hard to break even in farming. Most people, having no other recourse, planted more, driving the price down even further.

But I digress. The land at Longbourn has had its rest now, and is probably ready for planting again, as long as we rotate the crops. I know you despise farming, Thomas, but it would be a way to support your family until a teaching position could be found. Additionally, there is the farmhouse where Fanny, Agnes and I grew up. It is in some disrepair, and has little in the way of modern conveniences, but it is structurally sound and would be big enough to house your brood of chicks. I jest with you — you know how I love your girls.

I will neither charge, nor accept, any rent on the fields or the house. I think it unfair that property is generally handed down only to sons, and my father was old-fashioned in that way. It was Fanny's childhood home after all, even though it was left in my care. She has as much right to live there as any of us. Therefore, I only ask for you to split the profit from the farm with me — half for each of us. I will help you with any start-up costs, seed tools, etc. — as I am able. You are a smart man, and if my memory serves, you have quite a wealth of knowledge regarding farming, having grown up on one yourself.

I think this arrangement would suit us both. The farm would be put to good use and cared for, and your family would be sheltered and fed. Having a large number of mouths to feed can be an advantage in that you have willing hands available as well. Who knows, perhaps my sister will even learn to practice some economy when she is back around her old stomping ground!

I joke, Thomas, but I truly would be happy to have you here. My love for my sister and for you and your children requires me to assist you in any way I can. Please consider it most carefully. I await your answer, brother.

Sincerely,
Edward Gardiner

Dr. Bennet got up and walked around his desk, sitting on the edge and reaching for his daughter's hand. "I have decided to accept your uncle's generous offer. We leave for Longbourn in two weeks."

"Two weeks! So soon?"

"We must vacate the house by the end of the month, Lizzy."

Tears streamed down her cheeks and her lip trembled, but she nodded.

He gripped her hands in his and looked pleadingly into her face. "Please, Princess, I will need your help, your level head, and your strength if we are to come out on the other side of this." His voice broke. "I know it is not fair to ask it of you..." Lizzy put her arms around her father and felt his shoulders shake with silent sobs. His grief and despair frightened her more than anything else he had said during their entire conversation. He released her with a quick embrace, and stood up straight and tall. Wiping the tears out of his eyes, he laughed mirthlessly. "I am not looking forward to my next conversation with your mother."

"It has been a while since Uncle Ed was around us for any length of time, hasn't it?"

"I suppose. What made you think of that?"

"Oh, just something he wrote." She tried to cover her fear with an impertinent grin. "He must not know us very well, if he thinks Kitty and Lydia will ever have 'willing hands' for farm work."

Dr. Bennet chuckled and expelled a big breath. "You may be right." He paused for several seconds, thinking. Finally, he gently patted her on the shoulder. "I know things look bleak right now, but try not to worry yourself, my child. I believe, all will be well."

Chapter 2

A Journey

August 2, 1932

The train whistle sounded and the passenger car lurched slowly forward, bringing a welcome breeze through the open windows.

"I hate those bank men! Vicious, conniving...vultures! Turning us out of our own home to starve in the streets!"

Jane gazed beseechingly at Elizabeth, who looked up from her novel.

"Hush, Mama! I'm sure there's at least one banker on this train who will hear you." Elizabeth spoke in a low, urgent voice, glancing at the stern-looking gentleman three rows back. He stared at the back of her mother's head with a scowl that should have burned a hole in her felt hat.

"And so what if they do?" Mrs. Bennet's shrill voice resounded through the passenger car. "I hope they do hear me!" She sat back and huffed, fanning herself with a tattered copy of *Harper's Bazaar*.

Elizabeth rolled her eyes and smiled at the scowling man apologetically. He started, looking alarmed when he realized she saw him, and hurriedly ducked back behind his *Courier-Journal. Well, how rude!* Elizabeth tossed the man a haughty glare, which he missed entirely, and turned back to her book.

"Lydia!" Kitty shrieked, making Elizabeth jump and several people around them turn and stare. Mary elbowed Kitty in the ribs, eliciting an "Ow!" that nevertheless had the desired effect. Kitty lowered her voice. "That is *my* hair ribbon."

Lydia snatched her hand away from Kitty, holding the ribbon just out of reach. "You should just give it to me, because you know you don't look well in it."

"Mama!" Kitty whined, ending with a hacking cough.

"Oh, for heaven's sake, Kitty, let her have it and be done. And stop that dreadful coughing!" Mrs. Bennet leaned her head against the back of the seat, rolling it side to side as if trying to shake a horrible headache.

"I don't cough for my own amusement." Kitty reached for the ribbon again, and Lydia held it to the open window.

"No!"

"Kitty, please!" Mrs. Bennet said through clenched teeth.

"But it's mine! You let her have everything that is mine!"

"Girls! Have some compassion on me…"

Elizabeth tuned out the strife in the seats across the aisle and busied herself with looking out the window at the passing scenery. The Knobs — big, round hills scattered around Bardstown — had given way to a gently rolling ground, the Pennyrile region of the state. A summer haze covered everything, making the forests appear a dull green. Fields of corn, and some other big leafy crop that her father said was tobacco, littered the landscape. The clackety-clack of the train wheels against the rails and the to-and-fro movement of the car lulled Elizabeth into slumber.

SHE JERKED AWAKE TO THE sound of the train whistle. The train was slowing, and peering ahead, Elizabeth could just barely make out the edges of a train station. Her father folded his paper, and turned to them all. "Well, girls, it looks as though we have finally arrived at Meryton."

"Thank goodness!" Mrs. Bennet exhaled loudly.

"Yes, Kitty…" he replied dryly, "I think once we are stopped, you may cough as much as you choose." The train slowed and gradually stopped. "Let's see if you can exit this train without making a spectacle of yourselves." He looked around. "There's a bench over by the ticket window. Wait there while I deal with our luggage. Mary, dear, can you assist me?"

"Of course, Papa." She looked at her younger sisters haughtily. "I would be *glad* to be helpful."

Lydia sighed in disgust. Kitty collected her belongings and scurried after Lydia and their mother, bumping her hip on one of the seat arm rests as she walked. "Ouch!" she squeaked, causing several people to turn and look at her. Elizabeth and Jane brought up the rear, putting some space between them and their scolding mother.

Once she stepped on the platform, Elizabeth wandered away from the bench where her mother and sisters were waiting.

"Lizzy!" her mother called. "Where are you off to, girl?"

"I'm just going to stretch my legs a little. Be right back."

Elizabeth ambled past the ticket window. Several dozen people were milling about, greeting loved ones or saying good-bye, clustered together in embraces. The air had a thick, sweet smell, and she was aware of the drawled out, Southern vowels in the conversations around her. She turned in amusement to the sound of a small voice yelling, "Baa-baa." A little girl, perhaps two years old, was toddling toward the train, waving at some unseen passenger. Corn-silk blond curls swirled around her shoulders. As she neared the edge of the platform, Elizabeth glanced around for the girl's parents, but saw no one coming to retrieve her. The little one had stepped perilously close to the train when Elizabeth sprang forward and caught her hand.

She squatted down to the girl's eye-level and smiled at her. "Whoa there, sweet pea. You can't go over there all by yourself."

The girl looked at her quizzically. "Choo-choo. Baa-baa!"

"Baa?" Elizabeth said, amused. "I don't see any sheep anywhere." She had noticed a chorus of "baa's" from the passengers and their families, as they stood and waved good-bye to each other.

"Where's your mama?"

"Mama!" the girl parroted.

Elizabeth stood, picking the girl up and looking around. She heard a woman's anxious voice calling, "Ruth! Ruth?"

A child's voice joined in. "Ruth!" Elizabeth saw a young woman hurry through the crowd and scan the platform frantically. She was dragging another girl along by the hand.

Elizabeth called to her. "Ma'am, is this who you're looking for?" The woman stopped, and a look of relief washed over her features. She put a hand to her heart and closed her eyes briefly. Taking a deep breath, she began moving toward them. Elizabeth set the little girl on her feet and watched her toddle back to her mother, calling, "Mama!" The woman scooped the girl up into her arms, and hugged her fiercely, wrapping a protective hand around her blonde head.

"Ruth Anne Darcy! You mustn't run from Mama like that, darling." She approached Elizabeth, moving the girl to her hip. "Thank you so much for catching her, Miss. She's quick as lightning. I looked away for a moment, and she was gone."

"I tried to tell you Mama, but you shushed me," a little voice piped up from below.

Elizabeth looked down; dark brown eyes with long sooty lashes were blinking up at her curiously. The girl's face was framed with a shock of glossy brown hair, red and gold highlights catching the sun's light. Elizabeth gave her a sympathetic smile. "You watch out for your sister, don't you?"

The girl sighed dramatically. "I try. But she just gets in troubles all the time anyway."

Elizabeth stifled a chuckle and put on a serious-looking face. "I know exactly what you mean," she returned gravely. "My little sisters are always getting into troubles too." She looked back at the girls' mother, who seemed embarrassed at her daughter's frank assessment of the situation. Her cheeks were pink in her gaunt face. She was about Elizabeth's height, but thinner, with dark blond hair and sad, grey eyes. She smiled shyly and changed the topic. "Are you meeting someone here, miss?"

"Oh," Elizabeth started. "No, I've just arrived. I've come here with my family to live."

"How nice. Do you have children too?"

Elizabeth looked at the woman in confusion and then hurriedly shook her head. "Ah. I'm not married. My family is my parents and sisters." She felt a tug on her skirt.

"What's your name?"

"Maggie! That's a little forward; you haven't been introduced." The woman admonished her older daughter, placing her free arm around the girl's shoulders.

"I want to *be* introduced, Mama, that's why I asked her."

Elizabeth did chuckle this time. "Makes sense to me." She bent down to look the girl in the face and held out her hand. "My name is Elizabeth Bennet."

The little hand shook hers. "I'm Maggie. My middle name is Elizabeth, just like yours. I'm Margaret Elizabeth Darcy, and I'm four years old."

"Good to meet you, Margaret Elizabeth Darcy." She stood up and smiled gently at the girls' mother. "Do you live here?"

"Yes, we live on a farm out in the country. The girls are so excited. We've come to meet..."

A loud squeal erupted from Maggie's lips as she pulled loose from her mother's hold and ran down the platform, yelling something incomprehensible. The young mother turned and a smile broke over her face. "There he is!" Ruth was wriggling in her mother's arms, trying to get down. After being set free, she followed along behind her sister. Elizabeth glanced up and saw a tall, dark-haired gentleman with a small suitcase in one hand. He stopped and smiled at the girls' squeals and held both arms wide, kneeling and gathering them into a hug.

The mother turned back to Elizabeth. "I guess I should go. It was good to meet you Miss Bennet, and thank you so much for catching Ruth."

"I hope to see you again soon," Elizabeth returned.

The woman cocked her head to one side and smiled cautiously at Elizabeth, as though she was deciding if that were indeed a true statement.

"Good-bye Mrs…" Elizabeth paused expectantly.

"Oh," the young woman said, "I'm Georgiana. Georgiana Darcy." She began walking backward toward her family and smiled broadly before she turned around, striding swiftly away.

Elizabeth watched the man reach for Georgiana and give her a quick embrace. As they chatted, Georgiana turned and indicated Elizabeth. The man stopped and frowned. Elizabeth recognized him then from the passenger car, three rows behind her family. It was the grim, dour banker who had scowled at her and then retreated behind his paper.

The family turned to go, and Georgiana held up a hand to Elizabeth in farewell, which Lizzy returned. *What a sweet little family. The children are precious, and the mother seems friendly, if not a little shy. But the father! Rude and unpleasant indeed.*

Elizabeth turned away, going back the way she had come. She sighed. From the looks of things, her father had found the luggage. It was piled all around the bench, and she could hear her sisters quibbling over who would have to carry it. Her mother was lamenting that they could not afford a porter to perform that service for them. Her father's face looked tight and strained, the way it always did when he spent any significant amount of time with his wife and two youngest daughters.

"Come, Lizzy," he called to her. "Uncle Ed's brought the wagon and his car to carry us to the house."

She stopped and hoisted up her suitcase with both hands. As she exited the train station, she saw the tall, grinning form of her Uncle Ed, his arm around her Aunt Madeline and both of them waving frantically.

"Here we are," he shouted, as the couple separated and began walking toward them. He held out his arms to Mrs. Bennet and drew her into a bear hug.

"Oh, Ed!" she wailed as she returned the embrace. "I don't know what we would've done without you to take care of us."

Ed looked embarrassed. "There, there, Fanny." He turned and extended his hand. "Good to see you, Thomas." The two shook hands, clapping each other on the shoulder in a gesture of brotherly affection. "How was the trip down?"

"Well, we're all here. Didn't lose anyone on the way."

Ed laughed. "Glad to hear it; glad to hear it. We've brought the horse and wagon and the car so we could fit everyone and their luggage for the trip home. Madeline can drive Fanny and some of the girls in the car, and we can take the rest in the wagon with the luggage. It'll be slow going, but that way, we won't have to leave anyone waiting here while we make two trips."

"Excellent," Mr. Bennet returned. "Jane, Lizzy, Mary, as the oldest three, I suppose you can take the back seat of the car.

A chorus of protests went up from the two youngest Bennets. "Papa, that's not fair!" Lydia complained. "They shouldn't get to ride only because they're older."

"We should at least draw straws," Kitty chimed in.

"I think we can probably fit four of the girls across the back seat," Ed mused. "They're so small."

"So who gets to ride in the wagon?" Lydia asked. "I volunteer Mary." She snorted and giggled behind her hand.

Mary looked scandalized at the thought of riding in the hot sun among the suitcases and the hay. Jane opened her mouth to volunteer, but Elizabeth put a restraining hand on her arm.

"Oh, for heaven's sake, I'll go in the wagon."

"Lizzy!" her mother replied, "You'll get all sunburned and brown."

"I have a hat, Mama. I'll be fine."

"Are you sure?" Jane asked anxiously. "I don't mind at all."

"Yes, Jane, I'm sure. I'd much rather ride in the wagon than play peacemaker all the way to the farm. You're so much better at that anyway."

Jane's lips twitched into an amused smile. "How did you manage to make riding in a wagon sound so appealing?"

Elizabeth laughed. "I'll see you at the house."

ELIZABETH LOOKED AROUND FROM HER perch atop her mother's large trunk. The sun was hot; she felt the heat through her hat, and sweat trickled down her back and between her breasts. The wagon was not fast enough to kick up a breeze, and afternoons in the South could be brutal for a Northern girl. She heard her uncle yell, "Whoa!" and the horse slowed down and finally stopped.

Muffled voices were heard, and then her uncle shouted again, "Thank ye kindly, Mr. Darcy," and the horses began walking again, jostling Elizabeth from her perch and nearly sending her to the wagon floor. She scrambled up, just in time to see the Darcys sitting in their open car at the intersection while they let the wagon pass by. A little dark head popped up from the back seat, pointing at her and shouting excitedly. "Mama! Look! It's Elizabeth!" Maggie waved, bouncing up and down on the seat. Georgiana also smiled and waved, but Mr. Darcy only watched her, a serious, forbidding look on his face.

Ed turned back and spoke over his shoulder. "You know the Darcys?"

"I met them at the station, while we were waiting for you. Is Mr. Darcy the banker here?"

"Banker? Oh no, he's no banker. Darcy owns the biggest farm around these parts. Lots of livestock. Big, nice house about two miles that way." He pointed.

"Oh." Elizabeth felt mildly embarrassed to be caught riding in a luggage wagon by people, who, from the looks of their car, rarely had to use such humble transportation. But she shrugged her shoulders and tried to put the thought out of her mind. Such was her reality now, and the sooner she accepted it, the better off she would be. That kind of pride in appearances was a luxury she could no longer afford.

Chapter 3

Home Sweet Home

The wagon pulled up in front of Mrs. Bennet's childhood home. Elizabeth hopped down and made her way around to look at her new residence. She stopped dead in her tracks, staring back and forth between the white clapboard house in front of her and the row of Bennet women — speechless and standing in a line, staring at the house. In another lifetime, it would have been comical. Elizabeth heard her mother sniff.

Aunt Madeline put an arm around her sister-in-law's shoulder. "It shouldn't take more than a few days to clean it up real nice, Fanny." She turned around and looked helplessly at her husband. "You can stay with us until then. We have one guest room, and the girls can make pallets on the floor in the parlor."

Mrs. Bennet seemed to come back to herself then. She pursed her lips and let out an "hmm" that was neither high-pitched nor loud. "Well, girls, let's get your things up to Ed's. Make sure you get a good night's sleep. First thing tomorrow, we start."

THE NEXT MORNING, ELIZABETH PICKED her way across the floorboards of the Bennets' new parlor. Several of them had loose nails; some had come off the floor joists altogether. The plaster on the walls was cracked and the paint was peeling.

"Lizzy, come look," Jane called from the other room. Elizabeth went through the doorway into the kitchen. The wide floorboards continued; metal cabinets lined the far wall. A long wooden table with one chair at the end and two long benches down the sides sat to her right.

"Here," Jane continued. "It's a hand water pump." In the place where the kitchen faucet should be, a large water pump was installed. Jane pushed the pump up and down a few times, and a stream of water flowed into the basin.

"At least we don't have to fetch water," Elizabeth reasoned.

Jane smiled. "Yes, thank goodness for small mercies."

In the far corner was a door that led to a mud room along the back of the house. A bench ran the length of one wall, and the opposite wall contained a row of a dozen or so wooden pegs.

Elizabeth wandered back to the parlor and circled the potbelly stove, ducking under the large pipe that disappeared into the ceiling to carry the smoke out of the house. She went through the door at one end into the master bedroom, if it could be called such a thing. It was half the size of Mr. and Mrs. Bennet's old room, and there was no closet. There was one window in the corner. Next, she traipsed through the door at the other end of the parlor. It led upstairs, where there were two bedrooms with sloped ceilings. One was slightly larger than the other, and each had a window. *And good thing too. It's sweltering up here.*

She headed downstairs, only to be nearly flattened in the stairwell by Lydia and Kitty on a mission to scout out the bigger bedroom. She encountered her mother and Jane standing in the kitchen in front of an open icebox.

"Mama?" Elizabeth ventured. "Where's the bathroom?"

Mrs. Bennet sighed. "Oh, Lizzy, dear, there's no bathroom in this house."

Elizabeth stared at her mother. "No bathroom?"

"No."

"Then how…"

"The outhouse, of course," Mrs. Bennet rolled her eyes and pointed out the back door.

"And where do we bathe? In the pond?"

"Don't be silly! We heat water on the stove and bathe in the mud room or here in the kitchen if it's too cold out there."

"What! In front of everyone?"

"There are hooks; we'll hang a curtain."

Mrs. Bennet looked from one shocked daughter to the other. "Don't worry, you'll get used to it." She turned around and headed back to the front door, sticking her head out and calling toward the truck. "Thomas, there are two beds already here, an old sofa and a chair, an icebox, and a kitchen table. You need to make sure the kitchen stove and the heating stove both work. Madeline says she has another bed and a cot that we can use for the girls."

A resigned "Yes, dear," was heard from the front yard.

Jane and Elizabeth looked at each other in shock. There was neither a whine nor a wail in their mother's tone. They had never heard her sound so reasonable before. She poked her head back in the kitchen doorway. "Don't just stand there, Lizzy! Get a piece of paper and a pencil so I can make a list of things to do and things we'll need. Jane, grab that bucket in the mudroom and draw some water from the sink, and start wiping down the kitchen appliances with the cleaning rags Aunt Maddie brought. Mary's going to see what tools are in the shed. I'm going to send Kitty and Lydia up to your uncle's to bring us some more cleaning supplies."

Then she was gone. Elizabeth shrugged at Jane and went to retrieve her paper and pencil. It seemed as if more things than just their location and the heat index had changed.

Chapter 4

New friends and ice cream

September 4, 1932

By the first of September, the Longbourn family home was inhabited once more. Nails, plaster and whitewash, soap and water, and wood varnish had made the house livable again. It was still warm enough to go without a fire in the black potbelly stove, but Mr. Bennet had already begun chopping and collecting firewood in a pile beside the storage shed for the coming winter.

The family had been introduced at the Harvey's Ridge Methodist Church, where Mrs. Bennet had attended as a young girl. Several of the families out in the county belonged to that church, including the Darcys, the Lucases, and the Longs. Mrs. Bennet's sister, Agnes Phillips, and her husband attended the First Baptist Church in town.

Elizabeth quickly found a kindred spirit in Charlotte Lucas, the oldest of the Lucas children. She was hardly a child; in fact, she was three years older than Jane, but she had a cheerful, practical disposition that made her seem more youthful. She was also the best source for gossip in the county. She knew everyone's stories and had no qualms about sharing them with the Bennet girls, taking it as her personal responsibility to inform them as much as possible about their new surroundings.

She and Elizabeth were sitting in church one hot September Sunday morning engaged in just such a conversation.

"Watch out for those Long boys; they're rough as cobs. Lewis, the second oldest, he spent some time in jail last year — carousing and gambling and drinking down in Franklin, Tennessee." She accented the first syllable, giving the state name a Southern lilt to it. "The girls are nice though, if a little dim."

"What about the Darcys?" Elizabeth asked cautiously, looking down at her hymnal and thumbing through it.

Charlotte looked at her with an amused smile. "Set your cap for William Darcy already, have ya?"

Elizabeth's head shot up. "What?" she asked too loudly, as she looked around and caught a warning glare from her mother.

"I have not 'set my cap' for him," she hissed. "Charlotte Lucas, I'm ashamed of you. He's married!"

It was Charlotte's turn to look shocked. "He's not married."

Lizzy frowned. "But Georgiana and the little girls…"

"Oh, I see what you mean," Charlotte nodded. "But Georgiana's not his wife; she's his sister."

Elizabeth's eyes and mouth all made perfectly round 'O's. "But where's her husband? And why are the girls' last names Darcy? Are they…you know?"

Charlotte shook her head. "No, you've got it all wrong. Georgiana Darcy *was* married, and she lived off somewhere far away for awhile, but then about a year and a half ago, she came back, with them two little girls in tow. She and Mr. Darcy told everyone her husband was gone, and she took back her maiden name."

"Whatever happened?"

"No one knows for sure. Some say the husband died. Some say he was a criminal and Mr. Darcy didn't want the girls to have a jailbird's name, so he legally changed their name to Darcy. Some say the husband just up and left her, and she had to come back home so she could feed the babies."

"That's terrible!"

Charlotte nodded her head solemnly. "And then," she leaned in, "some say that Mr. Darcy just didn't like the husband, so he made her get a divorce and take back her name, or he'd cut her off without a penny."

"Which story is the truth?"

"Don't guess any of us will ever know. Poor Georgiana had an awful time when she first came back. Some of the older ladies weren't too nice to her, but over time, people kind of forget, you know. Or, maybe not forget — but accept. Georgiana's very sweet and shy. Most people began to feel sorry for her unfortunate past, no matter what it was. They don't talk too much about it anymore. Lots of folks got problems of their own these days."

Elizabeth gave a noncommittal 'hmm' and turned back to her hymnal.

"So you can set your cap for him," Charlotte went on. "Every other woman within twenty miles has — even the older ones, like Caroline Bingley — not that it'll do any of 'em any good." The object of their conversation had just entered the back of the church, ushering his sister and nieces in front of him. His dark brown suit seemed to match his dark, serious disposition. He paused at the back to shake hands with Mr. Lucas, and the girls made their way down to the pew in the third row from the front. Maggie gave Elizabeth a shy little wave from the aisle, which Elizabeth returned with an indulgent grin. She then turned back to Charlotte.

"So, is he too good to stoop to the mortal institution of marriage?" she snickered.

"That's another mystery — why isn't Mr. Darcy married? He could certainly afford to marry."

"He's so stern; I can't imagine him courting anyone. I mean, just look at him." Darcy was walking down the aisle now, frowning to himself. He shot a haughty look at the two women watching him. Elizabeth gave a little gasp and looked away, but Charlotte kept him in her frank, discriminating gaze.

"Yes, but he's handsome too. A lot of girls would put up with a serious feller if he was tall and rich, and had those pretty eyes and that wavy hair."

"Maybe," Elizabeth answered in a bored voice.

There was a lull in the conversation as Elizabeth and Charlotte scooted down the pew to make room for Mary and Jane. After a minute or two, Charlotte leaned back over toward her new friend. "He sure looks at you a lot." Charlotte remarked casually.

"Who, Mr. Darcy? He does not!"

"Just look over there and see for yourself." Charlotte looked innocently through her Bible, finding the morning's verse that was posted at the front of the church.

Elizabeth couldn't stop her eyes darting in front of her and to the left. Indeed, Charlotte was right. The old stodgy puss was looking right at her, with those brown pools of opaque darkness. When their eyes met, he twisted his lips into a grimace that, on him, looked almost friendly. She returned it and looked back down at her hymnal. "He looks at me as if I had a smudge on my face, or smelled bad or something. He looks down on all of us—the Bennets, I mean."

Charlotte looked at her curiously and then back at Darcy. She shrugged her shoulders. "He's tall enough that he looks down on everyone," she joked. "Oh, are you coming to the ice cream social after church today?"

"Mm-hmm. Mama says they've been having those since she was a little girl. She insisted we go and maybe we'd meet some 'nice young church-going boys.'" Elizabeth rolled her eyes, and Charlotte giggled.

Mrs. Bennet shushed her second oldest daughter from farther down the pew, and Lizzy quieted in preparation for the service. She looked up and caught Mr. Darcy staring at her once more. He turned quickly when she saw him. Elizabeth self-consciously rubbed an imaginary ink smudge from her cheek and returned her attention to Reverend Adams.

"STRAWBERRY IS MY VERY FAVORITE ice cream, but Unca says there's no strawberry today because it's 'outta season.' Do you know what 'outta season' means?"

Elizabeth smiled down into the warm, dark eyes. "Why yes, I do."

"I do too," Maggie Darcy continued. "It means the strawberries all come in May and June, and now it's September, and there's none left in the strawberry patch." She swung her feet, rhythmically kicking the log upon which she was perched. "So now there's just plain vanilla. You can put syrup on it though, and nuts and cherries."

Elizabeth dipped her spoon into her bowl and took a bite of her ice cream.

Maggie looked intently at the young woman sitting beside her. "I didn't know if you knew that, 'cause you're new here."

"Oh, yes, I knew," Elizabeth responded. "Did I tell you there was an ice cream parlor in the town where I used to live?"

Maggie shook her head.

"And they sold ice cream every day, all year round." Elizabeth leaned down and whispered in her ear, "We could even get strawberry when it was out of season."

Maggie's eyes were round. "Ooh, I would like that. Why did you leave there?"

Elizabeth shrugged. "My family came here, so I came with them."

"To your farm?"

"Yes, to my farm."

"Did you live on a farm before — where you used ta' live?"

"No, I, we … well, my father was a professor … " She looked down at Maggie, who was blinking at her, uncomprehending. "Mmm … my father was a teacher, for grown people, but he couldn't do that work anymore, so we came here to live on the farm."

Maggie nodded solemnly. "It's the 'Pression."

"Pardon me?"

"The 'Pression. Mama says lots of people have to move to get a new job, 'cause of the 'Pression. I heard her and Unca talk about it at the supper table."

Elizabeth blinked and stared at the girl in wonder. *She's a precocious little thing.* The sound of a throat clearing behind her made her jump. Maggie turned and her face lit up like a sunrise. "Unca!"

"Hello, Maggie." Elizabeth's pulse gave a little jolt in response to the smooth, deep baritone voice of William Darcy. She realized she'd never heard him speak before. His voice was surprisingly…pleasant. *I wonder how long he's been standing behind us?*

Maggie hopped down and took his hand. "Unca, this is my new friend, Elizabeth Bennet."

"Really?" he asked, a twitch of his lips indicating amusement.

Maggie went on formally. "Miss Bennet, this is my Unca…" she shook her head, "I mean, my uncle, William Darcy."

"Pleased to meet you…Miss Bennet." He nodded to her.

"And you," Elizabeth gave him a cool, refined smile.

Maggie went on, trying to start a conversation. "Elizabeth saved Ruth from the train, on that other day."

He looked at Maggie seriously. "Yes, I remember that." His eyes drifted to Elizabeth's face. "I haven't thanked you properly, have I?"

"No thanks necessary." Elizabeth met his intense gaze straight on, and they looked at each other for a second too long. Suddenly, as if realizing he was staring, he glanced down at Maggie. "Could you take my bowl back over to the big table? If you're all finished too, that is."

"Yes, sir." She reached out and stacked her bowl inside his.

"Thank you, Maggie Moo." He smiled, which made him actually look handsome in Elizabeth's opinion.

The little girl rolled her eyes. "Uncaaa!" she drawled and giggled, skipping away toward the table.

"She is precious," Elizabeth ventured.

"I hope she wasn't disturbing you."

"Of course not — I love talking to her."

He looked down at his shoes. "She thinks she's a little adult." He paused.

"My fault, I suppose. There aren't many children around for her to play with, so I try to keep her company. She's more used to adults than little ones, except for Ruth, of course." He looked up.

"She seems very bright."

"Mmm. I think so, but then, I'm hardly objective."

There was a pause, and Elizabeth thought she might try to excuse herself somehow, when he spoke again.

"Where did your father teach?"

"Hmm?"

"Your father — at what university did he teach?"

Elizabeth looked at him, puzzled.

"I didn't mean to eavesdrop, but I heard you tell Maggie he was a professor."

"Oh, it was Northwestern University…English Literature Department."

He nodded. "I see. Did you attend university there — at Northwestern?"

"Yes."

"What did you study?"

"Some English, some history. I thought I might like to be a teacher." *Why am I telling him this?* "I couldn't go back this year, well, for obvious reasons."

"So you weren't able to finish your degree." It was a quiet statement he made, almost to himself.

Elizabeth felt herself being scrutinized and found wanting. She was pretty sure Mr. Darcy had been to college — and finished too. She took a deep breath and lifted her chin. "My life is here now with my family, so I am here as well. If you'll excuse me, Mr. Darcy?"

He nodded and gestured with his arm for her to leave if she wished. "Of course."

Elizabeth strode over and returned her bowl, not noticing when Charlotte sidled up to her.

"Mm-hmm," Charlotte pursed her lips, barely quelling a smile. "Told you. He's been looking at you."

Elizabeth sighed in exasperation. "We were talking about Maggie."

"And he promptly sent her off so he could get you on your own."

Elizabeth rolled her eyes. "You're imagining things."

"Good strategy, by the way, making nice with Maggie. He's crazy about those girls."

Elizabeth turned to Charlotte. "Look, I'm not trying any…strategy. I'm not interested in Mr. Darcy, and he's certainly not going to stoop to show any interest in me." Elizabeth walked away, leaving Charlotte smiling at her back.

MR. BENNET WIPED HIS MOUTH on his napkin and placed his spoon carefully beside his bowl of soup beans. He looked around the table and cleared his throat.

"Girls, I have an announcement."

All sets of female eyes turned toward the head of the table.

"I see I have your undivided attention." He smiled wryly. "Well, as you know, we arrived too late in the growing season to plant a garden, or corn or tobacco. Thanks to your uncle, we have a cow, a few pigs and chickens and," his mouth twitched, "a mama goat, much to your mother's delight."

Mrs. Bennet harrumphed. "That creature..." she began, but he held up a hand to stop her.

"At any rate," he continued, "we will be hard pressed to make it through this first winter. We will have very little stored up, and very little money, so I have taken the liberty of finding suitable work for you all. Hopefully, this will help defray the costs of food and other necessities until we can begin farming in earnest next spring, and be more self-sufficient."

Lydia scoffed but quickly subdued her derision at a fierce glare from her father.

"You, young lady, and Kitty will be selling eggs. There is a market of local farmers in Meryton on Saturdays. I think you will be able to find buyers there, and perhaps be able to sell them on more than just Saturdays eventually. Mary, I haven't found anything for you yet, so for now, you will be assisting your mother with the house and animals each day. Elizabeth, your uncle has agreed to your helping out in the vet office, cleaning, assisting, record keeping and such in exchange for cash, when he can pay you, and bartered items when he can't."

"Yes, Papa." Spending her days with her aunt and uncle seemed very pleasant to her at this point.

"And that leaves you, Jane."

"Yes, Papa?" Jane looked seriously at her father.

"I have secured a clerk's job for you at the dry goods store."

"Netherfield's?"

"The very one. I told Mr. Bingley that you had some college education and had an excellent grasp of figures and ciphering. I also told him you were a fair seamstress, and he said there were some people in need of mending and tailoring, including his own two maiden aunts. You'll start there next week."

Mrs. Bennet looked at her husband forlornly. "To think, Thomas, our girls, having to eke out a living like servants. It's almost criminal, what that university has done to this family."

"Yes, well, I'm sure there are girls everywhere who are eking out a living now who didn't have to before. We will have to make the best of things," he offered lightly, picking up a piece of cornbread and sopping up the remains of his soup with it.

"They don't know what we suffer," she returned vehemently.

"I'm sure they don't." He stood. "Well, I'm off to the parlor to read, and I don't want to be disturbed."

"Papa," Kitty asked pleadingly, "may we listen to *Amos and Andy* on the radio tonight?"

"I suppose I will allow that, if you can manage to clear the supper dishes without arguing with your sister."

Kitty shot Lydia a threatening look, and Lydia stuck out her tongue.

"Mrs. Bennet, perhaps we have few pleasures in life, but I can safely say that here we have two of the silliest girls in the all of these United States." He laid his napkin beside his bowl and disappeared into the other room.

Chapter 5

Jane the Angel

October 4, 1932

"Did I tell you I hired a new clerk for the store?"

"No."

Elizabeth's ears pricked up as she stood just inside the screen door of the unusually crowded butcher's shop. That must be Mr. Bingley's voice; he and another man were waiting just outside for their orders.

"Yes, she's quite the find," Bingley continued. "Learns quickly, according to Caroline, good at counting change, and pleasant to the customers."

"Mmphh…"

Elizabeth smiled at Mr. Bingley's praise of Jane and peeked out the door to see who he was talking to. She rolled her eyes. *Of course, the grumble emanates from Mr. Darcy. Who else?*

"She's awfully pretty too, and very sweet. She has some sisters. If they're all as angelic as this girl is, you should have a look, Darcy."

"I'm too old to be ogling skinny former flapper girls down on their luck."

Elizabeth heard Bingley's patronizing smile in his voice. "Now, now, you're never too old to look. You might find a woman to suit you yet."

Darcy snorted. "Unlikely." He leaned against the porch rail, hands crammed in his trouser pockets. "Take care, Bingley," he went on, "times are hard. There are plenty of desperate women out there who would do their royal best to snare a gullible man with a little money. You'd do well to keep that in mind."

Elizabeth's eyebrows raised into her hairline. She was incredulous. *That man is insufferable, conceited, and arrogant beyond all belief! To say those things about Jane, without even meeting her first!*

"Miss Bennet?" the butcher called. "Your order." He laid the package wrapped in heavy paper on the counter and winked at her flirtatiously. "I put an extra soup bone in there."

Elizabeth reached over grabbed it, and gave him a prim, "Thank you very much." She punched the screen door and went outside where both men jumped at the sight of her. Bingley gave her a nervous smile as she went past, which she returned, but she shot Darcy her fiercest glare. He started, but stared after her as she reached the end of the porch and descended the steps. She turned back to give him one last haughty look, and was surprised to see him still watching her. Bingley's cheeks were red, and he was whispering urgently to his friend. Elizabeth marched off down the street toward her uncle's vet office with an air of confidence that she certainly didn't feel.

"Lizzy?" Jane called. "Are you up there?"

"Yes."

She heard Jane running up the stairs. She opened the door and sat down on the bed, looking at Elizabeth with shining eyes.

"You'll never believe what's happened!"

Elizabeth laid her book down and sighed. "Probably not. Did the pigs get in the garden again? Or did Kitty and Lydia drop the eggs?"

"No, you goose. I've got a message." She waved a piece of paper in the air.

"From who?" Elizabeth was interested in spite of herself.

"Miss Caroline."

"Mr. Bingley's aunt? Good Lord, Jane, does she really make you call her 'Miss Caroline'? She can't be any more than thirty-five or forty years old."

"I can't very well call her Miss Bingley, can I? Then I'd always be confusing her with Miss Louisa." Jane shook her head, batting that topic away. "Anyway, the Bingleys are giving a dance at their home on November twenty-sixth. Apparently they do that every year around Thanksgiving, and Miss Louisa and Miss Caroline hired me to sew their new dresses for the party."

"A seamstress job; that's good."

"Yes! They want us to come out to Netherfield Hall and stay the week while we work on them."

"We?"

"Well, I said it might take me quite a while, and Miss Caroline suggested I bring one of my sisters to help. Please, will you come?"

"Oh, Jane, I don't know...I..."

"Please? It won't be a lot of hand sewing; they have a treadle sewing machine."

"What about my job at Uncle Ed's office?"

"I bet he can spare you for a few days at least. I don't want to go alone."

"Are you afraid of being alone with the dashing Mr. Bingley?" Elizabeth teased.

Jane blushed. "No. I just want some company and some help. Come on, say you'll do it."

Elizabeth considered. She would love to see the inside of the Bingleys' home; it had been described to her as a mansion for this part of the country.

"Well, all right."

Jane clapped her hands and bounced on the bed, dislodging Elizabeth and almost making her fall to the floor.

"Wonderful! I know you won't be sorry." She ran downstairs to give the news to her mother.

Chapter 6

Netherfield Hall

October 12, 1932

"Please, do come in." Caroline oozed insincere hospitality. "Nan? Could you please bring some refreshments for Dr. Gardiner and his nieces? Sir, may I offer you something?"

"Oh, no, no, thank you. I need to get back to my office. Just wanted to bring the girls out in the car. It's quite a walk."

Caroline gave him an artificial smile. "Yes, quite." She looked Elizabeth up and down. "Is this your young sister, Jane?"

Jane nodded and replied graciously. "Yes, this is Elizabeth. She is my next younger sister. Elizabeth, this is Miss Caroline Bingley."

Elizabeth nodded. "Good to meet you, Miss Bingley."

"Likewise, I'm sure."

Jane looked around. "Is Miss Louisa here?"

Caroline waved her hand. "Oh, she's around here somewhere, probably off puttering around in that rose garden of hers. I'm sure we'll see her at supper."

"And will Mr. Bingley be at supper as well?" Jane inquired softly.

Elizabeth noticed a slight narrowing of Caroline's eyes as she looked at Jane. "Perhaps. He is working at the store, so we may not see him until later."

"Oh, of course."

"Well, I assume you'll want to put your things away, and see the dress materials we bought in Nashville. The fabric is just marvelous, and we found the

32

most darling bias cut dress patterns."

"I suppose that's my cue," Edward grinned, "to ask where to put these bags."

"Oh, Henry will take care of that."

"Very well, then." He laid a fatherly hand on Jane's shoulder. "Just send word when you're ready to come back."

"Thank you, Uncle Ed."

"Don't work too hard!" He held up his hand in farewell as he made his way to the front door.

ELIZABETH RUBBED A BLISTER ON her forefinger. "I'm not used to cutting fabric anymore."

Jane held up a pattern piece, eyeing it carefully. "It's because you cut with your left hand. The scissors are made for right-handed people. You know, I think I'll need to fit this piece carefully. Miss Louisa has more bosom than this bodice style accommodates." She pursed her lips and tilted her head, imagining.

Both girls turned abruptly at the sound of a door opening.

"Mr. Bingley!"

"Aunt Caro said you were back here, so I thought I'd come say hello. So...erm...hello."

Jane's cheeks were pink, but her eyes shone. "Hello. Oh, you remember Elizabeth, don't you?"

"Yes, of course." He turned a charming smile on her. "How are you?"

"I'm doing well, thank you." She turned away, giving Jane and her handsome employer a modicum of privacy.

"How's the dressmaking going?" he asked politely.

"Very well, I think. Your aunts were very kind to think of me for this job."

"Yes, well, I just hope you save some time to make yourselves something nice to wear for that night."

Elizabeth froze. Jane turned slightly pale.

He noticed her change of expression and continued earnestly. "You are planning on coming to the party, aren't you?"

"Um...unless you've spoken to my father recently, we haven't received an invitation." Jane glanced nervously at Elizabeth.

Bingley looked shocked, then embarrassed, and finally, annoyed. "But of course, you are invited."

Elizabeth spoke up. "Please don't feel obligated to..."

"Nonsense!" Bingley was adamant. "You're new to the community, so of course you didn't know that everyone is invited. My aunts should have made that clear, but they must have been so focused on their apparel that they forgot their manners." He smiled, but his blue eyes held a pointed look. "I would be very disappointed if you didn't attend. If you're able, of course. I'll send your father a note tomorrow."

Jane smiled graciously. "We would love to come. Thank you for your kind invitation."

Bingley nodded and a silence settled over the room. Elizabeth returned to marking the pattern pieces, leaving Jane and Bingley to continue their tête-à-tête.

"It's been very busy at the store the past couple of days."

"Oh?"

"Yes, I've missed you."

Elizabeth smiled to herself.

Mr. Bingley blushed slightly. "I missed your being there — at the store. I've gotten used to how smoothly things run when you're working."

Jane flushed and looked down at the fabric in her hand.

"Anyway," Charles grinned. "The main reason I came to find you was to make sure you were coming downstairs for supper tonight."

Jane kept her head lowered. Elizabeth sighed. *Goodness, Jane! At least, look up at him.* She realized she was thinking like her mother, but Jane actually liked this man, and he seemed to like her too.

"I invited my friend, William Darcy, to dine with us. Of course, Caroline went all out and ordered an expensive roast from the butcher. She's downstairs fussing at the staff as we speak. Poor Nan!"

"Mr. Darcy is coming here? For dinner?" Elizabeth asked, surprised.

Bingley looked almost gleeful at her expression. He nodded. "Should make for an interesting evening, don't you think?" He turned toward Jane. "Darcy is a good friend and quite the conversationalist."

Elizabeth looked at him in shock, and he glanced back at her, biting his lip in a futile effort to keep his expression blank. "I mentioned that you were staying here and working on a project for Caroline. He seemed interested in talking with you and Jane, so I invited him over."

"Oh." Elizabeth tried not to let her disbelief show. Obviously, Mr. Bingley was just trying to entertain his aunts' overnight help.

"William, dear," Miss Bingley said unctuously, "would you like a glass of our whiskey?" She sent him a flirtatious smile.

"No, thank you, Caroline." He looked over at the Bennet sisters, resting on the brocade-covered sofa and engaged in soft conversation of their own. Elizabeth was holding up a book and pointing out a certain passage to Jane as she talked animatedly, eyes sparkling and hands gesturing.

"I'll just have some coffee, cream, no sugar," he answered, not taking his eyes off the young woman on the couch.

The housekeeper moved to serve him, but Caroline was too quick for her. "No!" she said a little too loudly, before she brought her voice back under control. "I'll pour for Mr. Darcy, Nan. You can just help clear up the dining room." Caroline took the tray from her and set it on the sideboard.

"May I use the telephone for a minute, Charles?" Darcy asked quietly. Charles nodded in consent. "Of course, Darcy. Help yourself."

"Who would you telephone so secretly, sir?" Caroline made her nosy comment almost sound like pleasant after-dinner conversation.

"It's no secret. I told my niece Maggie I would call and tell her good night. I typically read to her before she goes to bed, but I won't be home tonight until after she falls asleep."

"Dear, precious, little Margaret. How old is she now?"

"She is four years old."

"How devoted you are! How gracefully you bear the burden of father to your little nieces."

"It's no burden," he replied curtly.

"I still say your generosity to them is laudable. I know they will have many opportunities they would not have had otherwise, because of you."

"I would hope so."

"They will have the best home, the best medical care, the best education. Will you send the little dears to the private boarding school Georgiana attended?"

"That has not been decided. Maggie is only four, after all. Her mother is uncomfortable with the idea of parting from her so that she can attend boarding school. Although I would, of course, miss her very much, I think a private education would be good for her. Children need structure in order to learn effectively."

"There are some well-respected educators who would not agree." Elizabeth piped up. She and Jane had finished their conversation, and Elizabeth was casually perusing her book.

"What?" Darcy's eyes snapped to her spot on the couch. Jane looked at Elizabeth, round-eyed. Caroline smirked. Charles looked nervously from one to the other.

"Have you read Dr. Montessori's work?"

"Who?"

"Maria Montessori. She is an Italian doctor who has developed some different methods of teaching children. She believes that children will seek out learning on their own, if they are allowed the freedom to experiment and learn hands-on."

"Rubbish," Darcy snorted. "Children have too much information to learn to let them play at it. A lackadaisical attitude toward education is the reason there are so few truly accomplished women these days. That is why we are currently saddled with a generation of females more interested in short skirts and speakeasies than in art and the classics. Or the Charleston, rather than in the development of virtues that would benefit society."

"My goodness, you certainly have strong opinions on the matter."

"I do, indeed. I have very specific ideas on the education I want for my nieces if they are to grow into thoughtful, interesting women."

"Oh, I agree with you completely, William," Caroline joined in, relishing her newfound alliance with her nephew's handsome friend. "Girls, especially, require a very strict course of instruction. A girl should learn to sing and play an instrument, to draw and paint, to dance, and to learn French, and above all, she must learn to conduct herself — by her speech and actions — as a proper young lady.

"I would add that she must develop her mind as well, by reading extensively." He glanced over at Elizabeth, who had shut her book with a snap.

Her eyes flared with the thrill of debate when she responded. "I now know why you've met so few accomplished women. Given your unrealistic expectations, I wonder whether you've ever met any."

"You are so critical of women in general?"

"I've never met this paragon of virtue you describe. It's a little much to ask of an ordinary human being, don't you think?"

"Miss Bennet," Caroline said haughtily. "Perhaps you have not had the social opportunities William and I have. I can assure you, dear, that *truly* accomplished women do exist."

Darcy frowned at Caroline but said nothing, and Elizabeth decided she had offended him enough for one evening. Miss Louisa began talking about her rose bushes, and all other topics of conversation came swiftly to an end.

DARCY PACED ACROSS THE FLOOR of the Bingley home, half-ready to kick himself. Or maybe he should run off before anyone but Nan knew he was there. He was taking a chance on encountering only Caroline. He knew that, but Charles had said the Misses Bennet were leaving tomorrow afternoon, and this might be his last chance to see and talk to Elizabeth without her uncle standing over her shoulder or that brood of sisters clustering around her. And if they weren't around, then Charlotte Lucas was with her, giving him that smug look that suggested she could see right through him. Damned nosy woman! At least Elizabeth seemed oblivious. Of course, why wouldn't she be? She didn't know him like busybody Charlotte who had lived in this little town all her life.

He blew out a sigh. What were his motives? He was behaving like a school-boy. Oh, he admitted he had been mildly intrigued when he saw her on the train that day. After all, she was just another pretty face to admire. Then she appeared at the station, watching the four Darcys with curiosity, but without passing judgment. Gigi certainly seemed to like her at any rate. Next, he saw her sitting there in the wagon as they waited at the crossroads, looking straight at him, bold as brass, like a queen amongst the suitcases and hay. Then, each Sunday at church — well, he had not been to church that many Sundays in a row since he was a boy.

Even after all that, he might have been able to keep her off his mind, if it had not been for Maggie. Every day, it seemed, his niece had something else to say about her. "Elizabeth is so pretty. Elizabeth is so nice. Elizabeth liked my dress. Elizabeth has the same name as me. Elizabeth, Elizabeth, Elizabeth ... "

What was it about Elizabeth? Beauty? Jane was actually more beautiful. Charles was right about that. Elizabeth was not beautiful in that limited, superficial way; she was more. Her eyes sparkled with wit and intelligence. Her smile was bright and open; he loved to see it, although she rarely turned one on him. She was good to people; even though Maggie was only four, she was a good judge of kindness and sincerity. After all, the little rascal avoided Caroline Bingley like the plague.

Elizabeth was also brave in very trying circumstances, demonstrating an admirable strength of character. He had asked around; he knew that Bennet was going to have a hard time making ends meet, at least this first year. And the man had seven mouths to feed. Her situation was even more tragic, because Elizabeth was smart enough to know what she had lost — what she could have been if her family had been able to stay in Chicago.

So why was he here, hoping to see her? Why would a bright, lively twenty-year-old girl want any attention from a thirty-year-old man—a man who felt old, older than thirty, older than fifty on some days? His days ran one into the other, broken only by smiles from his precious little nieces — and now by the wit and charm of a college girl down on her luck—a girl with fine eyes, soft brown hair, and creamy porcelain-like skin that glowed above the neckline of her dress. He berated himself for thinking of her in that lurid way when he knew he could not — and would not — ever act on those feelings.

Suddenly, he made up his mind. He was leaving before he made a complete ass of himself. He turned and grabbed his hat as he hurried out the front door, slamming it behind him. A bewildered Caroline hurried downstairs, primping as she came. "But...Where is he? Nan?"

"I dunno, Miss Caroline. Mr. Darcy was just here. I declare, what made him run off like that?"

DARCY WALKED BY THE HEDGE that separated the driveway from the flower garden, heading for his car, when he heard female voices. He froze. The last person he wanted to encounter now was Caroline Bingley without the protection of Charles. Louisa was less problematic; she actually seemed to realize she was too old for him. Caroline, though, was only a few years older than he. He might have even considered her had she not been such a cold, detached shrew.

As the voices continued, he realized that they did not belong to the Bingley sisters but to the Bennet sisters. Now he froze for a completely different reason. He strained to hear their conversation, chastising himself for eavesdropping on Elizabeth again.

"I sent a message to Uncle Ed this morning." It was Jane's soft, melodious voice. "He should be here around one o'clock tomorrow."

He heard a sigh from Elizabeth. He glanced around guiltily and closed his eyes. He was going to indulge himself in the sound of her voice, just this one last time. "I never thought I'd say this, but I'll be glad to get back to Longbourn."

"Oh, Lizzy, it hasn't been so bad, has it?"

"No, I suppose not. Your Mr. Bingley is very kind and attentive."

"He is not my Mr. Bingley."

"But, his aunts seem to want little company at all, except for Mr. Darcy. I keep waiting for 'Miss' Caroline to bark at me to serve her tea until I see poor sweet Nan appear. Boy, wouldn't you hate to have that job?"

Jane giggled.

Elizabeth lowered her voice. "I tell you one thing I will miss, though." Darcy leaned closer to the hedge, his hope rising.

"What?" Jane almost whispered.

"The bathtub." He could hear the smile in her voice, and unexpectedly, he smiled too. "I know the housekeeper must think I'm crazy. I've been in that tub every night: warm water, lavender soap, soaking as long as I want."

Darcy found himself visualizing the scene, sensations all but forgotten were running through his body.

Her throaty whisper drifted over him. "It's heavenly."

He audibly swallowed. *Yes, I bet it is.*

"That crunched-up little metal tub in the kitchen at home just won't be the same."

Darcy's eyes opened. *Of course, old farmhouse, not lived in for years. No indoor plumbing. No bath.* His hand reached up and touched the hedge. The wistfulness in her voice tugged some place deep inside him. He remained still, letting the rest of the conversation wash over him. Jane and Elizabeth's voices slowly moved away and he turned to head for his car, feeling all the heaviness of the world in his bones.

Chapter 7

Mr. Serious

November 14, 1932

Elizabeth was taking an inventory of medicinal supplies in the vet office when she heard a loud crash and men's voices yelling from the big treatment room in the back of the building. She hurried to see what had happened but was halted at the door by the scene in front of her.

A large, wild-eyed, brown horse was rearing, neighing and snorting as he stomped around frantically.

Dr. Gardiner tossed the other man a blindfold for the horse and turned back to the panicked animal. "Hold him still, Darcy!" Ed shouted over the din. "I can't even see the wound."

"I'm trying. He's—" Darcy broke off. Elizabeth turned to look at him. He was more disheveled than she had ever seen him, dressed in khaki trousers and a shirt, open at the collar. Mud stains adorned the trousers and he had rolled up the shirtsleeves to his elbows. His forearms were corded with the strain of trying to hold the horse's head still. He leaned in and began murmuring to the giant beast in deep, soft tones. A lock of his dark, wavy hair had fallen over his forehead, giving him a rugged look.

"Whatever happened?" Ed asked loudly as he tried again to inspect the leg.

"Snake spooked him," Darcy answered.

"Snake? This time of year?"

"He was moving slow, but he was there." Darcy raised his voice so he could be heard above the noise. "Horse threw me and took off like a shot, tried to jump a barbed wire fence, and almost cleared it too, except for this scrape."

"Lord! You're lucky he didn't break a leg. You all right?"

"Yep. Landed on my rump, fortunately. I managed to scramble clear before he kicked me. Be sore tomorrow, I'm sure."

Ed frowned. "Ah, I see the problem now; there's a tiny piece of wire stuck in there. Just let me . . ."

He reached over and the horse screamed and reared once more. Ed had kept himself away from the path of the kicking leg. Startled by the commotion, Elizabeth dropped the metal tray she was holding. It clattered noisily on the concrete floor.

Darcy whirled around. "Get the hell out of here," he shouted harshly, "before you get trampled to death!"

Elizabeth picked up her tray and dashed out of the room, leaning back against the hallway wall and trying to calm her pounding heart.

"Don't scare off my niece, young man," Ed said, amused. "She's the only help I've got right now."

"Sorry, Gardiner, she startled me."

Ed yelled out, "Lizzy, dear?"

Elizabeth stuck her head back in the door, not looking at Mr. Darcy.

"Can you get me some carbolic acid to clean this? Atta girl — thank you." He smiled reassuringly.

Elizabeth headed back into the front room, red-faced and fuming at Mr. Darcy for yelling at her like she was a child or a servant.

"Unca, we already been to Mr. Charles' store this week. Mama took us yesterday."

Elizabeth heard the singsong voice of Maggie Darcy over the doorbell at Netherfield's Dry Goods. She looked around for a shelf to hide behind; she was in no mood to put up with William Darcy after he scolded her about the horse yesterday.

She peeked around the corner of the aisle and took in the surprising scene before her. Maggie had trotted in, sporting a pretty red dress and a big red bow in her hair. What surprised Elizabeth was the man behind her. William Darcy was dressed as usual in his trousers, dress shirt and a jacket, and in his arms was a bundle of tow-headed energy, wriggling and giggling as she tried to put her fingers in his mouth. He pretended to devour them with lip-covered teeth, and she squealed with delight. He set her down and she took off toward the display of stick candy in the corner.

"Watch after Ruth, would you please, Maggie? I need to pick up a couple things."

The little girl sighed dramatically and headed over to the counter. "No Ruth! You can't have all those."

Caroline Bingley moved toward the girls, pasting an insincere smile on her face. "Good morning, Margaret," she began in a sticky voice, "and hello to you too, little Ruth Anne."

"Hullo, Miss Caroline," Maggie returned. Ruth stopped where she was, and looked wide-eyed at the woman towering over her. She put two of her fingers in her mouth, and twirled her hair with the other hand.

"Would you like a piece of stick candy?" she asked, bending over Ruth. "Hmm?" she demanded.

Maggie looked at her uncle. "We don't have permission, ma'am." She turned back around and gasped. "Ruth! Put your dress down!" Ruth had picked up the front hem of her dress and was covering her face with it. Miss Bingley looked mortified, as Ruth revealed her underthings and belly button to everyone in the shop. Maggie reached over and pushed Ruth's hands down. She looked apologetically at Caroline. "She's not 'apposed to do that. It makes Great Aunt Catherine really mad."

Caroline stood speechless. A chuckle escaped Elizabeth's mouth before she could stop it. Darcy whirled at the sound and strode over to the clique gathered at the candy counter.

"Miss Bennet!" He looked at her, smiling.

"Mr. Darcy," Elizabeth smiled in spite of herself. Underneath that stern demeanor, Mr. Serious had been hiding a pair of adorable dimples. Maggie ran up and grabbed her hand.

"Hi! I didn't know *you* were here."

"How are you, sweet pea?"

"I'm fine. Mama's at the drugstore. We came over here with Unca."

"I see that. I'm glad you did. That way, we got to meet up with each other today."

Caroline frowned as she watched this interchange. She cleared her throat, and Darcy turned toward her.

"Caroline, I've got the gloves I need up at the counter. Georgiana asked for some of those hooks and eyes for the girls' dresses, but I don't know what size. Could you find the right ones, please?" He turned to Maggie. "You may pick out some candy for you and Ruth."

"But Mama said we're not 'apposed to have too much…"

"It'll be all right with Mama. Tell her I said you could." He picked up several sticks in various flavors and handed them to Caroline. "We'll take these also."

Maggie muttered, "And Mama said you need to have your own children so you stop spoiling us with so much candy."

Elizabeth bit her lip to keep from laughing, and cautiously lifted her eyes to see how Darcy took to being reprimanded by a four-year-old. Darcy looked hastily at Elizabeth and said nothing, although his cheeks turned bright red. He scooped up Ruth and nodded to Elizabeth before turning abruptly and heading to the cash register.

Elizabeth followed them as Maggie was pulling on her hand and telling her about Unca losing his work gloves in the woods yesterday.

Caroline Bingley stopped suddenly and slowly turned toward Elizabeth. In a loud, carrying voice she announced, "Oh Miss Bennet. I'm supposed to send some empty flour sacks home with you. Your mother asked Jane if we had any extra. I think Jane said something about making dresses or aprons or something out of them. She's so frugal, your mother. But I suppose that has been very helpful since you came here, from… where was it again?"

"Chicago." Darcy was counting out his payment. He didn't look up, but ventured, "Frugality is a good trait to have in this day and time."

"Of course," Miss Bingley returned smugly, proud that she had effectively reminded Darcy just how beneath him the Bennets were.

Elizabeth clenched her jaw and lifted her chin in defiance. The nasty pettiness of Caroline Bingley had caught her off guard, but she would not let the shrew have the satisfaction of seeing that she had hurt her. "Thank you, ma'am."

Darcy picked up his gloves and handed the candy to Maggie. Ruth had already gotten a piece from him and was rubbing sticky fingers in her hair. He looked intently at Elizabeth. "Good day."

"And good day to you too, William," Caroline cooed.

Elizabeth was digging in her purse for coins. "Good-bye," she replied, not looking up, not wanting to see the disdain she predicted would be in those dark eyes.

The Darcys exited the shop, but seconds later, the door reopened and a little red blur came running up and pressed a stick of candy into Elizabeth's hand. "Bye!" She grinned, turned and was gone before Elizabeth could thank her.

Chapter 8

The 26th of November

Elizabeth looked up at the front entrance of the Bingleys' home. Lights shone from the windows, and gas lanterns lined the driveway. She ascended the steps to the front door, which was adorned with a festive evergreen wreath. She paused and looked behind her to smile encouragingly at Jane. It had been a long time since the Bennet girls had had an evening of fun. Elizabeth adjusted her wrap and smoothed the skirt of her dress. It was a remade version of last year's party dress, but the cranberry satin was flattering on her, and Jane had helped her curl her hair so it fell in glossy brown waves around her face. For days, the sisters had been lathering their hands with lard and the hand balm at Uncle Ed's office to keep rough, chapped skin at bay. It would not do for a girl to have work-worn hands when someone asked her to dance.

Jane's dress was a lovely true blue that brought out the blue in her eyes and contrasted with her flaxen hair. A string of pearls and her angelic smile set off the ensemble perfectly. Jane gave off an air of cool sophistication, even though she was wearing last year's fashion. Elizabeth's appearance, on the other hand, evoked an intriguing, spicy warmth. She leaned over to whisper in her sister's ear and took her arm as they walked into the foyer. The sisters presented a living, breathing contrast of female beauty that soon garnered the attention of Charles Bingley, as well as some of the other gentlemen in the room.

Jane's face brightened in response to the approach of their dashing host. He made his way toward them through the crush of party guests, sporting a charming smile and stopping briefly to shake a couple of hands as he went. Elizabeth greeted him warmly and then excused herself, ostensibly to get some punch and find Charlotte, but in truth, she wanted to let Charles talk to Jane on his own. Gazing across the room, she found her friend, and after giving her a wave, she gestured toward the punch table, indicating that they could meet there.

"I see Jane has caught Charles Bingley's eye; no mystery there," Charlotte whispered to Lizzy as she took a cup of punch from the serving girl. "She is beautiful and he is handsome. His admiration is written all over his face."

Elizabeth smiled. "I think she does like him quite a bit, and he seems to enjoy her company."

"Then she ought to snap him up before he changes his mind."

"Charlotte! She hardly knows him."

"Lizzy, he's rich and handsome and kind, and just about the best thing she'll find around these parts."

"You don't mean that. You would never act that way. It's almost…mercenary."

Charlotte shrugged. "Well, it seems Jane won't." She paused and took a sip of her punch. "Oops, look out, here comes Mr. Serious. I think he's on a mission."

"Who's on a mi —?" Elizabeth turned her head and looked straight into the finely tailored suit jacket of Mr. Serious himself.

WILLIAM DARCY HAD HELD HIS ground at the end of the room, using his height to scan the guests as they arrived. Finally, he saw the woman for whom he'd been searching. He saw her face break into a smile, and he started to return it, when he realized she was gesturing to Miss Lucas who was several feet to his right.

He had then watched her animated face and gestures, and before he was aware of what he was doing, he found himself beside her. She stopped mid-sentence and slowly raised her fine eyes to meet his.

"Good evening, Miss Bennet. Would you care to dance?"

Elizabeth stood like a deer in headlights before she felt a poke in her ribs and a nudge toward the man towering over her. She nodded. "Mmm…yes…thank you."

He took her punch and handed it to Charlotte, before clasping her hand and leading her to Bingley's impromptu dance floor. She gave Charlotte a surprised look and caught her friend's encouraging grin.

The band Bingley had hired was on a break and a large Victrola currently manned by the band's piano player was spinning records. Darcy pulled her toward him and put a large, warm hand securely at her waist, keeping a respectable distance between them. The other hand engulfed her small one. He had a farmer's hands — the skin on his palm was thick and somewhat rough and calloused. *Not a gentleman farmer, then.* Elizabeth thought, her respect for him rising slightly. *Odd what a difference a year makes. I wouldn't have even noticed that before I lived here.*

The "Tennessee Waltz" was playing as they moved around the floor amongst the other dancers. When the song ended, they stepped apart, clapping politely. Another song began, and Elizabeth was shocked when Darcy took her hand and waist again. Still, he said nothing to her, looking steadily over her shoulder, but apparently not seeing anything in particular.

"Are you counting?" she asked, deciding he needed a good tease.

"Pardon?" He seemed startled, as he looked down at her, dark eyes boring into her golden ones.

She raised one eyebrow impertinently. "I said, are you counting? Do you have to concentrate on the steps so much that there's nothing left over to make conversation?"

"Conversation?"

"Yes, Mr. Darcy, I believe it is common for two people dancing to have some conversation. Let's see, you could talk about what a nice evening it turned out to be, and I could…oh, I don't know, I could talk about how lovely Mr. Bingley's house looks all decorated for Christmas, how unusually warm the weather is, or how many people here are fond of dancing."

"So, these are the party rules according to Miss Elizabeth Bennet?" He pursed his lips in a thin line, but she thought she saw a sparkle of amusement in his eyes for just a second.

She laughed. "Well, sometimes it is best to have some conversation, when two people must endure each other's company."

He frowned for real this time. "Is that what we are doing — enduring each other's company?"

"Oh, never mind. It's probably for the best anyway. I have to crane my neck to look up at you." She smiled, and he couldn't help but smile in return. Her comments might sound acerbic coming from anyone else, but there was a sweetness to the way she spoke them, and it made it very difficult to be truly annoyed with her.

"My apologies for my height, Miss Bennet," he returned in a deep, warm voice.

She shrugged and looked back at his shoulder. "I suppose you cannot help it." She realized that his movements were less stilted now, and their bodies were closer, almost touching each other as he guided her about the floor. He was an unexpectedly good dancer, but a third dance would set people's tongues wagging, and she certainly did not need any more grief from Charlotte Lucas — or Mrs. Bennet, either. When this dance ended, she would excuse herself somehow, if he seemed to want to dance another song with her.

When that time came, Elizabeth stepped back and looked up at him. "Thank you for the dance, Mr. Darcy."

"Thank you," he replied, his face expressionless as always. He put a hand to her elbow as she turned to walk away and escorted her back to the punch table, where Charlotte and her sister, Maria, were talking with one of the Goulding girls from the other end of the county. He nodded to her solemnly. "Miss Bennet, have a good evening." He turned on his heel and left the room, striding past a table of young women who tittered as he went by.

"I wonder what that was all about," Elizabeth murmured.

"You make a very handsome couple," Charlotte observed wryly.

Lucy Goulding stared at Elizabeth, wide-eyed. "He *never* dances, ever. What did you do to make him like you?"

"Nothing," Elizabeth replied, exasperated. "I mean, he doesn't like me. He must have just been bored or something. You'll see; he'll ask someone else in a minute."

But Elizabeth was wrong. The rest of the evening passed without Mr. Darcy setting foot on the dance floor again.

"Miss Darcy, how are you this evening?"

Georgiana turned and smiled into the blue eyes directed her way. "Good evening, Sheriff. I'm well — and you?" She stood, knowing that her voice was too soft for him to hear otherwise. At five foot seven, she was almost as tall as Richard Fitzwilliam's five foot nine-inch frame, but he had a powerful wiry build that seemed to dwarf Georgiana's waif-like figure.

"Doin' fine, just fine." He looked around, fishing for a topic of conversation. "Lots of people here tonight."

"Yes, most of the county, I think."

"It's become a tradition around here, hasn't it?"

"Yes."

"Have you had some punch? Can I get you some?" He nudged her gently and whispered. "I don't think the Bingley sisters spiked it with their homemade liquor this year."

Georgiana looked at him, aghast.

Sheriff Fitzwilliam had the grace to look embarrassed. "Sorry, ma'am, I was just making a little joke."

Georgiana gave him a disconcerted smile. "Oh," she replied.

"I've heard tell that the government may repeal the Volstead Act."

"Oh?"

"Sure would make enforcing the law easier."

"I've never drunk a drop of liquor, or any other alcohol. It's been illegal since I was a young girl." Her face took on a slightly hardened expression. "But I have seen the damage drinking can do to some people. So I don't know how I feel about doing away with Prohibition."

He looked at her thoughtfully as she gazed out over the room. "A lot of evil come from drink, that's true enough, but I can't see as the law's really got rid of that. Seems to me evil will be around as long as there's men around to do it."

Georgiana sighed, retreating back behind the grey mist in her eyes. "You may be right, Sheriff. You'd certainly know more about it than I."

"Oh, I'm not so sure about that," he replied softly.

Georgiana turned and looked at him.

He cleared his throat and shuffled his feet. "I saw your brother asked that Bennet girl to dance."

Georgiana let out a soft incredulous laugh. "Dancing? *My* brother?"

Fitzwilliam smiled, relieved to get back to a more comfortable subject. "Tall feller? Dark hair? Scowls even though he's supposed to be having fun?"

Georgiana shook her head, smiling. "Shame on you, Richard Fitzwilliam! You're right though; he does scowl when he should be smiling."

"How 'bout you? You like to dance?"

"Me?" Georgiana looked around self-consciously. "Oh no, I…I don't want to draw attention to myself. After all, I'm not a young unmarried girl. I—"

"Miss Darcy," he said gently, "it's been over a year and a half since you come back. Folks wouldn't think nothin' about you dancing."

"I've probably forgotten how to dance; it's been a good long while." Georgiana looked down at her hands, and forced herself to stop wringing them.

"Well, maybe it's time to start dancing again."

She looked at him and smiled wistfully.

After a pause, he spoke again with a forced cheerfulness. "So, how's them little girls? Growin' like weeds, I expect."

"Yes, they are at that."

"Very sweet children."

"Thank you."

"Think I'll head over and speak to that scowling brother of yours. But first, I'm going to bring you a cup of punch."

"You needn't bother on my account..."

He laid his hand gently on her arm. "Ma'am, 'tis no bother...at all." He turned slowly and walked away. Georgiana sat down heavily and willed her hands to stop shaking.

Chapter 9

Encounter at the Kent County Library

December 27, 1932

Darcy slipped quietly into the library vestibule, shaking snow from his coat and hat before proceeding inside. The musty smell of old books, ink and paper, along with the heavy quiet, was like slipping into another world — far away from the noise and bustle of the little town's streets. He glanced around. Georgiana had told him Maggie would be finished with this new 'story hour' at eleven o'clock, and he needed to get her back to her mother at the Woolworth's lunch counter before his meeting with the attorney.

He pulled his hand out of his coat pocket and looked impatiently at his watch. *Where is the little imp anyway? It's five minutes after.*

He heard little voices and walked toward the sound. What he saw made him stop short. There, sitting in a chair, in front of an adoring audience of about a half-dozen four- and five-year-olds, was Elizabeth Bennet. He folded his arms and leaned his shoulder against the books in the stack, an unwilling smile twitching at the corners of his mouth.

Elizabeth was holding up a picture book for the children to see and reading *The Tale of Peter Rabbit* in lively character voices. She leaned forward, eyes vibrant, and asked them in hushed but exaggerated tones, "And what do you think happened then?"

The children chorused various answers, and she laughed, gesturing for them to lower their voices, "Shhh! Mr. Collins will make us all leave if we're too loud."

She turned the page. "Let's see what Peter did next..."

She finished the book and dismissed the children, saying, "Would you all like to hear some more stories next week?" They all nodded. "All right, then, I will be here next Wednesday at ten o'clock, and I hope you're here too."

"Good-bye, Miss Lizzy!" several voices called as the children collected coats and hats. She helped some with buttons and mittens, and sent them to their parents milling about the library.

Elizabeth stilled as if she had sensed Darcy's eyes on her, and turned around. "Oh, did you come to get Maggie? She's helping put the carpet mat back in the closet."

"I didn't know you were the 'story lady.'"

Elizabeth blushed. "I volunteered. I'll enjoy it as much as the children do, and it isn't really Mr. Collins' kind of fun."

"No, I would imagine not." He paused, wryly thinking about the short, balding, middle-aged man who ran the Kent County Library. He stood up straight, as if making a decision.

"I'm taking Maggie to have lunch at the Woolworth's counter with her mother. Would you like to join us?"

"Oh, yes, Elizabeth!" Maggie's voice rang out beside her. "Please come have lunch with me."

Elizabeth looked surprised and considered before she spoke to Maggie, so as not to hurt the little girl's feelings. "Thank you for the invitation, but I need to get back to my Uncle Ed's and finish my work for today." She looked up at Darcy. "He's been good enough to let me be away from the office for story hour, but I really do need to be back within a reasonable time."

"Aww," Maggie's face showed her disappointment. Darcy looked down at her sternly, and she pursed her lips together in an expression so like Mr. Darcy's that it brought a smile to Elizabeth's face.

"Of course, we understand," he replied.

"I will walk out with you though," she continued to Maggie. "I have to pass Woolworth's on the way."

"Good!" This seemed to appease the girl. "Will you hold my hand?"

"Of course."

Darcy's eyes followed Elizabeth as she picked up her coat. He stepped forward and held it for her as she slipped her arms into the sleeves. He opened the door for them, and Elizabeth thanked him, before setting off at a brisk pace through the snow, Maggie's hand swinging in hers.

"Well, Miss Darcy, what should we read next week at story hour?"

"I don't know." Maggie was silent for a minute, considering. "Maybe we should read a cowboy story."

"A cowboy story?"

"Yes, I think a cowboy story would be good."

"So you like cowboy stories?"

"Not particularly," Maggie replied. "But there was only one boy at the library today. Boys should come to story hour too, 'cuz boys need books just as much as girls."

"I agree."

"And boys like cowboy stories. So if we have one, they might ask their mamas if they can come."

Elizabeth nodded, amused, yet impressed with the little girl's reasoning. "I see what you mean. I will try to find a cowboy story for next week. But how will we let the boys know about it?"

"Hmm," Maggie pursed her lips seriously. Then her eyes lit up, and she turned her shining face up to Elizabeth. "I know! I will tell the boys at Sunday School and…"

Elizabeth smiled at her encouragingly. "And?"

"And you tell the boys and mamas that come in the vet office." A triumphant smile lit up Maggie's sweet face.

"That sounds like a good plan to me."

The little girl beamed. "Thank you." She laid her cheek against Elizabeth's forearm and squeezed her hand.

They stopped outside the Woolworth's, and Elizabeth turned to make her good-byes.

Darcy addressed his niece in a warm voice full of pride. "Run along inside, Maggie Moo. Your mama's over at that table, see?" He pointed inside to where Georgiana was waving at them. "Tell her I'll be right there; I'm going to escort Miss Bennet to her uncle's office."

"Yes, sir. Bye, Elizabeth!"

"Bye." She turned to him. "Mr. Darcy, you do not need to escort me; I know the way."

"Yes, I'm aware of that."

"Oh." He continually surprised her. They walked on in silence, until she dared a look up at the man beside her.

"Maggie is a very bright little girl, Mr. Darcy."

"Mm-hmm."

"She can retell the stories we read, and she's asking what sounds the letters make. I think she's ready to start learning to read."

"Honestly?" Surprise showed in his voice. "You don't think she's too young?"

Elizabeth shrugged. "Some children are ready to read at four. Like I said, she's very bright."

He did not reply, and Elizabeth wondered if somehow she had offended the man. She stole another look at him, but for once, he was not scowling. He was grinning.

"What do you find so amusing, sir?" she asked saucily.

"Not amusing, exactly. Although, your Farmer MacGregor voice was quite entertaining." He paused. "No, I just find your efforts at the library interesting...and commendable."

"Reading stories to children? It is hardly an onerous task."

"It's...well...I guess you found a way to be a teacher after all, didn't you?"

Elizabeth stopped, momentarily stunned. She hadn't considered that before. She looked at him intently. "I suppose I did."

"Reading like that, in different voices — is that one of Dr. Montessori's methods?"

"That? Oh no, not particularly. My father used to read to us like that when we were younger. I enjoyed it, so I figured these children would too."

"Ah."

"I'm surprised you remember that conversation about Montessori. Her work isn't very well-known because some educators here in America have been critical of her methods."

"I remember a great many things you've said, Miss Bennet. And, as I told you that day at Bingley's, education is an interesting topic to me because of my nieces."

"I was under the impression that you believed Montessori's ideas were 'rubbish.'"

"I hope I am always willing to listen to new ideas," he began carefully. "But I keep my own counsel as to whether the ideas are good ones."

"You seem to have a great amount faith in your judgment."

"Yes, I do. I believe I've lived a sufficient amount of time and seen enough of the world to earn that.

"So you're infallible?"

"No. Of course not; that would be impossible for anyone."

"I see."

"But I do make it a priority to carefully weigh my decisions. For example, I didn't build Pemberley by following the latest fads in agriculture without thinking them through."

"No, you didn't *build* Pemberley that way. If I understand correctly, it was left to you."

He stopped and looked at her, astounded at her blunt reply. Again, he felt a reluctant smile tug on his lips. "I could hardly argue with you about that, without sounding..."

"Arrogant?"

"I was going to say condescending."

"Well, I suppose you are responsible for maintaining Pemberley, which seems to be a big enough job," Elizabeth conceded. She looked up and realized they were standing outside the vet office. "We are here."

"Yes," Darcy paused, as if to say something else, but then he touched his hat. "Have a good afternoon, Miss Bennet." He turned, and Elizabeth watched him turn up the lapels of his finely made overcoat and hunch his shoulders against the cold wind as he trudged off down the street.

Chapter 10

It's Going to Be a Long Winter

January 9, 1933

Elizabeth started to call out to her uncle when she entered the shop, but she heard low, urgent voices coming from his office. Thinking that it was a client, she quietly hung up her coat and looked at the list of tasks Ed left for her. As she approached the office door, however, she recognized the other man's voice. It was her father. She slowed and finally stopped right outside the open door, feeling guilty for eavesdropping. She could hear the tension in her father's voice and could not tear herself away from it.

"I don't know exactly what I'm going to do, Ed. Spending what we have been for food, and adding what we'll need for additional firewood as the winter goes on, I figure I'll run out of savings about the end of February. It's months until we can get the garden and the crops going, and if we eat all the livestock, there will be no eggs or milk — except the goat's — and no sows to give us piglets next year."

"Thomas, we won't let you starve. Together we can think of something."

"No! You've done enough, more than you should have. As it is, I don't know how I'll ever repay you."

"Don't be nonsensical…"

"We can't live off you and Madeline. It isn't right. Is it not humiliating enough that I can't shelter my own family? At least leave me some of my dignity and let me figure out how to feed them."

Ed sounded uncomfortable. "I didn't mean to insult you..."

Mr. Bennet sighed. "I know you didn't. You're very generous, and I know your offer is made out of concern, but I simply can't take advantage of you. We'll make do somehow."

"What about the money the girls are bringing in?"

"Kitty and Lydia are still selling eggs; it's helpful but still just a drop in the bucket."

"I can pay Lizzy in cornmeal, soup beans, anything I have that you all need," Ed offered.

"That would help on the food end." He continued, after a pause, "I have a spinster aunt in Chattanooga. One of the girls might be able to go there and work. My sister says Aunt Irene might be in need of a caregiver. Perhaps Mary could go...or Kitty."

"You don't want to split up the family, Thomas. The girls need each other."

Mr. Bennet went on, murmuring almost to himself. "Lizzy would be the best suited for something like that, but even though I know it isn't right, I've come to rely on her these last few months for encouragement and...conversation. The other girls aren't too interested in English literature. Besides, Lizzy already has a job, and we haven't been able to find any work for Mary."

"I still think you should keep your family together."

"I may not have a choice. At any rate, some or all of them will eventually marry and split themselves up, I suppose. I have to admit, I was half-hoping young Bingley might make his move toward Jane. He seemed quite interested in her before Christmas. He's a nice enough fellow, and Jane seems to like him, but that appears to be going nowhere."

There was another awkward pause. "Damn it all! I sound more mercenary than my wife! I can't believe I'm actually considering marrying off my girls to any old Joe to try and make ends meet. I'm ashamed to know I can even think such a thing. Honestly, Ed, I would never do that to them."

"Of course you wouldn't. This is all just coming out of frustration. Try not to worry too much, Thomas; you'll make yourself sick. I've learned that things have a way of working out somehow. Something unexpected may turn up at any time."

"I hope you're right, Brother. I really do."

"Have you told Fanny about this? The shortfall of funds, I mean."

"I can't."

"She's tougher than you think."

"Perhaps. But I'm afraid she will worry to excess, and she'll take it out on the girls. I would tell Jane and Lizzy, but I hate to burden them when they have no control over our situation. They're lucky to have the jobs they do have, and they're helping out all they can. What's the point of worrying them any further?"

Elizabeth abruptly left her place outside the door and returned to the front office. She felt remorseful about listening in. Her father did not want to worry them, but goodness! *This affects us so profoundly. Do we not deserve to know? Surely knowing about impending hardship could not be worse than springing it on us the way he did in Chicago.* She felt her father's distress, but the more she thought about it, she began to feel another emotion — anger. She and Jane, and even their mother — they were adults, yet he did not think them capable of dealing with the truth. *I wonder how much of Mama's nerves is the result of him not being honest with her?*

She had had no idea things were so dire. What she would not give for a way out — for all of them! Was there no other way to give her father some relief and ease the strain on her family? She would think of something; she just had to.

Chapter 11

January Thaw

January 28, 1933

After a brief respite from the cold temperatures, winter had taken hold of Meryton again. The frigid, cloudy days lent themselves to sitting at home in front of the fireplace with a good book, not traipsing around town. William Darcy, lost in his own thoughts, made a half-sighing, half-snorting sound and wondered what he was doing here...again. Mr. Darcy and Sheriff Fitzwilliam were in the waiting room of Dr. Gardiner's vet office for the third time in two weeks.

"You didn't need to come with me, Richard." Darcy seemed actually irritated by the presence of his friend, Elizabeth noted. Mr. Serious shifted in his chair, leaned forward and rested his elbows on his knees, intermittently scowling at the sheriff, who was reading the local newspaper. "Didn't mean for you to go out of your way," he went on pointedly.

Fitzwilliam casually turned the page of his newspaper. "No matter. Nothin' going on at the station today and no garden to tend at my house, no 'baccer to work in. I'm glad for the company."

Darcy snorted, "Hmmph," and Elizabeth stifled a chuckle.

"Mr. Darcy," she began, "we've certainly seen you around here a lot lately. What are you doing to those animals out on that farm of yours? They seem to be meeting with an inordinate amount of illness." She eyed him appraisingly. "Shall I call on our dashing Sheriff Fitzwilliam here to investigate?" She passed them and patted the sheriff's arm, laughing, and he tipped his hat to her.

"At your service, Miss."

Darcy looked slightly taken aback, as he often did when Elizabeth teased him, but he answered with a small smile. "Do your worst. I am not afraid of you, Miss Bennet."

The sheriff grinned. "Don't mind my friend, Miss Bennet. He can be mighty stern and silent in the company of pretty ladies, although he is lively enough in other places."

"Truly?"

"Yes, ma'am."

Darcy sent the sheriff another glare.

"Then why can't he be lively in mixed company as well?" Elizabeth stopped and leaned on the counter, facing the two men. She rested her chin in her hand and drummed her other fingers on the countertop, in an exaggerated thoughtful gesture. "Let's see. Why should a well-educated man who has 'lived and seen enough of the world', as he once told me — why can't a man like that engage in a clever discussion with the people he meets?"

"Because he will not take the trouble?" the sheriff replied jovially.

Darcy frowned at Fitzwilliam, but he directed his answer to Elizabeth. His voice softened somewhat; his gaze became earnest and intense. "For some people, the ability to start a conversation with new acquaintances is a gift. However, I have always found it difficult to comfortably discuss trivial matters with people I have recently met, the way I see others do."

Elizabeth pulled out a cloth and carefully wiped the countertop in front of her. "When I came to work in this office, I was unable to fill a syringe or give an injection as I have seen my uncle do. But I had to learn, and it was only a matter of time until I could. Now, my fingers are not as competent as his, but it is not because my fingers are not as capable, but that he has had rather more time to practice. Would you not agree?"

Darcy looked at her steadily. "I agree perfectly. However, I think you have employed your time much better. No one who has seen you dance or read to children or sew a party dress could think you inadequate in any way."

Dr. Gardiner's voice sounded from the next room. "Can I get one of you fellas to give me a hand with these boxes?"

The sheriff looked at his friend, whose attention was completely absorbed in the sparkling gaze of the girl behind the counter. "Uh... I'll just go help Ed, then." He quickly exited the waiting room, an amused grin on his face, leaving the couple alone to continue their obvious flirtation.

Elizabeth cleared her throat. "I'm sure Uncle Ed will be back in a minute with your supplies. Is there anything else I can get you?"

"Not right now," he replied evenly, with a hint of a grin. "But, thank you."

Darcy sat for a bit and watched as she busied herself with some paperwork at the desk at the end of the room. She leaned over and frowned in a half-hearted attempt to concentrate. After a moment, he stood up and walked around, looking at the pictures and certificates on the wall. Out of the corner of her eye, Lizzy watched him. He moved gracefully for a man, each step confident and sure. Or maybe it was his height that drew her interest. He was about the tallest man she had ever met. Then he sat back down, and after a second, shifted in his seat. She surreptitiously watched him stretch out his long legs in front of him, and promptly flushed with embarrassment at her frank consideration of his person. Relieved that he could not read her mind, she startled when he finally got up and walked over to stand directly in front of her. Self-conscious about his looming presence, she put down her pencil. He was obviously not going to let her get any work done while he waited. Suddenly, it occurred to her that she might be able to learn some information about Mr. Bingley for Jane's sake.

"I haven't seen Mr. Bingley around the store much lately," she ventured.

"No, now that he has plenty of good employees here, he has been devoting more time to the store in Glasgow."

"Oh," Elizabeth replied coolly. "He has a house there as well?"

"Yes, he has a small house in town that he inherited from his mother. Bingley has been waiting to expand his business into that area, and this appeared to be a favorable time to do that. The dry goods store in Glasgow went out of business last year."

"It's unfortunate that he has to be away from Meryton so much."

"Not so unfortunate," Darcy answered. "It's not as if he has a wife and children depending on him. This is a time in his life when he can devote himself to business."

Elizabeth blushed, imagining Darcy must believe she was thinking about Jane being the mistress of Bingley's house, but she said nothing else.

Darcy walked around the desk, until he was sitting on a stool beside her. He leaned toward her, his dark eyes fixed on hers. "Would you think it unfortunate to be far away from your home? You appear to have a strong attachment to your family. Would you like to settle near them, do you think?"

Elizabeth looked at him in surprise and wondered what the point was of this conversation. "Well..." she stammered, "I mean it is possible to be too close to one's family, I guess, no matter how much you love them." She turned her head toward the footsteps approaching from the back office. Darcy straightened at the sound of Dr. Gardiner's and Sheriff Fitzwilliam's voices.

"Are you happy here in Meryton?" Darcy asked politely.

"I like the people I've met here. Life certainly moves slower here than in Chicago, but there are advantages to living at a more relaxed pace."

This answer seemed to please Darcy, and he let a slight, smug smile turn his mouth. By this time, however, Dr. Gardiner had returned, ending the opportunity for further conversation, at least as far as Darcy was concerned. He stood and paid his bill, shaking Ed's hand as he involuntarily cast a glance over his shoulder at Elizabeth. Unexpectedly, he then approached her, and left her with a softly spoken, "Good-bye, Miss Bennet," before he left the office.

"He is the strangest man I've ever met," Elizabeth commented as she watched him pass by the office window. "I can never predict what he's going to say next."

"He is reserved, but I've known him a long time. He's a good man." Ed snuck a look at his niece. "He's had some trying times, had a lot of responsibility on his shoulders at an early age. I suppose that might make a young man seem...a little serious."

Elizabeth smiled. "Mr. Serious."

"What?"

"Charlotte and I — sometimes we call him Mr. Serious."

"Lizzy..." he started, chiding gently.

She shrugged and turned back to her papers. "It's all in fun, Uncle, all in fun."

Dr. Gardiner looked at the dark head bent over the desk. "I wonder if the man himself would find it so amusing," he murmured. He had seen the look William Darcy had given his niece, and a suspicion was forming in his mind. After all, his nieces were nearly perfect girls in his eyes. Any young man would admire them. *But Darcy always seemed a confirmed bachelor. Could that be why I've seen him more in the last month than all of last year? I wonder what Madeline thinks.*

Chapter 12

An Offer You Can't Refuse?

February 5, 1933

The rattle of a car approaching the house pulled Elizabeth out of her silent reverie. The family had gone up the road to her uncle's for Sunday dinner but she had begged off, citing a headache. Her head did hurt, but truthfully, she could have gone to eat with them. It was just very nice to have the quiet parlor all to herself for a couple of hours: no Mama quizzing Jane about whether Mr. Bingley had been at the shop, no *Amos and Andy* on the radio, no Kitty and Lydia squabbling about heaven knows what. She had curled up in her father's chair and was reading a novel when the she heard the vehicle outside. There was a loud knock at the door and she got up, curious as to who could be coming to visit on a Sunday afternoon. Her curiosity turned to bewilderment when she reached the front door and opened it.

"Mr. Darcy!"

"Hello, Miss Bennet." He stood, looking at her across the threshold.

She recalled her manners. "Oh, come in," she said, stepping back and opening the door so he could step through. "It's freezing out there."

"Thank you." Darcy looked around, as if seeking someone.

"My father's not here."

He looked at her hesitantly. "He's not?"

"No, I'm afraid you find me all alone today. They've gone up to the Gardiners' for Sunday dinner. I'm sure they will be back soon if you'd like to wait." She indicated a chair.

He took it and looked at her, his eyes inquiring. "You didn't go with them?"

"No, I had a little bit of headache, I'm afraid."

"I hope you're feeling better."

"Yes, I am, thank you."

She sat back down in her chair, and he bounced right back up and began pacing. He turned and looked at her.

"Is there something I can help you with?" she asked.

"Hmm." A distracted smile floated across his face. He paced the room a few more times, stopped abruptly, then he approached her, halting just a few feet in front of her. She had to tilt her head upward to see his face. His cheeks were red, and his eyes were as dark as night. He looked her over, and finally, he began to speak.

"I was going to talk to your father first, but perhaps this is the better way."

"Better way for what?"

He bridged the remaining steps between them, and to Elizabeth's horror, he bent down on one knee and took her hand in his.

"I have struggled with my feelings, but I can't seem to put them aside. I'm compelled to . . . I have to . . . tell you how much I admire you and ask you . . . ask you . . . "

He took a deep breath as if he was about to dive under water. "I would like to marry you, Elizabeth." He exhaled the rest of his air, and stood up to resume his pacing.

"Before you say anything, hear me out. I realize that we haven't known each other very long, and you may not have the kind of feelings for me you think you should. I know girls have silly romantic notions about being in love before they marry. But you seem to have some sense about you, and I think you can see how this marriage would benefit both of us."

Elizabeth sat in complete and utter shock, her eyes round as saucers. Her blood was roaring in her ears. She started to speak, stopped, and was silent. Darcy took this as encouragement and went on.

"I'm thirty years old, and most likely tied to Pemberley for the rest of my life. I'm not complaining, mind you, but that is the reality of my situation. I have always wanted a family — I know you must have seen how I dote on my nieces — but I've never married because, quite frankly, since I returned from college, I haven't met anyone I thought I could tolerate who would also consider living at Pemberley. Your family is already in Meryton, so you could live here and be content. I know people will perhaps look askance at the difference in our social and financial stations, but I care little for other's opinions. I know what I am doing. You are a kind, Christian woman, with some education and intellect. I know that you will be a good mother; I've watched you with Maggie and Ruth. And you seem to be very accepting of Georgiana's past." He turned and looked at her closely. "That is very important to me. I could never allow my wife to treat my sister poorly. She and the girls will, after all, be living in the same house with us. You have lived with several sisters, some of whom are … well, let's just say that it wouldn't be too difficult for Georgiana to be a more pleasant companion for you."

Elizabeth felt her hackles rise and straightened up, ready to speak, when he interrupted her again.

"Excepting Jane, of course, who is very pleasant to talk to … and maybe that middle one — what is her name again?"

"Mary."

"Yes, of course, Mary." After an awkward pause, he carried on. "On your side, the advantages would be obvious: a good home, a respected standing in the community, financial security, and a family of your own, to name a few."

He seemed suddenly to sense some tension in the air and stopped to observe her. "You have nothing to say?"

"I'm not sure what to say…" she almost whispered.

He went on as if he had not heard her. "Oh, and I would like to marry as soon as possible. Spring is a very busy time, and I would like to take you somewhere on a short honeymoon before spring planting. I was thinking late February or early March would be a good time for a wedding ceremony."

"Mr. Darcy, I…"

"I can speak with your father as soon as he returns, if you like."

Elizabeth's initial reaction was to send him packing. This was the most un-romantic proposal she could imagine. Except for the brief stint down on one knee, he had botched the entire affair! Presumptuous, arrogant, high-handed… She looked up at him and the words died in her throat. He was watching her with an intensity that was unnerving at worst, and at best… well, it was somewhat stirring.

A lot of women would be willing to put up with a serious feller, if he were tall and rich, and had those pretty eyes and that wavy hair." Charlotte's words echoed in her head. It was almost unbelievable, but Charlotte had been right about him all along.

She looked away from his piercing gaze. It seemed as if he was trying to read her mind. Suddenly, it all made sense. The staring, the escorted walks around town, their one and only dance, the frequent trips he made to the vet office — to think, he had admired her all that time! Her mind whirled as she realized that she had inadvertently captured the interest of this man, whom everyone in town said was unobtainable.

"You look a little apprehensive," he ventured tentatively, "but you needn't be troubled. I would never treat you with anything less than respect. I think… I think… we would do well together. Please don't worry about the future."

The future. And there it was — the major reason she hadn't turned him down flat. The future.

"… *I'll run out of savings by the end of February.*"

"… *perhaps Mary could go, or Kitty.*"

"… *we won't let you starve…* "

"… *I've known him a long time. He's a good man.*"

Snippets of conversations flitted through Elizabeth's mind like a bird trapped indoors and trying to escape.

"Mr. Darcy," she began shakily. "I'm honored by your proposal, but I was wondering… might I have a day or so to think it over?"

He seemed surprised by this. "Think it over?" he repeated.

"Yes, it is a momentous decision. And while you have apparently been acclimating yourself to the idea for some time now, I have only just had it sprung upon me. I'd like to sleep on it, so as not to make an impulsive decision."

He smiled. "Ah, I understand. Of course. Very sensible — it's one of things I appreciate most about you."

"Be careful, sir. You will sweep me off my feet with your ardent declaration," Elizabeth muttered sarcastically as she stood.

He let out a bark of laughter, which startled her. "I also appreciate your quick wit and irreverent humor, even if, at times, I am the object of it."

Elizabeth had no idea how to respond to that, so she said nothing.

"I will call on you at your uncle's office — when? Tomorrow? The next day?"

"The day after tomorrow — I will let you know my decision by then."

"Until Tuesday." He reached out and took her hand, looking down at it and moving his thumb across her knuckles slowly. He then pulled her toward him, gazing down on her. He closed his eyes and swiftly brushed his lips across her temple. "Good-bye… Elizabeth."

Butterflies swirled around in her stomach at the low, hoarse voice in her ear.

He turned away and left before she could say another word.

"He did what!"

"Hush, Jane! You'll wake the entire house. The last thing I need is Mama putting in her two cents about this." Elizabeth paced back and forth in front of her sister. She wrung her hands and shook her head. "I couldn't believe it myself."

"And you had no idea?"

"Absolutely none. I thought he came over to ask me if I would teach Maggie to read! Apparently, he has been thinking about this marriage business for some time, enough time to have it all planned out."

Jane gave her a wry smile. "Why is it so hard for you to believe that someone might fall in love with you?"

"Oh Jane, he's not in love with me. It was the coldest, most practical exchange of words we have ever had. He wants to marry and have a family, and I'm simply the best option available."

"But then, if he isn't in love with you, why does he look at you the way he does? I overheard Mr. Bingley and his aunt talking about it several months ago when we were staying at Netherfield. He seemed to think Mr. Darcy was enamored of you, and Miss Caroline was of the opposite opinion. After that, I began to notice it more."

"I thought that he was staring because he disapproved of me."

"I guess he doesn't."

"Apparently not. What am I going to do?"

Elizabeth turned and plopped back on the bed beside Jane. She put her head in her hands, and Jane reached over and rubbed her back gently. "You don't have to say yes, Lizzy."

"It's not that simple." Elizabeth's mind waged an internal debate. She had decided to respect her father's wishes, in spite of her anger at him, and not tell Jane about their impending financial crisis. However, that was before Mr. Darcy had thrown her into this whirlwind of doubt. Hadn't she said she would do *anything* to get them out of this situation? Wouldn't it help her father to have one less mouth to feed? Perhaps, if she married, she could spare Mary or Kitty being sent away from home. Surely, Mr. Darcy would be willing to help his in-laws at least a little bit.

Should she tell Jane? She looked into her blue eyes; her older sister was naïve in so many ways — protected, sheltered — as Elizabeth herself had been before they moved from Chicago. No, she would not tell Jane about the conversation she overheard between their uncle and their father. She would make this decision on her own.

Elizabeth took a deep breath. "He is, in many ways, a 'good catch' for me. Aside from his financial situation, he is well-educated and seems to enjoy intelligent conversation, once he deigns to converse with the common-folk, that is. He is arrogant, that's true, but I don't think he would mistreat me. He will most likely be devoted to any children we have, judging from his commitment to his sister and his nieces. Uncle Ed says he is a good man, if a little serious." She gave Jane a sidelong glance. "He is handsome."

"He is that," Jane agreed. "And he seems enamored of you, which shows he has good taste."

Elizabeth looked down at the floor. "Right before he left this afternoon, he took my hand, and…he kissed me."

She looked up and saw Jane's look of astonishment. "What was *that* like?"

"It was just on the cheek…well, it was…not…unpleasant. It was certainly different than when Bobby Anderson tried to kiss me under the mistletoe at that college mixer. Then, I was just worried about someone catching us; this time, I couldn't think about anything at all, except how hot my face felt. So, I don't suppose being married to him would be *very* objectionable. I think we could be friends, in time."

"I'm not sure that's a good enough reason for getting married. Marriage is for the rest of your life."

"Let's be truthful. What are my options for the rest of my life? I have no education and no money. I can marry, or I can live with Mama and Papa, or I can strike out on my own and live God knows how. If I marry Mr. Darcy, I know what I'm getting into, and I will be close to my family." She reached out and took Jane's hand. "Perhaps I could even help Mama and Papa — if I were Mrs. Darcy."

Jane shook her head. "Papa will not let you do that; he is too proud to take charity from Mr. Darcy."

Elizabeth shrugged. "Perhaps," she said enigmatically.

"It sounds as though you have made up your mind already."

"I guess I have. He is going to call on me on Tuesday, and I said I would give him an answer then." She sat down close to Jane and laid her head on her shoulder. "I am so tired right now. I feel as if the weight of the world is on my shoulders, and has been since July. I just want all this worry to end."

Jane enclosed her in a sisterly hug. "As long as I am able, I will be here for you, little sister."

"Thank you. And Jane?"

"Yes?"

"Please pray for me."

Jane squeezed her one more time. "That you may rely upon."

Chapter 13

The Illusion of Courtship

February 8, 1933

"Lizzy, my dear, could you come into my library...I mean, the parlor for a moment?"

Elizabeth took a deep breath and steeled herself. She knew what was coming, and she was going to have to reassure her father that she knew what she was doing.

"Yes, Papa? What is it?"

"I had a most interesting visit this morning."

"Oh?"

"From Mr. Darcy."

"Oh."

"Don't be coy, Elizabeth," he said, irritated. "You know why he was here. I was in shock for a full minute when he told me that he had asked you to marry him, and that you had said yes."

"Is it so difficult to believe someone might want to marry me?" She turned Jane's words to herself, back out on him.

His expression softened. "Of course not, Princess." He sighed heavily. "But do you know what you're doing, accepting this man?" He stood up and went to the window to stare out into the bare, frozen garden. "He's rich, to be sure, but," he turned back around, eyeing her warily, "will he make you happy? I had the impression that you didn't care much for him, or even thought much about him at all."

Elizabeth leveled a direct look at her father. "Do you have any objection other than your belief in my indifference?"

"No, I mean, he is a stern, unpleasant sort of fellow, but this would be nothing if you really liked him."

"I do like him, Papa. He is a good man; you can ask Uncle Ed if you don't trust my judgment on the matter."

"I already have. He also says that Darcy has been stopping by the vet office and escorting you around town for the last several weeks. He didn't seem very shocked that the man had asked to marry you."

Elizabeth was truly surprised by this. Had everyone seen Mr. Darcy's intentions except her?

Dr. Bennet gave her a critical, almost accusatory look. "I'm a little disturbed that he has been covertly pursuing my daughter right under my nose." He studied Elizabeth's face, trying unsuccessfully to read her expression. Finally, he continued. "Well, he is his own man, used to having his way, but that doesn't mean I approve of his behavior."

Elizabeth said nothing.

He considered a minute more before sighing in resignation. "Well, if you're sure, Lizzy, I'll give my blessing. I hope you and your uncle are right about him. It would grieve me to part with you to anyone unworthy."

Elizabeth looked her father straight in the eye, hoping she sounded more confident than she felt. "I'm sure, Papa. This is what's right for me."

He leaned over to kiss her forehead. "I will miss you terribly, my Princess."

She almost felt her resolve give way when she thought about leaving her family's home. "I'll be close by," she said in a choked voice. "I'll get to see you very often."

"Yes, but your life will be there now. You'll have responsibilities — running your own house, being a wife and a mother."

"I will never be too busy for you," she insisted, covering the wrinkled, work-worn hand on her shoulder with her own and pressing it gently.

He responded only with a wistful smile.

February 15, 1933
ELIZABETH HEARD THE DOOR TO her uncle's waiting room open and felt the cold air on her back before she turned around to see who had entered so late in the afternoon.

"Darcy!" Dr. Gardiner greeted him heartily. "How are you? Cold enough for ya?"

"Dr. Gardiner," he replied politely. "Yes it's chilly enough, although I would expect it to be cold in the middle of February." His eyes shot over to where his bride-to-be was standing behind the counter.

"Good afternoon," she answered in a cheerful voice. "What brings you here?" she smiled teasingly.

"Umm... Elizabeth, may I talk to you for a few minutes?"

"This sounds ominous." She tossed her uncle a wink.

"No..." Darcy looked at her, momentarily shocked, but then he smiled at her teasing remark. "Would you like to take a little walk?"

"Oh, Lizzy, he tempts you with a walk!" Gardiner boomed. "He knows you well, my dear."

"Yes, he's learned I will never turn down the offer of a walk." She reached for her coat, and Darcy promptly moved up behind her to hold it while she finished putting it on.

They stepped out into the cold, dry, winter air and began to stroll up the street.

"Your father came to see me today."

"He said he would."

"He said we'll need to talk to Reverend Adams and discuss the church arrangements, but most of the other arrangements for the reception have been made."

"Yes, my mother has been busy," she said wryly.

"I thought we might travel to Nashville for a few days after the wedding; there are several nice hotels there to choose from and good restaurants and jazz clubs. Do you like jazz music?" he inquired, looking at her a little anxiously.

She smiled at his attempt to please her. He was trying to treat her well, at least. "Yes, I do. It all sounds very fine."

"Good."

"Have you told many people about the wedding?"

"No, actually. Have you?"

"No, but people seem to know anyway. I received some pretty interesting looks at church last Sunday."

"And many kind congratulations, I assume?" He raised a questioning eyebrow at her.

"Mostly, yes. I think people are wondering why you decided to marry all of a sudden."

"It wasn't an impulsive decision as I think you are well aware."

"You're quite the mystery of the county, Mr. Darcy," she ribbed him good-naturedly.

"Hmmpphh," he muttered.

"According to Charlotte Lucas, everyone has always wondered, 'Why isn't the elusive Mr. Darcy married?' Have you never considered it before?"

"Yes, I have."

"Do tell." Elizabeth was intrigued in spite of herself.

He looked away uncomfortably. "I was engaged once."

Elizabeth stopped in her tracks. "Really?"

"Do you doubt the possibility?" His voice was stern.

"No, of course not." She looked directly at him, determined not to let his intimidating scowl frighten her. *It's harder to believe that you would be moved enough to ever ask someone.* "When was this?"

"Several years ago — I was in my last year of college at Vanderbilt."

"Should I be worried about an unrequited love interrupting the wedding?" she teased, trying to lighten the atmosphere.

He paused. "No."

"Married someone else, did she?"

"No."

Elizabeth looked at him expectantly.

He returned her gaze briefly, before glancing ahead of them. "She died, actually, of pneumonia — the winter before we were to get married."

Elizabeth closed her eyes, completely mortified. Would she never stop saying the wrong thing at the worst time? She reached out and touched his arm. "I'm so sorry, William. I didn't mean ... I shouldn't have ... "

He was looking down at her hand on his arm. "Don't worry about it."

She put her other hand over her eyes. "I feel so awful."

He took her hand, turning her toward him. "There was no way for you to know. It was long ago; even Georgiana doesn't know very much about it. She was away at school at the time." He looked down at the slender hand in his, and squeezed it reassuringly. "Honestly, Elizabeth, it's all right."

She smiled sheepishly. "You're very gracious with my faux-pas. Unfortunately, I'm sure it won't be the last one I make."

To her surprise, he gave her one of his wide, heart-stopping dimpled smiles, then turned them around and began walking back toward her uncle's office, keeping hold of her hand.

"Tell me about her ... your fiancée, I mean."

72

"Why do you want to know? Won't this upset you?"

"No, I just want to learn some more about you."

He hesitated, looking at her intently, his thumb rubbing distracting circles across her knuckles. Suddenly, he pulled her hand into the crook of his arm and resumed a leisurely pace.

"Her name was Anne, Anne de Bourgh. We met at Vandy in a history class. She was from an old Tennessee family; my mother would have approved of her. We both liked the same authors, the same music. She was willing to come back with me to Pemberley. Her parents weren't pleased about that; she was frail and they wanted her close by." He gazed, unseeing, into the distance, his thoughts obviously far away. Elizabeth waited patiently for him to continue, eventually squeezing his arm. He started and looked down at her with a smile. "You're different from her. She was shy and very quiet."

"Whereas I am certainly not," she said with a wry smile. Her expression turned serious when she asked, "What happened?"

"There was an outbreak of influenza that winter. She was never very strong, and she contracted the flu. It developed into pneumonia, and within two weeks, she was gone."

Compassion and empathy diffused over Elizabeth's face at this revelation. "How sad for you."

"Yes, it was sad. She was a very kind person, a very interesting person. I felt especially grieved for her parents; she was their only child."

They walked on in silence, until he finally spoke again.

"You shouldn't be concerned that I've pined for her all these years; or that I never married because of some romantic notion that there would never be another woman for me. I mean I did care for her, but it was so long ago, and I was quite young. I'm... I'm a different person now. The harsh experiences of life have a way of altering a man."

"Or a woman," Elizabeth agreed. "I may not have your years, but I feel that in the last six months I've had enough harsh experiences to last a lifetime."

He nodded slowly in agreement. "I've said it before; I think we will do well together." He smiled down at her again, releasing her hand from the crook of his arm.

They had reached Dr. Gardiner's office, and the setting sun cast a cold, pink light on the snow around them. In the gathering dusk, Darcy faced the woman who was to be his wife. Her nose and cheeks were rosy from the cold, and her eyes sparkled like stars. She really was quite lovely, he thought. He removed a glove and lifted his bare hand to caress her face gently. Leaning down, he cautiously touched his cold lips to her red ones. Her eyes fluttered closed, and she looked disappointed when he pulled away, almost as quickly as he had approached her.

"I'll see you tomorrow," he said softly. "Good night, Elizabeth." He opened the office door for her and held it until she was inside. Holding up his hand in farewell, he climbed into his truck and drove away. Elizabeth watched him drive off, the brilliant winter sunset blazing all around him. "You're full of surprises, William Darcy," she murmured, "but I think I'll like you just fine."

Chapter 14

The Wedding of the Year

February 25, 1933

News of Miss Elizabeth Bennet's and Mr. Darcy's upcoming marriage quickly spread around the county, thanks to the all-knowing Charlotte Lucas, who smugly commented that she had seen Mr. Darcy's interest as far back as last September.

As the big day approached, Elizabeth found herself with a fit of nerves the likes of which she had never experienced before. Oddly enough, though, as the day of her marriage drew closer, she also became more reconciled to her decision to marry Mr. Darcy. Their families and the community at large considered them a typical engaged couple. His intense gazes and courtly manners, and her friendly compliance, gave the world the illusion of two happy people in love. Generally, people wished them well, although several young women suggested behind her back that Elizabeth was luckier than she probably deserved.

The wedding morning dawned clear and cold. In the quiet Sunday School room off the main hall at Harvey's Ridge Methodist Church, Georgiana was putting the finishing touches on her soon-to-be sister's hair and using hairpins to secure her mother's lace finger tip veil. She stepped back to look and directed Elizabeth's attention to the mirror they had propped against the wall.

"What do you think?" she asked.

"It's lovely. Thank you so much for finding it. It's my 'something borrowed.' And the dress is 'new', thanks to Uncle Ed and Aunt Madeline."

"What's old?"

"My stockings."

Georgiana looked her over. "And what's blue?"

Elizabeth smiled. "Kitty gave me one of her hair ribbons. It was a big sacrifice for her; she loves hair ribbons and hasn't had a new one in quite a while. Jane trimmed my underskirt with it."

Georgiana turned to the chair that contained her handbag. "I brought a gift for you too."

"You didn't have to get me a gift."

"I wanted to get you something nice for your wedding, but this gift also has a history."

Elizabeth opened the pale green box tied with a white ribbon, and looked up at Georgiana with a question in her eyes. "It's perfume, isn't it?" She lifted the dainty engraved bottle out of its silk-lined package.

Georgiana nodded, her eyes shining.

Elizabeth dabbed some behind her ear and on her wrists, sniffing delicately. "Oooh, it smells wonderful. Tell me the story behind it."

"My brother came to see me once when I was at boarding school. I was often lonely there, and I guess William wanted to cheer me a little, so he took me shopping in Nashville — that's where my school was. One of the places I wanted to go was a little perfume shop that mixed custom fragrances."

Elizabeth stifled a giggle and Georgiana looked at her questioningly.

"I'm having trouble imagining your brother in a perfume store."

Georgiana's face broke into a smile. "Yes, it does seem out of character doesn't it? But I wanted to go, so he took me.

I was trying the different scents and after I smelled each one, I would ask him what he thought. When I came to this one — it's infused with jasmine, by the way — and asked him about it, he paused and got this distracted look on his face.

I asked him again, 'William, how about that one?' He shook his head and said, 'No. It's very nice but not for sisters.' So I said, 'For who then?' And he smiled and said, 'I don't know yet, but I'll let you know when I find her.'" Georgiana smiled shyly. "So I think this scent must belong to you. He's quite smitten with you, and I'm glad to see it. I didn't think I would ever see him happy again."

Elizabeth was incredulous. The thought of her austere husband-to-be even *thinking* about something as frivolous as women's perfume was unimaginable. "Thank you, Georgiana. How on Earth did you ever find it again?"

"I wrote to the shop and ordered it, of course. Richard Fitzwilliam went down there and picked it up for me."

"Sheriff Fitzwilliam?"

"Yes, we were talking about wedding gifts, and I mentioned to him that I wasn't sure I would be able to get it here in time, so he offered. Wasn't that nice?"

"He must think a lot of you to go that far," Elizabeth replied.

Georgiana looked away, her expression somber. "He thinks a lot of *William*. They have been friends for many years."

"Oh."

The door opened and Mrs. Bennet plowed in with Bennet girls trailing behind her. "Oh! My poor nerves! Will I ever get through this day? We found Jane's tortoise shell hair comb. Poor dear had dropped it right outside the car door. It's a wonder someone didn't step on it! Are you ready, Lizzy? Your hair looks very nice, by the way. You'll never be as beautiful as Jane, but every bride shines on her wedding day."

Elizabeth rolled her eyes. "Why, thank you, Mama. Such high praise!"

"You're welcome," Mrs. Bennet continued, turning Mary around and smoothing a wrinkle out of the back of her skirt. "Well, we'll head out to the foyer and wait to be escorted to our seats. Miss Darcy, are you coming too?"

"Yes, ma'am," Georgiana said softly. She pressed Elizabeth's hand and quietly exited the room.

"All right then. Jane, you stay here with Lizzy and your father will come get you when it's time." She bustled out, herding the other girls in front of her.

Elizabeth sighed. Jane looked at her warily.

"Lizzy?"

"Yes, I'm fine, to answer your question."

Jane reached over and squeezed her hand. "Your hands are like ice; are you nervous?"

"Yes, but I'm ready."

Mr. Bennet stuck his head in the door and smiled at her. "If you're sure you don't want to slip out the back door, then it's time to go, Lizzy."

Elizabeth drew in a deep breath and headed out to face her destiny.

When asked later, Elizabeth Bennet Darcy would say she could remember very little about her wedding day. She recalled her mother telling her how pretty her hair looked for a change; her sister told her how beautiful her dress was; her father teased her that he had to cover her hand with his own to keep it from shaking when she walked down the aisle. But of the actual ceremony, she had only an impression, an image. It was the sight of her soon-to-be husband standing at the front of the church, hands clasped in front him, dark eyes seizing her from across the room. His lips curved ever so slightly into a barely perceptible smile. He was larger than life, and her feet propelled her toward him involuntarily.

When she reached the altar, her father leaned over, kissed her cheek, and put her hand in William's. His large hand enveloped hers, and she could hardly concentrate on her vows because he kept rubbing slow, rhythmic circles on the back of it. Somehow, the words were uttered, the promises made, and next thing she knew, she was being kissed as carefully and tenderly as if she were a delicate china cup. He led her back up the aisle and pushed open the door of the sanctuary, ushering her into the blinding winter sunlight.

Chapter 15

The First Night

The wedding took place at one-thirty in the afternoon. It was a small, intimate affair, with a short reception, held in the basement of the church. The groom was anxious for them to be on their way, so by four o'clock, Elizabeth had said her good-byes to her family and they were in Darcy's roadster, heading out of town. Their wedding night would be spent in the Hermitage, a fine Nashville hotel, and they would remain there for five days before returning to begin their married life at Pemberley.

Nashville was sixty-one miles away, lengthier than any car trip Elizabeth had ever taken, but they would arrive there by evening. During the trip, the newly formed Mr. and Mrs. Darcy sat either awkwardly in silence, or engaged in stilted conversation about the wedding, the reception, anything but the strange situation in which they had put themselves.

After a quiet dinner at the Grille Room, housed at the hotel, they retired for the evening. Darcy unlocked the door with his key and Elizabeth noticed his hand shaking slightly. *Now what does* he *have to be nervous about? I'm the blushing bride here.* She shuddered, remembering her mother's instructions: *'Let him do what he will to you. It will hurt some, but it's necessary. And whatever you do, don't cry. We don't want him to have regrets about marrying you.'*

Thank goodness for Aunt Madeline's advice. She was practical, explaining exactly what would happen. Elizabeth wasn't really shocked; working in the vet's office had certainly exposed her to a lot of things she would never encounter in a sheltered Chicago neighborhood. It did seem rather bizarre for humans to act that way though. She hoped she could make it through the act without laughing. When she'd said as much to her aunt, Madeline had smiled wryly and told her laughing was probably not advisable, at least the first time, lest she completely obliterate her husband's masculinity. They had shared a good giggle over it, and that conversation had relieved most of Elizabeth's anxiety — until she actually got to the hotel room.

William held the door for her and she smiled a brief thanks. He looked about as grim and forbidding as she'd ever seen him.

Elizabeth stopped once inside the suite. There was a round table adorned with flowers, two overstuffed chairs, an armoire, and a bed, already turned down, with big white fluffy pillows that looked quite inviting. She walked through the room, taking it all in, and stepped into the bath. A claw foot tub with various soaps and lotions was at one end. Elizabeth also saw a sink with a mirror above it. Lights were mounted all around it; she had never seen such a thing before and gasped in admiration.

"Do you like it?" his deep voice rumbled behind her. "It's supposed to be one of the nicer rooms."

"I've never been anywhere so luxurious; it's beautiful."

He looked pleased. "I'm glad you like it; I wanted you to, ah…well, I wanted you to be comfortable."

She blushed. "Thank you. You're very thoughtful."

"Do you want some time alone? Or we could sit for a while? I think it's too late to go out anywhere, but…"

"I don't want to go out. I think I just want to go to bed." She stopped, blushing even hotter, if that was possible. "What I mean is…"

He tried unsuccessfully to suppress a grin. "I know what you mean, Elizabeth." He took a deep breath. "Why don't you go ahead and get ready for bed, and then we'll sit over there and talk for a bit." He looked at her seriously. "There's no rush."

She gifted him with a grateful smile. "I won't be but a few minutes." She closed the door and leaned against it, jumping half out of her skin when a knock sounded at her back.

"Do you want your bag?"

"Oh, yes, thanks." She opened the door and took the carpetbag from him, their hands brushing as he handed it to her. They looked at each other, startled, when static electricity passed between them. He gave her an apologetic smile. She grabbed the bag from him, and closed the door in his face, murmuring another brief thanks.

Elizabeth emerged, wearing a white floor-length nightgown in a soft, draping fabric. The sleeveless bodice was designed with a low v-neckline. Jane had made it for her as a wedding gift, along with a matching robe, which she also wore. She had washed her face and cleaned her teeth, and looked about as presentable as she could. Opening the door and peering out into the room, she saw William, sitting on the sofa. He was sipping from a glass and staring into the gas logs of the fireplace. She walked out, set her bag down, and proceeded over to him. He turned at her approach and sat very still. His expression was unreadable except for a widening of his eyes.

"You look beautiful," he said hoarsely.

She looked down, smoothing the skirt of her gown. "Jane made it for me."

"I wasn't speaking of the gown; it's lovely, but I meant the woman in it."

She flushed and said nothing.

She sat in the chair opposite him and saw that he had doffed his jacket and tie, and his shoes, leaving him in his stocking feet. The top two or three buttons of his shirt were undone, but to her immediate relief, all his parts were still clothed.

"Would you like a glass of champagne?" he indicated another champagne flute sitting on the little table beside him.

"Champagne? Where...?"

"It was a wedding gift."

Elizabeth remembered sipping on her father's champagne one New Year's Eve when she was very small, but she had long forgotten what it tasted like. He held out a glass to her. She started to take a sip, but he spoke and stopped her. "To my wife, and her health and happiness. Cheers." He nodded and clinked his glass against hers.

"Cheers," she responded, and took a sip. Bubbly like a soda, and stronger tasting, but it was not unpleasant. She took another drink.

He patted the sofa. "Could I convince you to sit beside me?"

She moved over obediently, her heart thudding so loudly she was sure he could hear it. His arm was lying on the back of the sofa and he reached over to gently touch her shoulder. "Are you all right, Elizabeth?"

"I'm nervous," she admitted. It seemed pointless to deny it.

"How can I put you at ease?"

She looked at him in disbelief, but no, he was actually serious about it. She let out a rueful laugh. "I'm not sure that's possible."

"Do you know what's to happen? What to expect?"

"Yes, I...I mean my mother told me."

"Oh, no..." he grumbled.

She laughed again. "But then, Aunt Maddie talked with me too."

"I see."

"Maybe we can talk for a while first."

"If you like."

"Or maybe it's just better to get it over with, I don't know. Do you know?"

He looked at her, startled, and let out one of his sharp bursts of laughter. "No, I don't. I've never done this before either."

"You what? You mean neither of us knows what they're doing? I was counting on you..." Elizabeth was dismayed. "You've never...no wild night in college?" He raised an eyebrow at her.

"Of course not, remember who you're talking to, Lizzy," she muttered under her breath.

"Never with Anne?"

"Certainly not!" he exclaimed indignantly. "She was a lady! And fornication is a sin."

"Oh, well, sorry to offend your gentlemanly sensibilities." Although this fact strangely relieved her.

"Don't fret, Elizabeth. I may not be experienced, but that doesn't mean I'm not educated."

She arched an eyebrow at him.

"I...good Lord! I can't believe I'm talking about this with you!"

"I am your wife, William. This concerns me as well as you."

"Yes, well..." His cheeks were a dark red. Elizabeth was actually a little charmed by his embarrassment.

"So? Who did you talk to?" Her eyes opened wide. "Not my father!"

"No!"

"Or my uncle?"

"No."

"Thank goodness."

"Yes."

"So who?"

"Richard."

"You asked the sheriff?" she squeaked.

He looked defensive. "He was the only married man I knew well enough to discuss it. And I didn't ask; he offered his...advice."

"The sheriff is married?" Elizabeth's mind was reeling from this new information.

"He's a widower."

"Oh." The bluster went out of her voice, but it was quickly replaced with curiosity. "What happened to his wife?"

"She died giving birth almost six years ago."

"And the child?"

"The baby boy died a few hours after."

"Oh, how awful!"

"This is not a good conversation to be having right now," he muttered to himself, wondering how Elizabeth managed to get him off on these tangents.

She gave him a direct look. "Do you think I don't know about the dangers of bearing a child? Any girl who pays attention to women's talk knows about that."

He was incredulous at her frank reply. She was so direct, so starkly honest, so impertinent, so compelling, so enticing...beguiling...enchanting...He found himself leaning toward her, losing his awkwardness in her warm, shining eyes.

Elizabeth felt him kiss her lips, gingerly, tentatively, like dipping a bare toe into a bath or taking a small sip of hot soup from a spoon. He kissed her cheeks, her jaw, the place behind her ear, her now closed eyelids. She felt him right her hand that held the champagne flute, before he took it from her and drained the glass. He set it on the low table in front of the sofa and drew her up to her feet. He kissed her hand and pulled her into a gentle embrace, his hands roaming over her back in gentle, rhythmic strokes. She felt something hard pressing into her tummy.

"Is this when we..."

"Shh," he whispered. "No more talking." He didn't want to veer off on any more tangents. He needed to concentrate if he wasn't going to hurt her, and he couldn't let her distract him anymore.

He held her closer, the strokes of his hands becoming stronger and more urgent. He ran his hands over her hair, her shoulders, her hips. He eased her robe off her shoulders and laid it carefully over the back of the sofa. Her arms were covered in gooseflesh from the sudden rush of cool air on her skin, and he saw that her nipples had pebbled under the thin satin of her gown. He felt an answering pull in his groin, and pulled her back to him to kiss her some more.

After a few more minutes of this, he took her hand and led her to the bed. Her eyes were round and dark, reminding him of a deer he had surprised once out on the farm. Strange that he should think of hunting at a time like this. He smiled at her reassuringly and lifted the covers. She obediently slid between them and lay very still, her dark hair contrasting sharply with the white silken pillowcase. He turned off the lamp because he didn't think he could do this if he had to see those anxious eyes boring into his soul. After he undressed, he slid in beside her, reaching for her and pulling her toward him. He found her lips again and kissed them softly. Her gown had gathered up around her knees and he slipped his hand down and slid underneath it to feel the soft skin of her legs. She gasped, but, as he had requested, said nothing. She was obviously going to let him run the whole show. He was terrified.

Directing her with his touch to sit, he eased the gown up so he could pull it over her head before he threw it, somewhere, he wasn't sure where, and gently laid her back down, leaning over her. He could feel the softness of her breath and the rapid patter of her heart against his chest. This was the important part, when he had to go slowly. He found the idea of hurting her deeply distressing, but he knew he would carry this out to its completion — if not, he thought he would go mad.

So he bought himself time, kissing her face and mouth, running his hands down the keel of her body, shoulder to hip, repeatedly. He found himself fascinated with the soft flesh of her breasts and returned to them again and again. When he realized he was moaning, he made himself stop.

Deciding it was time, he moved over her, settling himself between her legs. He remembered to push himself up on his elbows so as not to crush her with his weight, and he reached down between them to guide himself to her. When the tip of him touched her, he nearly came on the spot, and rolled away quickly.

"William?"

"Unuh," he said in hoarse whisper..

"Was that all there is to it?"

He chuckled mirthlessly. "No, I just … need … a minute."

"Oh." She lay there for a bit, and then without words, she reached for him, pulling him to her and stroking his back as he had done to her. She leaned in to kiss him, and he realized she was aware of his distress and was trying, in her own way, to comfort him. A tiny burst of tenderness flared in his heart and melted another little corner of it.

He rolled over and tried again. He pushed a little way in and stopped against her barrier. A shudder ran through his body, not of revulsion, but of desire, and he pushed a little harder.

"William," she gasped, "stop."

He managed to croak out, "Can't," before, of their own volition, his hips thrust forward and broke through.

He heard a squeak and pulled back to look at her. Her eyes were squeezed shut and her lips were pressed together. "Lizzy?" He brought his hand up to stroke her face gently. "I'm sorry."

"Are you inside me?" He could barely hear her timid question.

"Yes," he groaned. "Oh God, yes." She fit all around him like a glove; he thought he would expire from the pleasure of it.

She opened her eyes. "I'm all right." She smiled in tentative relief, and he bent to kiss her. She wiggled a little under him.

"Sweet Jesus!" he cried, and promptly spilled himself inside her.

HOURS LATER, AS THE SUN rose and shone through the window, he lay awake, nuzzling the jasmine scented skin at the nape of her neck. He had awakened with his arms protectively around her, lying on his side with her back and backside pulled tight against him. He felt her stir and then her body stiffened. She turned over and looked at him.

"Good morning." His low, gravelly voice sounded strange to him.

"Good morning," she replied.

"How are you?" he asked, meaningfully.

"I'm fine."

He paused, not quite sure what to say next. "About last night...what we did...It's supposed to get better."

"Oh?"

"Yes, especially for you. The first time can be a little..." he trailed off. "I'm sorry if I hurt you."

Elizabeth had overheard stories about wedding nights that were much worse; she figured, all things considered, she'd had a fairly easy time of it. At least her husband seemed to care about what he did to her. "I'm not worried; you shouldn't be either."

"What would you like to do today, Mrs. Darcy?" He reached up and twirled a wayward curl around his finger. He knew what he would like to do, and it did not involve anything outside the four-poster bed.

She tilted her head, considering. After several seconds, she had an idea. "Well, first, I think I'd like to take a bath," she looked up at him through her lashes.

He smiled, remembering how much she liked the bathtub at Netherfield Hall. This one was at least as fine. He opened his arms wider to let her go. "Of course." She got up and found her gown beside the bed. Clutching it to her, she grabbed her bag as she disappeared into the bathroom.

After several minutes of dozing, he got up and put on his trousers. Maybe later tonight, he could try again. He was amazed at himself; after living celibate for all these years, he was surprised that only one foray into the marriage bed had led him to the point where he thought about little else.

"Elizabeth?" he called through the door.

"Yes?"

"I'm going to order some breakfast. Then I had planned to take you shopping. You'll need some new clothes, and this may be the last time we'll get to town for a while."

Elizabeth leaned back in the tub. *Bathtubs, shopping, dinners out, handsome Mr. Serious as my escort. Gee whiz, I could really get used to this.* She smiled dreamily.

Chapter 16

Night and Day

February 26, 1933

Elizabeth stood before the lighted mirror, fascinated by the bright incandescence that flooded the room even after dark. She combed and pulled her hair into waves and curls about her face, trying to imitate the style Gigi had created yesterday morning for the wedding. She reached up, pinched her cheeks, and bit her lips in an effort to give them more color. She rarely wore makeup of any kind because she was gifted with a natural blush, thanks to a complexion inherited from her mother. Additionally, there was absolutely no money in the Bennet family budget for cosmetics. Georgiana had gone with her to the Meryton drugstore and bought a few things: shampoo softly scented with lavender, soap that did not contain lye, some kind of lotion that made her skin soft in spite of the dry winter air. At her mother's insistence, Elizabeth had also splurged on a little bit of mascara and lipstick, bought with the wages earned at Ed's office. However, guilt had prevented her from purchasing anything else for herself. At any rate, William apparently meant to spoil her beyond all imagining if their excursion earlier today was any indication.

He had escorted her around to three or four dress shops, some of Georgiana's favorite haunts in downtown Nashville. Elizabeth was somewhat surprised when the dressmakers recognized him at every place. Either Georgiana was a very good customer, or her husband's tall, handsome form attracted its own attention. The young shop girls were quite solicitous, although slightly less enthusiastic when they discovered he was buying a trousseau for his new wife.

Darcy was as stern and forbidding as ever in company. Elizabeth was beginning to learn that this was his way in the presence of people outside his circle of family and friends. She had found that particular trait off-putting when she first met him, but it did not seem to bother others as much as it had her. At the dress shops, he sat in the politely offered chairs located near the mirrors, uncomfortably folding his large frame into the small wooden seats, frowning or nodding his disapproval or approval at the clerks' choices. Sometimes, he simply shrugged as if to say, 'whatever you like.' Elizabeth had grown up listening to strong opinions about her appearance from her mother, but a male perspective on her clothes was a novel experience. It was a particularly odd feeling having her person appraised so closely, especially by a man who had a very good idea of what she looked like without any clothing at all.

This line of thinking led her back to images of the previous evening. She didn't know what she was supposed to think about *that* situation. It was not the horrific experience her mother had predicted nor the tender, warm interlude Aunt Maddie had intimated. If she had to put a word on it, it would be...tolerable. In any event, it was part of being married, and she had best accustom herself to it. She was very thankful that her husband seemed concerned for her comfort. In fact, except for that one moment last night, when he pushed into her, he had treated her with kid gloves, as if she were a delicate flower that would crumble under the slightest pressure. He was very attentive, and it pleased and yet slightly embarrassed her. She wondered if his consideration would last once they returned home. Special treatment seemed unnecessary to her. She was now a farmer's wife after all, and had no expectations of leading a pampered existence that might have been hers, if her family had remained in Chicago. That future was long lost now.

She stood back and looked at her reflection in the mirror. The dress was undeniably beautiful; she had to admit his taste was exquisite in regards to her clothing. The plum-colored silk gown had a boat neck and capped sleeves, and the skirt was cut on the bias, so it flared out jauntily at her feet. The back plunged almost to her waist, leaving her feeling somewhat bare and indecent. She had blushed furiously when the dressmaker pulled her aside and asked her if she had 'foundation garments' that would 'accommodate the lines of the bodice'. Elizabeth had no idea such underthings even existed.

They had ended up with four everyday and two Sunday dresses bought off the rack, the evening gown and a wrap and gloves to go with it, two pairs of shoes, two nightgowns, a new coat and other cold weather items, some lingerie, and three pairs of stockings. Orders had been placed for more clothing, over Elizabeth's protestations at the expense. But then Darcy had frowned and murmured something about 'fitting for your position' and 'my wife', and she had sighed in resignation, not wanting him to think her ungrateful. Did he realize that she would be working mostly in the garden and the barn? Levi denim trousers and work boots, or at least a simple work dress and apron would be more appropriate for those tasks.

This idea led her to speculate what she might actually be doing with her days now. She and Uncle Ed had given Mary her job at the vet office. When she told William this, he had looked at her as if she were stating something painfully obvious. Apparently, her new 'position' as 'his wife' did not include gainful employment. This produced mixed feelings as well. She had become used to contributing monetarily to her family, and had grown to like the idea that she was providing for people who needed her. Now, she existed only to please her husband and run his house, and her recently discovered usefulness was null and void. What was there for her to do at Pemberley? She had met the extremely efficient and hard-working Mrs. Reynolds, who had been running the house without a hitch since Georgiana was an infant. Again, she reproached herself. As Charlotte said, every woman 'within twenty miles' would love to be in her brand new leather shoes right now. Why could she not feel appreciative?

She heard the door to the suite open and close, followed by heavy footfalls. Her husband had returned from his own shopping excursion. She drew in a deep breath, checked her appearance one more time, and tried on a graceful smile. He seemed to like it when she smiled at him. She was superficially pleased with her appearance, but the glamorous woman who stared back at her was a stranger, a façade covering the woman she had come to know in the last seven months.

WILLIAM WAS PULLING OUT HIS suit and tie, when the bathroom door opened. He turned his head at the sound, and his jaw promptly dropped open. He had seen Elizabeth's new evening dress on her earlier in the day, had asked the clerk for that color specifically in fact because he thought it would flatter her. But then they had been in public view and in the harsh light of day. Now the low lamplight gave her hair a soft shimmer and her porcelain skin a warm glow. A slow smile graced her lips and lit up her eyes. She looked like a femme fatale who had walked right off the silver screen and into his bedroom. He shut his mouth self-consciously and turned away from her. He wished now he had ordered dinner served in their room tonight.

"The dress suits you," he murmured, understating the point. He did not want to sound as inane and foolish as he felt or be accused of flattering her with empty praise. "I made reservations for seven o'clock at the restaurant. They have a jazz band that plays after dinner." He poured himself a glass of water and drank it in one long series of swallows.

"That sounds lovely," she replied in a soft voice that set his blood to simmering.

"Be ready in a bit," he said tersely and disappeared behind the bathroom door.

Darcy leaned against the sink with both hands and took several deep breaths in an effort to get control of himself. He looked up at his face in the mirror and saw his pulse hammering against his neck. After a minute or so, he thought he was calm enough to shave without slitting his throat and began assembling his razor.

Spending all day with her had been a blissful torture. The worst had been the dress shops — his eyes gliding over her form, devouring every detail, visualizing her without the garment on at all. He knew she had to wonder why he cared so much about what she wore. In truth, he couldn't care less about the clothes; he just wanted to look at her, constantly. And that thought mortified and terrified him.

Never had he felt this way about anyone. This overwhelming desire to control and possess her, and then sink and drown in her power over him made his tender feelings for Anne seem fraternal in comparison. Had he ever loved Anne at all? Perhaps not if this was what love was like. And he knew he had gone way beyond the admiration and respect he told her about when he proposed; he was falling in love with her, and the pain of it was acute because he knew she didn't return his feelings. He thought after the wedding night he would stop obsessing about her. He told himself it was just infatuation or beginner's nerves, but the actual experience had done nothing to quell the urge to disrobe her, subdue her and demand that she love him in return. He imagined her curls in rumpled disarray, her eyes warm and inviting, her red lips speaking the words, and felt himself rousing to the call of his imagination.

"Mmphh!" he growled, deep in his throat, and threw the razor down on the sink. He stepped over to the tub; washing with cold water would temporarily get his rutting mind off *that*.

Darcy was standing before the mirror once again, getting ready to shave, his mind calmed by water and quiet, physical hunger beginning to replace hunger of another, more carnal kind. He told himself that he must keep control of his emotions. He saw the pain his father suffered when his mother died; the man was almost incapacitated with grief. He had seen that pain in the wrinkled face of Mrs. Reynolds years after Mr. Reynolds had passed. He knew what love cost those who were left behind. Hadn't he experienced it to some degree after Anne? Additionally, he knew how Richard had suffered after the death of his wife. Look what love had done to him. He considered soberly. Look what it had done to Gi.

Darcy reminded himself he was certifiable to risk loving a woman who held him in no special regard. She was a good person; she was kind to him, but she didn't love him back. Perhaps in time... No, he shook his head. He could not think that far into the future. First, he had to get through this honeymoon; first, he had to make it through this night.

He had just covered his face in lather, when a faint knock on the door startled him.

"William? I left my comb in there; may I come in and get it?"

He opened the door and grinned slightly at her gasp of surprise.

"I'm sorry I'm not quite presentable, but I am decent." He was wearing his trousers and a ribbed sleeveless undershirt, although his feet were still bare. A lock of wet hair fell over his forehead.

She blushed profusely and lowered her eyes. "It's no matter." She walked around him, keeping her eyes averted, but after she found the comb, she dared a look up at him. He was drawing the razor down his face in a way she found fascinating, and she continued to watch him intently.

He looked at her, reflected in the mirror behind him, perched on the edge of the tub. "Did you never watch your father shave?" he asked, mildly amused.

His question broke her concentration and she smiled. "Not for many years." She paused as he went on shaving absentmindedly. "It's different, isn't it?"

"What is?" he asked, reaching down and rinsing out the razor before drying it and placing it back in its case. He toweled off his face.

"Living with someone else, I mean, living with a man — or a woman. Getting used to their ways, their things." She stood up and reached around him, running a finger down the handle of the razor.

He turned to her, leaning back against the sink and crossing his arms over his chest. "Yes, it's different. Do you think it will be unbearable?"

She gave him one of her brilliant smiles and his heart exploded. "No, not unbearable. Unbearable is Kitty and Lydia fighting over who gets the bath water first while they're standing in the mud room where we can all hear them."

He shuddered dramatically for effect, and she laughed. How he loved to hear her laugh! She tilted her head and reached over to take the towel from the rack. He raised an eyebrow in question, and she leaned close to him and dabbed some shaving cream from behind his ear.

"There you go — spic and span." She trailed a finger tentatively down his jaw.

William closed his eyes, basking in the pleasure of her touch, but his earlier savage thoughts had given way to more familiar, tender feelings. "Thank you."

She gave him an odd look and brought her hand down suddenly. "You're welcome," she replied hastily and hurried out of the room.

WILLIAM SIPPED HIS COFFEE AND scanned the dining room's entrance for his wife. She had left him sitting there and had gone to the ladies' room a few minutes ago. The band was warming up, and people were milling about between the tables and near the edges of the dance floor. The crowd had picked up considerably since the dinner hour. Abruptly, she reappeared, and he met her searching gaze with a lift of his hand. She smiled brightly and headed toward him, weaving through the throng of people and making her excuses as she went. When she was only a couple of tables away, she accidentally backed into a tall man, perhaps in his early twenties. She turned around rapidly and he caught her elbow to keep her from stumbling. Darcy saw her flush and bumble out an apology, which the young man accepted with a handsome smile. Darcy frowned as the man turned back around to watch her walk away and almost sputtered in indignation when the young pup's eyes traveled down and stopped right below the back of her dress. He bolted to his feet, but by the time she reached the table, the man had disappeared into the crowd, leaving Darcy feeling angry and slightly foolish. *Surely, you realized men were going to look at her in that dress. After all, you looked at her too.* He tried to hide his expression, but it was too late; she had seen him scowling.

"What's the matter?" she asked innocently.

"Nothing," he replied in a clipped tone.

"Are we leaving?" She sounded a little wistful.

"No, I..." he fished around for some reason for standing so suddenly. "I thought you'd like to dance, that's all." He held out his hand.

"Oh," she answered, "Yes, I'd love to."

Darcy looked around, wanting to show the unwelcome trespasser that this lady was taken, but the man was nowhere to be seen.

They danced in silence through several songs. Then, as the strains of "Stormy Weather" began, Darcy pulled Elizabeth close, his mood beginning to match his expression. The torch singer's sultry alto was plaintively crooning about separation and loneliness. He traced a sure, possessive circle on her bare back, and he breathed in the vaguely familiar scent of jasmine. He had not remembered her wearing that fragrance before yesterday, but now, it immediately invoked memories of their wedding night. *Let the cad look,* he thought smugly. *She's my wife, and she's going home with me.*

Elizabeth pulled back and looked up at him. "William, are you all right?"

He looked down at her searchingly. "Yes, why?"

"You seem... worried or distracted."

He consciously relaxed his furrowed brow and tried a brief smile. "I'm fine."

"Good." She brought her eyes back level with his shoulder, wishing she could see over it and look around the room. A change in music caught her attention, and she listened to a few bars to see if she recognized the tune.

"What is this song? I don't think I've heard it before."

"Really?" he answered. "Cole Porter wrote it. It's called "Night and Day.""

"The melody is beautiful." She sighed, relaxing into his arms a little further and he felt her curls brush his downturned cheek. He was unconsciously humming, and he felt her smile. He pulled back, realizing he was nearly embracing her in front of all these people, but she didn't seem concerned.

"I'd..." he began softly, "I'm... ready to go back to the hotel. If you are," he added hastily.

She looked in his eyes a long moment, as if trying to discern what she saw there. "All right. Just let me step over to the table and grab my wrap."

"I'll get it," he volunteered. Before she could respond, he had turned away and stridden over to fetch her fur-lined wrap from the back of her chair. As he slowly made his way back to her, he halted at the sight of the trespasser, approaching Elizabeth with two glasses in his hand and a smooth grin on his face. Darcy quickened his pace and managed to cut the man off, looking down on him with a fierce glare. He turned toward Elizabeth and held the wrap for her, covertly lifting her left hand and displaying her wedding ring with a pointed look at the man. The fellow looked slightly shocked, but then nodded in understanding with an 'aha' on his lips and gave Darcy an approving smirk — which he was tempted to wipe forcibly off the nitwit's face.

The ride to the hotel was a quiet one. Elizabeth stifled a little yawn and leaned her head against the car window. William kept his eyes focused on the road, and wondered if there would always be this awkwardness between them.

ELIZABETH APPROACHED THE BED SLOWLY. William looked up at her from where he was sitting with his back against the headboard, reading the newspaper. He gave her a gentle smile.

"Coming to bed, Mrs. Darcy?"

She startled at the appellation, but then she nodded. She rounded the foot of the bed, hurriedly slipped her robe off and laid it on the chair, before climbing in on her side. She pulled the covers up to her chin and stared up at the ceiling, wondering what he would do next. Her mother and Maddie had both suggested that he would want to…well, more often than not.

He looked at her, noting her wide-eyed uncertainty. This was not a good situation. He regretted anew his inability to control himself the night before. He looked casually back at the newspaper.

"Roosevelt's inauguration is next week," he remarked, turning the page. "I wonder what he will say in his inaugural address."

Elizabeth rolled to her side and propped her head on her hand. "Do you think he can help? End the Depression, that is?"

He smiled. "Oh, I don't know, perhaps. The situation will right itself at some point anyway."

He looked at her, and was surprised by the earnest expression on her face. He found himself a little pleased too; she was asking for and interested in his honest opinion of the matter. He put the paper down. "The markets run in cycles, see? It's typical for them to go up and down."

"And men who invest try to buy stocks when the prices are low and sell them when the prices are high," she added.

He gave her a slightly puzzled glance and nodded his head in admiration. "That's right. But in this case, a sort of fever took over — some men even borrowed money to start buying stocks that were priced too high. When the prices started falling so rapidly — the Crash — many people panicked and tried to sell all their stocks at once and there was no one to buy. The prices kept going lower, to the point where they couldn't sell their stocks for what they had borrowed."

"And so they couldn't pay the loans back," she mused.

"Basically. I mean, that was one reason for the Depression."

She looked at him and blurted out, "That's what happened to my father. He also borrowed money to buy our house and then when he lost his job, he couldn't pay the mortgage because his savings — what little there was — was gone. The bank took the house, and we came here." Her eyes were shiny.

William slid down, facing her, and propped his own head on his hand. He reached for her hand and intertwined their fingers.

"There were other factors too. One was the bad droughts, which made growing food almost impossible in some areas. So people who were poor had no money, and then they had no food either. Also there was a decrease in crop prices; in some areas the markets were flooded with extra goods like corn and grain, so the prices went down. Many farmers depleted their soil because they planted the same things year after year with less and less success. That's one of the reasons I'm so careful about rotating crops. You know what that means, right?"

"Oh yes, my uncle and my father discussed crop rotation when we moved here."

"Ah."

"How did you escape?" she inquired solemnly.

"Escape?"

"The Depression."

"I didn't 'escape' the Depression; very few people did — maybe some of the very rich. I lost some money in the stock market, like most everyone else. But I didn't have all my money in stocks, or in one bank. I was diligent about checking on my investments, so when things started to turn, I did pull some out of the market."

"So you were smarter than everyone else?"

He smiled wryly. "No, you won't trap me into an arrogant statement like that, my wife." He rolled to his back and pulled her with him, resting her hand over his heart. "I *was* diligent, but luck also played a role. If you could call it 'luck.'" He lowered his voice. "A lot of the bank trouble occurred about the time Gigi came home; my expenses went up suddenly, having a family in the house, so I needed more cash at the ready."

He twisted his head around to look at her. "Also, you were right when you said Pemberley was left to me; it was, but most of my money was inherited from my mother's family."

"Really?"

"She was the only heiress to a small railroad fortune. Her family was from upstate New York."

"She was a Northern girl, like me?"

"Yes," he smiled slightly, settling his cheek against her hair and breathing in the delicious scent of her. "My grandfather was not pleased when she decided to marry a farmer, even a well-to-do one. He never forgave my mother for that, never spoke to her again. She was their only surviving child though, and both of my grandparents were only children too. So in the end, there was no other heir to their fortune, except her."

Elizabeth rose up on her elbow, her face animated with indignation. "That is...terrible! How could someone disown a child for following her heart?"

"It was a different world then, a different generation. I think she made her peace with it, although it did always grieve her a little." He shrugged.

She was silent for a minute, and he realized he was running his fingers up and down her arm. She seemed less nervous now, and didn't stiffen when he put his arms around her and drew her close. A warm, contented feeling had suffused throughout his body, but it was quickly being replaced with an even warmer urgency. He leaned close to her ear and murmured in a husky voice, "You looked very beautiful tonight, Elizabeth." He kissed her behind the ear and she shivered. "I should have told you before now. I...I'm not used to saying what's on my mind. You'll be patient with me, yes?"

She nodded breathlessly, and he turned her face to kiss her. Still pressing his lips to hers, he reached a long arm behind him and turned out the bedside lamp, bringing a comforting dark. The moonlight shone through the curtain, illuminating her gown as he eased it off her shoulders. He said not another word as he moved over and within her in gentle, rhythmic strokes, touching her hair, her face, her shoulders and breasts and sides, in a tender assault on her senses.

She gasped when he pushed inside her, his breath warm and harsh in her ear. She felt an odd sense of power when he finally shuddered and surrendered to her. A strange warmth flickered inside her like the glow of a tiny candle flame when she came back to bed after visiting the bathroom. He was already asleep, a peaceful smile on his lips and that lock of dark wavy hair over his forehead. She brushed it back tenderly, and he rolled toward her, drawing her close and mumbling "Lizzy" before he settled into a deep, restful slumber.

March 2, 1933
"GOOD LORD, WILLIAM! DON'T YOU think ten pounds of candy is enough for two little girls?" Elizabeth shook her head in amusement.

William turned his severe frown on her, but she caught the glimmer of mischief in his eyes. "We have to stock up; I don't know when I'll get back to town."

She chuckled. He had been using that excuse in every clothing, book, jewelry, toy and candy shop they had entered in the last four days. She supposed that if he truly did not come into town that often, he would not spend himself in the ground. The extravagance seemed almost obscene.

"You better stock up on toothbrushes and baking soda to wash their teeth, too."

He looked at her haughtily. "Well, of course, I will."

"Gigi's going to have kittens when she sees all this," she muttered.

"What's your favorite chocolate, Elizabeth?" he called from the glass counter a few feet away.

"Hmm?"

"Your favorite?"

"Oh, I don't need any."

"Of course you don't *need* any; what do you *like?*"

"Just a variety, I guess." She had a favorite — caramels — but a variety would suit all her sisters. Jane liked creams, Mary favored mints, Kitty liked pecan nut clusters and Lydia liked anything fruity. He had the confectioner assemble a foil box full of various chocolates and joined her near the door.

They exited the shop, walking slowly up Church Street before ducking into a diner for a meat and three lunch.

"Will you be glad to get home?" he asked, looking thoughtfully at her from across the table.

She nodded.

"It will be good to settle in, begin to make Pemberley your home. Now remember, Mrs. Reynolds is very efficient, and she's used to having her own way, but if there's something you want to change, you have my backing. Don't be afraid to tell her so."

Elizabeth shrugged and waved him off. "Oh, I'm sure the house is just fine the way it is."

He frowned. It disturbed him that she seemed to have such little interest in her new home. He had vaguely wondered if she might be like Caroline Bingley and completely redecorate the entire house. A thought occurred to him, and brought a tiny smile to lips. *So much for all the gossips who thought she married me for my money. I can't even get her to change the curtains in the kitchen.*

"Will you be glad to see the girls? And rot their teeth with candy?"

He gave her a grimace of a smile, but then his face softened. "Yes, I've missed them, and Gigi too."

Her heart warmed at his obvious affection; it bode well for their own children, when they came. A father's devotion and attention were important for raising them healthy and happy. She wondered, not for the first time, what had happened with the girls' father. It was as if he vanished into the mist. Her newfound connection with her husband gave her the nerve to ask.

"William?"

"Hmm," he muffled, through a mouthful of mashed potatoes and fried pork tenderloin.

"What happened to Gigi's husband?"

He froze in mid-bite and looked at her with a flash of…was it fear? And what on Earth did the powerful man before her have to be afraid of? As suddenly as it had appeared, it was gone, replaced with a dark, forbidding frown. He sat up straight and swallowed slowly.

"Why…would you ask me that?"

She met his gaze evenly. "Gigi and the girls are my family now. Don't you think I should know?"

"No, I don't," he snapped.

She was startled, confused at the vehemence in his voice. Perhaps it was a painful memory.

"Did he die?" She reached across the table, hand outstretched to comfort him on his loss, but he just stared at her.

After a long minute, he replied. "No, he did not."

She withdrew her hand. "Why doesn't anybody talk about him?"

"He is not to be mentioned in my house…ever. Do you understand me, Elizabeth?"

She stared at him, open-mouthed and not a little angry.

"I will not subject Georgiana to the pain of remembering what happened, and under no circumstances are you to discuss this with the girls. Even if they ask you, which I doubt, do not say anything, make any speculation, or even have them ask their mother. Send them to me. I will take care of it." His eyes focused over her shoulder. He was obviously seeing something or someone from the past. "Ruth was too young to remember, but Maggie may have some…" He drifted off for a few minutes before returning to the present and skewering Elizabeth with a dangerously cold-blooded look. It felt as if the temperature in the room actually dropped several degrees.

"Do not ever mention it again. I forbid it." He sat back, and pushed his plate from the edge of the table. "When you finish your lunch, we'll head over to the hotel to pack. We need to leave for Meryton by three o'clock. We're expected at Pemberley for supper."

Elizabeth took a bite of her lunch, but it tasted like sawdust in her mouth.

"I'm finished," she replied slowly, her stomach churning with shock and anger. *I don't know why I thought he had changed. Why should he suddenly grow a conscience and some feelings, just because we married?* The sting of being berated like a child was almost too much to take. Yet she had agreed to this life, and she was dependent on his good will now. She had chosen to marry him, even knowing what he was. *But did I know what he truly was? Why won't he just tell me about the man? What is he afraid I will find out?*

DARCY SHIFTED HIS GAZE OVER to his new wife. She was looking steadfastly out the passenger side window. He groaned inwardly. He knew he had upset her earlier with his harsh words. She was perfectly polite after they returned to the hotel, but the beautiful smiles, the ones that set his blood ablaze, were gone. He would have to apologize for his manner, but the substance of what he said was not to be questioned. Even talk of that man poisoned everyone within earshot of the conversation. But how to apologize, without stirring up more questions? He wasn't sure. Perhaps he should just not say anything else about it. Yes, just go on from here. She would forget all about it in a day or two. And he would be more careful how he spoke to her from now on. He glanced over at her again out of the corner of his eye. She was leaning against the door with her chin on her hand. Her hair was swept up and showed off the delicate shell of her ear and the ivory curve of her neck. He shifted uncomfortably, and reached for the hand that was closest to him. He lifted it to his lips and kissed it gently, giving her a meaningful look. She looked back in surprise, and then smiled — a brief quirk of lips that did not make her eyes light up. He let go of her and took hold of the wheel again with both hands.

"We should be home in about an hour. I'm sure you'll want to rest up before supper."

She hesitated, but then in a resigned voice, she replied, "Yes, thank you, that would be nice."

Chapter 17

Changes at home

March 7, 1933

"William, may I speak with you a minute?"

"Of course." He indicated a chair, and Georgiana sat down. He smiled ruefully. "I had no idea that being gone for a few days would put me this far behind with correspondence and other mundane tasks. When I do them a little at a time, they don't seem like much, but I guess things add up."

She smiled, a little nervously, he thought. "You work too hard, William. It was good for you to get away and spend some time with Elizabeth. These tasks will get done in time."

"Yes, well…" He paused and looked at her expectantly. "What is it, Gi?"

She braced herself and delicately cleared her throat. "I've decided to move out of the big house."

William sat and looked at her, too surprised to utter a word.

"While you were in Nashville, Mrs. Reynolds and I went down and cleared out the foreman's cottage. It cleaned up real nice. Richard helped me find someone to install some indoor plumbing and electricity. I've gotten spoiled with modern conveniences, living here again. It just makes taking care of the girls so much easier if there's a real bathroom and hot water. I hope you don't mind the expense."

"Of course I don't mind, but…"

"I'm quite determined, William, so please don't try to talk me out of it. I've been considering this for a while, and now, with your marriage, it seems like a good time to carry it out. You know what Aunt Catherine says, *'It doesn't work to have two families living in the same house.'*"

William rolled his eyes, and Georgiana laughed.

"Yes, I know she has some odd opinions about things, but she's right about that one."

"Just because Elizabeth is here, it doesn't mean you have to leave. She knows that this is your home; she's not territorial, and I think she likes your company."

"I like hers too, but this is the way it should be. You're starting your own family now." He opened his mouth to contradict her, but she held up her hand. "No, it's wonderful that you're going on with your life. I'm happy for you. And now, I need to get on with mine."

He sat in silence, scowling. Then, another thought occurred to him, and he looked up at her with a doleful expression. "What about the girls?"

"They will adapt, as they always do. Ruth will not know the difference after a week or so, and Maggie has been bribed with the possibility of getting a cousin or two out of the deal." She gave him a wry smile. "I made no promises for you, though, so you can relax for now. Although I can't guarantee she won't ask you about it at some point, so be planning what you'll say to her."

"But who will read to Maggie at bedtime?" he whispered, almost to himself.

"I will. I am her mother, after all. And I am perfectly capable of taking care of her and Ruth."

William startled. "No, I didn't mean you weren't a good mother, Gi..."

She smiled. "I know." She let the silence sit between them for a minute, and then went on. "You will never be able to understand the depth of my gratitude for what you have done for us. Taking us in when we had no home, feeding us, clothing us, helping us escape that horrible situation. And what you've done for the girls! Especially Maggie. Do you remember what she was like when we first came here? She wouldn't even speak! You cared for my daughters as if they were your own... but, William, they aren't your own. They are my children, my responsibility, and I want to raise them my way. Can you understand at all?"

William's frown returned. "No."

She sighed. "Maybe you will understand when you become a father."

"Who put this idea in your head? Fitzwilliam? What is he about anyway — interfering with my family!"

Georgiana lifted her chin. "Richard did not put me up to this; don't take your anger out on him. He only helped me find someone to do the repair work — after I asked him for assistance. The work should be finished by the end of next week, and the cottage will be ready for us to move in."

"You know, I could freeze your trust fund; you don't have control over the disbursement of interest until you're twenty-five."

"You would want to control me that way?"

He didn't reply.

Her grey eyes glinted like steel. "It wouldn't matter; I would still go. I'd get a job in town. I can still live in the cottage; you can't make me leave Pemberley. I do own part of it."

He sighed dejectedly. "No, I wouldn't do that; the trust fund is your money. I would have let you have it all those years you were gone if I had known what kind of circumstances you were in or how to find you."

Her expression softened.

"Honestly, it will be all right. Think of it as an opportunity, a way of opening up possibilities. I do. There weren't many things I liked when I lived so far away, but one thing I did like was running my own house — such as it was."

He looked at her dubiously.

"When I first came home, I was physically weak from having Ruth, and emotionally weak from guilt and a broken heart, but because you took care of me, I'm strong again. And now, thanks to you, I can be the mother I should be, the kind of mother I want to be."

There was a long pause. Finally, William spoke in a resigned voice as he stood up. "Well, I guess you are just down the road a piece."

Georgiana smiled brightly and put her arms around her brother's neck for a fierce hug. "Exactly right."

"I'll want to see them most every day."

"You will. You'll continue to spoil them like you always have." She grinned, but it faded to a soft look of affection. "You're a good man. I hope Elizabeth realizes the treasure she's found." Her eyes grew misty. "Thank you, William, for everything." She turned away before he could see her tears.

William sat down heavily in his chair. The dusk settled around him as he stayed at his desk, not working, not moving, but alone with his thoughts.

WILLIAM SAT ON THE BED and reached down to remove his boots. As he unlaced them, he looked over his shoulder. "Georgiana and the girls are moving."

Elizabeth looked up from her book. "What? Why?"

102

Darcy detailed the conversation he had with his sister as he moved about the room, getting ready for bed.

"I can see her point, but..." She paused, her eyes opening wide. "Wait a minute! William, this isn't because of me, is it? Because I live here now? I love having her live with us, and the little ones too." Elizabeth gave him a worried frown.

"She says she's been thinking about it for a while, and I believe her." Darcy suddenly threw his boot into the corner of the room, making Elizabeth jump. She sat very still, eyeing him warily. Was this a previously unseen side of him? A temper?

"But it's damned foolish and unnecessary if you ask me." He roughly yanked the quilts and crawled between the sheets. He lay on his side with his back to his wife.

Elizabeth lowered her voice to a gentle lull. "William, are you upset about Maggie and Ruth not living with you anymore?"

"No," he replied shortly.

She leaned over and put her hand on his shoulder. "The foreman's cottage is very close."

He replied to her in sharp tones. "I don't know what Georgiana is thinking; they're all much better off living here, but it's what she wants."

Elizabeth withdrew her hand. Her husband obviously didn't want her sympathy. Maybe he didn't need it. Still, she felt sad, for him — because even if he wouldn't admit it to her, she knew he would miss them, and also for herself — having Georgiana in the house meant there was someone to talk to, someone to laugh with. She had grown quite fond of her sister-in-law. With her and the little girls gone, there would be no one to talk to except Mrs. Reynolds and... him.

She heard the low sound of his breathing, but she could tell he wasn't asleep. She turned out the lamp and rolled over on her side, facing away from him. *I have a feeling it's about to get very lonely in this house.*

Chapter 18

Thunder and Lightning

April 9, 1933

Outside the dining room window, lightning streaked across the sky, followed by a loud boom of thunder a few seconds later. The lights flickered, and Elizabeth stopped with her fork half-way to her mouth, watching. Darcy frowned as he chewed, which Elizabeth thought was quite a feat.

Ruth let out a fearful wail, and Georgiana hurried over to her highchair, cooing and consoling her while she wiped off her hands and face.

Elizabeth stole a glance at Maggie, wondering if the girl was also afraid of storms. There she sat, tucking into mashed potatoes and fried chicken seemingly without a care in the world. Elizabeth smiled at her and got a friendly grin in return. Over time, Elizabeth had come to realize that Maggie rarely cried or was frightened. She was verbally precocious and could be reasoned out of any typical childhood fear. As a result, she appeared wise beyond her years. She was gifted and cursed with what Elizabeth's Aunt Madeline called 'an old soul.' Her dark brown eyes fixed on Elizabeth's face.

"Ruth is afraid of thunderstorms, but I'm not."

Elizabeth started to reply, but was surprised when Sheriff Fitzwilliam, who had joined them for Sunday dinner, ventured a reply. "Ruth is very little, sugar bean, and loud noises scare little children. But you're a big girl, and you understand about thunderstorms, so you're not afraid of them anymore."

"Nope, I'm not."

"So maybe Ruth will watch you and see that you're not afraid, and someday you can tell her all about 'em so she'll understand. And then, maybe she won't be so scairt of 'em."

Maggie looked at him skeptically as if trying to decide if he was teasing or serious. He met her direct gaze with his own and gave her a kindly smile. Then he took a bite of biscuit and turned toward Darcy.

"Guess you won't be doin' no plantin' today. Bet it'll rain all afternoon."

"Mmph," Darcy grunted, scowling.

Richard grinned as he chewed, also quite a feat in Elizabeth's opinion. He swallowed his bite of biscuit. "Serves you right, tryin' to work on the Lord's Day."

Darcy leaned toward his friend, giving him a scathing glare. "My ox is in the ditch," he said slowly.

At that, Richard tipped his head back and let out a cheerful laugh. He turned to Elizabeth. "Mrs. Darcy, were you aware that your husband is an awful curmudgeon when he is at his own house on a Sunday afternoon with nothing to do?"

Elizabeth only smiled and took another bite of green beans, sneaking a look under her lashes at the object of the sheriff's teasing to see how he took it.

"He would not get away with it either if he weren't such a big, tall son-of-a-gun."

"I am not a 'curmudgeon.' Am I, Gi?"

Georgiana's lips twitched. "Hmm, let me think about it … I have to say — as your adoring sister — that you definitely are … a curmudgeon." She smiled brightly across the table at Fitzwilliam, and they caught each other's eyes for a long moment before quickly looking away. Elizabeth, however, saw the wordless exchange.

Interesting. She filed that information away to consider at a later time.

Darcy frowned at his plate. "I need to get that back field planted if we're going to have corn 'knee-high by the Fourth of July.'"

Richard set his napkin beside his empty plate. "Well, there's no use worrying about that today," he said with finality. "Excellent dinner, Mrs. Darcy."

"Thank you, Sheriff. You can thank Mrs. Reynolds too; she's been teaching me some of her wonderful cooking skills. I'm learning them because I wanted her to have Sundays off." Elizabeth's eyes flitted across the table to her husband. He was staring at her with an intense, but unreadable look. That, at least, had not changed since their marriage.

"Oh, and thank Georgiana too. She made the biscuits … and the pecan pie.

We'll have some later with coffee."

"Pecan pie is my favorite," he returned, winking at Georgiana. "So what should we do this afternoon, Darcy, since you can't plant your cornfield?"

Darcy shrugged noncommittally.

"How about a game of Rook? I know Georgiana will play and you too, Mrs. Darcy. You'll play, won't you? We'll need a fourth."

"I don't know how, I'm afraid."

"So we'll teach you," he insisted.

"Yes, Mrs. Darcy, you should play," William ventured in his smooth, deep voice. "I have discovered that you're very adept at learning new skills. You're a very accomplished woman and take pleasure in many things." His lips twitched, and there was a glimmer of teasing humor in his eyes.

Elizabeth looked at him curiously, wondering what he was about. "Well, I suppose I can't turn down such a blatant challenge to my intellect, can I? My pride would not allow otherwise." She gave him a bewitching, impudent smile.

Georgiana put the girls down for naps while Elizabeth cleared the table, and the next couple of hours were devoted to teaching Elizabeth the subtleties of card playing. William offered to be her partner, of course, and although Richard and Georgiana beat them soundly, she learned how to bid her hand and count trumps and what 'shoot the moon' meant. She couldn't remember the last time she had laughed so much, or enjoyed her company more. More than once, she looked up and caught her husband staring at her in a way that made her spine tingle and her face feel hot. The rain poured steadily throughout the afternoon, but the atmosphere inside was cheerful and warm. Even the stoic William Darcy was coaxed into an occasional smile.

Later, Richard volunteered to take Georgiana and the girls back to the cottage in his truck. After they left, a gentle quiet settled over the house. The Darcys enjoyed a light supper, and Elizabeth sat down to read in the parlor, as she did many nights. William disappeared into his study, as he also did many nights, but after about a half an hour, he returned with a bottle and two old-fashioned glasses in his hands.

The glasses clinked as he set them on the table, causing Elizabeth to look up. "What is that?"

"Why, Mrs. Darcy, that is a glass and that is another glass — I've already used that one — and this is a bottle of Kentucky's finest bourbon."

"Bourbon? You mean bourbon whiskey?"

"Yes, ma'am. I thought perhaps you'd like to have a drink with me."

"I've never had a drink before."

"No, I would imagine not. It's illegal, you know, to buy and sell whiskey in these United States. But never fear, I did not buy this bottle illegally. And I'm sure as hell not going to sell it — I like the bourbon too much."

"However did you get it then?" she asked, more curious than shocked.

Her serious, staid husband's voice was cloaked in amusement. "Inquisitive, aren't we?" He opened the bottle and poured one glass about two fingers deep. The other he barely splashed with the amber liquid. Elizabeth could smell it from where she was sitting — a sweet, thick, pungent scent. He handed her the glass with a little in it, and sat down beside her on the couch.

"Fitzwilliam gave it to me."

"The sheriff?" Her expression was incredulous.

"He confiscated it during an arrest, and knowing how much I enjoy a glass of bourbon now and then, he brought it to me. Very neighborly of him, I thought. Go ahead, try some — just a little now; it's strong."

Elizabeth brought the glass to her lips, sniffing daintily. She wrinkled her nose, and he laughed. She took a tiny sip and carefully swallowed.

"Not bad — in small quantities."

"A Northern girl who can drink bourbon — what an anomaly you are…Mrs. Darcy." He looked at her steadily over the rim of his glass as he took a somewhat larger sip of his own. Then he slid back to sit on the brocade-covered sofa, laying his arm across the top of it. He crossed his ankle over one knee and rested his drink on the other.

They sat in silence for a minute. She took another, larger sip.

"Come Mrs. Darcy, we must have some conversation."

"Some conversation?" she smiled, remembering their dance at Bingley's — was it only last fall? It seemed so long ago now. "Hmm…let's see…" She took another sip. Very quietly, she asked, "Well, maybe you could tell me how long Georgiana has been in love with Richard Fitzwilliam."

He choked and sputtered. "What?"

"You heard me. Didn't you notice today, the way she looked at him?"

"Georgiana's not in love with Fitzwilliam. She couldn't be; he's fifteen years older than she is."

Her voice was filled with amusement. "Why would that matter?"

He shook his head vigorously. "No, you're wrong. When she first came home, he helped us with…some legal things. I'm sure she's fond of him, but she views him as a close family friend, that's all."

Elizabeth leveled a direct look at him. "I think I know a woman in love when I see one."

He set his glass on the end table and leaned toward her. "And how would you know that?" he asked in a condescending voice. Then he paused. "Have you ever been in love? Perhaps with some all-star football player or handsome med student at Northwestern?"

"Me? Heavens, no, I was never in love before." She looked down. "I wasn't particularly interested when I was in school, and after we moved here…well, girls like me don't have the luxury of infatuation."

"Girls like you?"

"Girls in my circumstances…poor girls." She shrugged and looked down into her glass, self-consciously taking another sip. "How about you?" she returned, eager to turn the conversation away from herself. "Have you ever been in love? Oh yes, of course you were — with Anne de Bourgh."

He sought and held her gaze. He seemed at once both far away and yet focused completely on her. "I thought I was…but now…" He drifted off.

"Now?" she prompted, not knowing if she wanted to hear his answer or not.

He shook his head. "Never mind. That was a long, long time ago. Would you like a little more whiskey?" He stood up to fetch the bottle.

"Maybe a little more," she nodded and held out her glass.

"All right, but this should probably be it for you. We don't want you waking up with a headache tomorrow."

William stopped, holding the bottle in mid-air. "Listen," he said reverently. He walked over to the radio and turned the volume up a little. Elizabeth heard the strains of "Night and Day" coming through the speaker. It was a thin, tinny sound compared to the band's live rendition they heard in the Nashville jazz club. He took the glass from her hand and pulled her up into a dancing embrace anyway.

He clasped her hand gently and moved her in small smooth steps. She was a little light-headed from the whiskey, just enough to let him guide her effortlessly to the music. His cheek rested against her hair, and she felt his warm, bourbon infused breath in her ear as he sang softly:

…in the roaring traffic's boom, in the silence of my lonely room,
I think of you…night and day

Elizabeth felt warm and tingly all over. She tried to pull away slightly, but he only flattened his hand against her lower back and drew her closer.

…and this torment won't be through,
till you let me spend my life making love to you…

There was a brilliant lightning flash, and the lights flickered once, twice and went out, surrounding them with a close, intimate darkness. Darcy had stopped when the music and lights went off, but still he held her, waiting. He pulled back as if to look at her face, and his low, smooth voice slowly covered her, like sugar cane molasses running down a bottle. He sang the rest of the line.

…day and night, night and day

The room was silent then, and his mouth was coming closer to her, closer, closer…and his lips were on hers, not tentatively like he usually kissed her, as if she were made of glass, but surely, confidently. Her hand slid from his, and she wrapped it around his neck, feeling the soft dark waves of his hair between her fingers. His lips slid over hers, drawing her lower lip between them. She gasped and he proceeded to plunder her mouth in rhythmic, devouring kisses. Elizabeth had never imagined kissing could be like this. This made her feel the way some of her dreams did: wanting something, just something — and then she always woke up gulping air and with her skin on fire. She made a weak noise in the back of her throat and he broke away, resting his forehead against hers.

"William, the lights," she whispered breathlessly after a few seconds.

"Will probably be off until tomorrow." He led her to a cabinet by the stair, where he reached into a drawer and drew out a candle, a candlestick holder and a book of matches. He struck the match and it hissed, the smell of sulfur wafting through the air. The candle flame cast a warm light and threw shadows about the room. The flame's light gave William a mysterious, intriguing appearance as he backed toward the stair, pulling her gently by the hand.

"Come." His husky voice seemed to emanate from all around her. Slowly, they made their way upstairs to the bedroom. He set the candle on the nightstand and turned the bed down. Then he approached her, stopping when there were just a few inches between them. His hands slid up her arms and around her shoulders. He drew a finger around the neckline of her dress and dipped it into the space between her breasts. She sighed, and he looked at her, as if asking permission. She smiled shakily, and his fingers began undoing the buttons down the front. When he reached her waist, he slid his hands under the fabric, caressing her sides before he returned to her shoulders to push the dress off.

Elizabeth felt as skittish as a newborn foal. He had never tried to undress her before; she always came to bed with her nightgown and robe already on. But he was different tonight...she was different. It was as if they had some new understanding, some connection that allowed them to know each other's thoughts, each other's wishes. While she was pondering how this could possibly have happened, she realized he had divested her of her bra and she was naked to the waist. He ran his hands over her, studiously cataloging each nook and cranny, dip and swell. His palm curved around one firm breast and he held it in his hand, his thumb gliding across it, making her shiver in response. He studied her face, and then slowly, he sat down on the edge of the bed and lowered his mouth to her breast, bestowing on it a kiss and a gentle taste from his tongue. Heat surged through her body and settled down below her belly. Her knees nearly buckled.

He returned to her waist and unbuttoned just enough to let the dress slide down and pool around her feet. He pushed her undergarments to the floor. She opened her mouth to protest, to protect her modesty; after all, he surely would not want to look at that part of her!

He put a finger over her lips as he stood back up. "Ssshh," he whispered. That was all he said, but it spoke volumes; he was calling the shots tonight. He picked up her hands and laid them on his chest, bringing her fingers to his shirt buttons. She took his unspoken cue and began working the buttons open, while his head dropped back and his eyes fluttered closed. When the shirt was off, he guided her hands to the front of his trousers. She could feel his arousal pushing on the fabric, trying to escape. She undid the buckle and drew the zipper down, pushing the clothing down over his legs. She tried to pull his boxers down too, but they were caught on him.

"Whoa, there!" he gasped. "Let me do that, a little more carefully."

She giggled a "sorry."

"Get in bed."

She slipped between the sheets and wondered what he would do next. Before she could turn back around, she felt him, warm and close behind her. She started to face him, but he stayed her motion. "No," he ordered softly. He ran a hand over her hair and held it in his hand for a second, and then he pushed it over her shoulder. She felt his fingers trailing down her spine, followed by his lips, bestowing soft, hot kisses on the paths his fingers had taken. When he reached the swell of her bottom, he filled his palm with her cheek and kneaded it with strong, steady strokes. His tongue traveled back up her spine, and he nipped at the juncture of her neck and shoulder. An unladylike sound escaped her mouth, and she could feel his lips curving into a smile against her shoulder. "Yes," he murmured.

She was momentarily embarrassed, even wondered if he was laughing at her, but her thoughts were distracted when he reached down to her hips and turned them so she was lying face down on the bed. She lifted her head to look over her shoulder at him, but she only saw his silhouette against the candlelight. He scooted closer to her, and she felt his hand reach down between her ankles. He ran his hand surely up between her legs, and by the time he reached her knees, she knew what she wanted. She wanted those warm, rough hands to touch her in the most private places of her body. She spread her legs a little way apart to encourage him, and when he reached her with gentle fingers, she let out a long shuddering sigh. Her head dropped to the pillow and she lost herself to the sensations coursing around her body and settling where his fingers were. He continued, stroking, probing, and she realized that her hips were moving of their own volition against his hand. She no longer cared if he laughed at her; actually, she cared about nothing at all except that he not stop. But he did stop, and when he pulled his hand away, she whimpered softly in despair.

"William, what are you doing?" Her voice was unrecognizable to her, for how low and hoarse it was.

"Mmm," was his only response, and he took hold of her hips again and turned her over to finally face him.

This was more familiar territory for her, and yet, something was very different about it. When he entered her, it was in one long stroke as if she had pulled him into her. She felt like sobbing from relief. And when he moved, she moved with him, starting slowly and then faster, faster. He rose up on one elbow to look at her and the other arm slid under her hips, pulling her even closer. She cried out and her body trembled with the force of release. He put her down and reared up on both hands, arching his back and uttering a triumphant roar to accompany a release of his own.

She lay very still; she couldn't move anyway because she was reasonably sure all her bones had melted. William rested on her heavily, his face in her neck. She could feel his harsh breathing on her skin before he rolled off her onto his back, his forearm across his eyes.

"William? I...I'm not...Do you know what just happened to me?" Her voice was small and uncertain.

He peeked out at her from under his arm. "Yes."

She looked at him with large, round eyes.

He smiled and rolled toward her, propping his head up on his hand, then he reached out tentatively and brushed a piece of hair behind her ear. "It's what I want to happen every time I love you."

She knew he was talking about the act and not the feeling, but when the three words 'I love you' washed over her in his deep, pleasant voice, her heart burned and fluttered.

"Oh." She smiled timidly.

His dimples made an appearance, mere shadows in the candlelight. He reached over and pulled her to him, chest to back, resting his hand on her breast. "It's been a long day, my wife. Go to sleep now."

She yawned and snuggled into him, feeling herself enveloped in warmth and safety. As her eyes fluttered closed, she thought she heard him whisper into her hair, "My Lizzy."

She awoke the next morning shortly after dawn. Sunlight was streaming in the window, nearly blinding her. She stretched languorously and permitted herself a satisfied grin. She turned over, eager to see her husband and face the new day with him, but he was gone. His pillow and the sheets were rumpled, which indicated he had truly slept there with her, but now in the harsh, cold morning light, she realized, once again, she was alone.

Chapter 19

Mother's Day

May 14, 1933

"What a lovely room this is, Mr. Darcy!" Mrs. Bennet gushed, looking around the dining room with awe.

"Thank you," he replied, curtly, silently cursing Mrs. Reynolds for seating him next to his mother-in-law. He could almost see the mischievous twinkle in her eyes when she indicated the chair to Mrs. Bennet. The world saw a sweet, kindly, grey-haired housekeeper, but he knew the truth: Underneath that motherly demeanor, there was an imp who took a naughty delight in making him squirm. Oh, she was loyal as the day was long, and discreet, and efficient, and she loved Gigi and the girls to distraction. And that, William decided, was what would save her from getting fired for subjecting him to the raptures of Mrs. Bennet.

He scowled, watching his wife's mother pick up her spoon and turn it over, eyeing it with the astute appraisal of a dedicated jeweler — or a seasoned gold-digger.

"Was this your mother's silver?"

"Yes."

"I thought so. It's much too fine for Lizzy to have picked it out."

He frowned, and Mrs. Bennet, taking it as indication he might be questioning his choice in spouse, hurriedly replied, "Oh, you know, Lizzy's just so young. She doesn't always think about things like that and how they reflect on a household. I'm sure she'll learn quickly, though. She's clever, I'll give her that." She giggled nervously. "She'd rather buy a leather-bound book than a pretty hat or a piece of china for the house." She leaned toward him and whispered, "It's her father's influence, I'm afraid."

"Mrs. Darcy is not required to decorate the house or her person to 'reflect well' on this household," he said sternly.

Mrs. Bennet, sensing she had annoyed her rich son-in-law but not knowing how, grasped for another topic. "Youth has its own benefits though. Lizzy is healthy and strong, and pretty — if I do say so myself."

He looked down the table at his wife, engaged in a private conversation with Jane.

"But I've been very fortunate; all my girls are attractive — Jane and Lydia are the most beautiful of course..." she stopped, as if suddenly realizing that she had not flattered Mr. Darcy's vanity by suggesting he had chosen the plain daughter.

"How is your sister, Mr. Darcy? She is such a lovely young lady. I saw her the other day at Netherfield's..."

William tuned out his mother-in-law and focused instead on admiring his wife. Mrs. Bennet was right; she was young and pretty, and bursting with health. Her eyes danced as she made a joke to Jane; her cheeks were just the color of a perfectly ripe peach. That lavender dress was so becoming on her. He imagined it sliding off her and squirmed uncomfortably, chastising himself for mentally undressing his wife while her mother sat prattling in his ear.

"...do you know, Mr. Darcy?"

"Hmm?" He jerked himself back to his dinnertime conversation. "Pardon?"

"I was wondering if you knew when Mr. Bingley would return from Glasgow."

"Oh. Probably not for a while. He is working on opening the store there. His aunts seem to have the Meryton store well in hand, so there is no need for him to be here."

"Hmm," Mrs. Bennet sniffed delicately, casting a blatant look at Jane.

He turned his attention to Jane too, and squirmed again, but for a different reason. He remembered his conversation with Bingley back before Christmas.

"Darcy, old man, I need some advice." Charles looked up at his friend uncertainly. "I'm thinking about trying to open a store in Glasgow; the dry goods place there closed last year, so there's a building already established and it's for sale. The store here and the one in Franklin have been doing well, so I have some capital

to invest in start-up."

"Sounds like you've got it all planned out."

"Then there's the personnel issue. I'm sure there are people there looking for work, but I was thinking it would be good to have someone in charge that I knew was capable and responsible. Caroline has already said she doesn't want to move."

Bingley looked up anxiously at his friend. "I was thinking about offering the job to Jane Bennet."

"Jane Bennet?"

"Yes, now, I know what you think about the Bennets, but Jane's very sharp. She's good at designing displays and what she orders from the suppliers always sells. And the customers love her." He fidgeted, shuffling his feet and looking down. "I mean, what's not to love? She's kind, and helpful, and easy to talk with... and beautiful... "

"Charles," Darcy's voice carried a warning tone.

"What?"

"What are you thinking? Don't tell me I have to warn you about trifling with the employees."

Charles looked up at him, offended. "I'm not 'trifling' with Jane Bennet. I really like her. If I could spend some time with her, I think... well, she might be just the girl for me."

Darcy snorted. "How many times have you said those same words about some other woman?"

Bingley grinned sheepishly. "Perhaps. But this time I really mean it. Come on, admit it, man — she's an angel."

"She smiles too much."

Bingley rolled his eyes.

"She is quite pretty, I suppose. But Charles, think very carefully — are you sure she wants your attention?"

Bingley looked taken aback. "What do you mean?"

"What I mean is — have you ever seen any indication that she welcomes your advances?"

"I've hardly made any kind of 'advances' — what kind of man do you think I am?"

"I know that you're a gentleman. But does Jane Bennet know you well enough to know that?"

"Well... "

"And how do you think she might react to what she sees as advances from her boss... given that she needs this job to help support her family? Do you really want

to put her in that position?"

"I never thought about it like that."

"I just think you need to be sure before you consider courting a woman who works for you."

"Exactly." A haughty voice sounded from the doorway. The men turned quickly, alarmed to find Caroline Bingley standing in the doorway, listening to every word they said. Darcy cringed for Charles' sake. He was glad he didn't have to deal with that meddling woman; Charles was much more patient than he would ever be. Too patient, probably.

"William," she cooed. "You always give Charles such good advice. Very sensible. Besides, I like Jane Bennet very much; she is valuable to us at the shop here in Meryton as an employee," *she said, emphasizing the word 'employee' and making it quite clear she didn't want to think of Jane Bennet as anything else — certainly not a member of her family. "And I would hate for you to frighten her off, Charles."*

Perhaps he had overstepped the bounds of friendship on that one. Then again, if Charles had felt what he should have for Jane Bennet, he would not have given up so easily.

His thoughts were interrupted by a shriek from the other end of the table. Lydia Bennet was giggling hysterically. "We should go down and call on Denny at the feed store; maybe we can catch him with his shirt off when he unloads the truck."

Kitty snorted, choking on her food. She grabbed her water and was trying to take a sip, when Mary reached over and gave her a sharp slap between the shoulder blades that sent water all over Kitty's plate.

He looked over at Elizabeth, who was sending her father a pleading look and looking humiliated. Mr. Bennet chewed his food thoughtfully, as if he hadn't heard or seen a thing amiss.

Darcy glanced back at Jane, whose face was frozen in a smile. A woman who would not react to this cacophony must not be affected by much. Charles was probably better off without a woman whose feelings could not be touched.

Chapter 20

In which seeds are planted

May 31, 1933

The Darcys settled into the busy routine of a large farm in the springtime. There was tilling, planting, and fertilizing to be done. Elizabeth learned the rhythms of housekeeping as designed by Mrs. Reynolds. And she discovered an affinity and unexpected talent for gardening.

One evening, as she was returning to the house after weeding, hoeing and otherwise hobnobbing with her precious plants, she saw her husband watching her from the front porch. He looked at her from his perch on the porch swing and shook his head with a 'hmmph'.

"Is that a 'hmmph' of disapproval, or are you speechless at my previously untapped gift for horticulture?" Elizabeth gave him a bright, pride-filled grin. She was very pleased with her first agricultural exploits. She started to walk past him into the house, when he caught her hand and tugged her toward the spot beside him on the swing.

"Oh no, William, I'm filthy. I'll get the cushions all dirty."

"I don't care about the cushions. I've been waiting for you to come up and sit on the swing with me for half an hour, so filthy or not, you're sitting down." He patted the seat beside him and pulled her hand, settling her so her leg touched his and his arm was around her shoulders.

She sat beside him in the gathering dusk, as his foot moved the swing to and fro. The sounds of nighttime were beginning to filter out over the farm. Off in the distance, she heard the low, plaintive maw of a cow, and the rhythmic chirp of crickets. The coolness of the night air chilled her sweaty skin, and she shivered. William's hand slid up and down her arm, giving her some of his warmth. For several minutes, they sat in the blissful silence that comes at the end of a long day.

"The strawberries are ripe."

"Mmm?" he replied.

"Georgiana, Maggie, Ruth and I are going out to the strawberry patch to pick them tomorrow."

"Mmm."

"Mrs. Reynolds is getting too old to do all that bending, so I'm going instead. But she's going to teach me how to make preserves."

"Mmm."

"Do you say anything but 'hmmph' and 'mmm?'"

"Mmm?" he answered, but he was smiling. He drew her gently to his shoulder and looked out over the top of her head toward the woods at the edge of the road. "You don't have to do this, you know," his voice was soft and deep, and it vibrated through her ear from his chest.

"Do what?"

"All this...farming."

She lifted her head and met his eyes directly. "Don't you do farming?"

"When I need to, yes, but it's not something you have to do. We have field hands who could pick the strawberries, for example. Mrs. Reynolds wouldn't have to; in fact, she didn't last year. Gigi and the girls pitch in because Maggie loves strawberries and it's a fun outing for them, but they don't have to either." He rubbed a dirt smudge off her nose and then kissed it.

"Oh, I didn't know."

"I never expected you to do as much as you have. That garden of yours is enormous."

She stiffened slightly. "What did you expect me to do with myself all day? Sit around and do nothing?"

"Well, no. But I thought you might still enjoy reading. If I remember correctly, you did a lot of that last fall and winter."

"I still read in the evenings before I go to bed."

She looked at him pensively. "Do you think it's below you for your wife to work on the farm? Are you ashamed of me?"

His eyebrows rose in surprise. "Of course not, it's just...I'm surprised that's all." He put his other arm around her, inhaling deeply the scent of grass and fresh dirt and her. "There will be enough food to feed an army from that garden. We'll never be able to eat it all," he teased.

She disentangled herself from his embrace and looked away. She had plans for all that extra, but she wasn't sure he would approve of them. As busy as he was, she had not expected him to notice the size of her garden. She set her lips in a thin, determined line. If she had anything to do with it, her family would not have another winter like last, eating soup beans and cornbread most nights for dinner.

He looked at her, puzzled. "What's wrong, Elizabeth? I was only teasing. If the garden makes you happy, then..."

She pasted on a smile. "Oh, nothing's the matter; I'm just tired I suppose — and grimy."

He looked at her intently, but it was hard to read her expression in the soft lamplight that came from inside the front room. He stood up and held out his hand. "Let's go then, can't have you falling asleep all grimy, can we?"

She followed him in, grateful he had not questioned her further.

So IT WAS THAT ONE morning, about a week after that evening's conversation, Elizabeth spent the hours before noon in her garden, weeding. She straightened up, arching her back and stretching to relieve the ache she had acquired from bending over her plants. Gardening challenged her body and mind and was a good substitute for the workload to which she had grown accustomed at her uncle's office. Armed with books from the library, advice from Mrs. Reynolds, and all the seeds, fertilizer and gardening tools her husband and his money could supply, she had laid in a three-season vegetable and herb garden that covered more than half an acre. She had big plans for this garden, but she wondered what her husband really thought about her growing it. Part of her felt guilty for keeping her plans from him, but he had so much money and so much food stored already, and he couldn't really complain about her taking labor from the farm; she was doing the work herself.

She turned at the splutter of a truck making its way up the road toward the big house. Shielding her eyes from the sun, she squinted to try and see who was approaching. When the driver got out and looked around, she recognized Sheriff Fitzwilliam and called to him. He held up his hand in greeting and began walking toward her.

She met him halfway to the house and wiped her hands on her apron.

He touched his hat. "Good morning, Mrs. Darcy."

"Hello. What brings you out here so early in the day?" she smiled brightly.

Fitzwilliam gave her a quick, distracted smile. "Need to see your man if he's around."

Odd for him to be so direct. He's usually full of pleasantries and little anecdotes. I wonder what's going on?

"I'm sorry, Sheriff, he's out in the back field today. They were a few hands short, so he went out to help. I don't expect him before lunch, I mean, dinner." She still had trouble thinking of the midday meal as 'dinner'.

"Ah, well…hmm…I need to get back to town."

"If it's important, I can go find him. Is anything wrong?"

"No, no, nothing wrong, but I do need to talk to him today. When he comes in, could you have him get a hold of me?"

Elizabeth looked at him quizzically. "Sure, I'll tell him."

"I thank ye." He turned to leave.

"If you stop at the house, Mrs. Reynolds will fix you something cool to drink."

He called back to her: "I appreciate that, but I do need to get back. Maybe next time."

"Of course." Elizabeth watched him walk away and get in the truck, while she sipped water from her canteen and considered. The sun was getting high in the sky, but still a couple of hours were left until lunch. Should she go find William? Richard had made a special trip, after all. *No, he said it could wait till lunch. I'll just tell him then.* She corked her canteen and returned to her plants.

When dinner rolled around, though, her husband was nowhere to be seen. The other hands stopped at the water pump outside, talking and laughing while they washed face and hands. As they crowded into the big, eat-in kitchen and seated themselves around the table, she inquired after William.

"He said he was gonna stop at the barn loft and pitch some hay down for the horses 'fore he come in to eat, ma'am."

Mrs. Reynolds pursed her lips and looked at Elizabeth, who smiled at the older woman's expression.

"How about I go fetch him, or at least take him something?"

Mrs. Reynolds' eyes lit up in approval, and before Elizabeth could turn around three times, she was out the door with a picnic lunch for two in a basket.

She entered the barn, waiting for her eyes to adjust to the darkened stalls. Both sets of doors were open, allowing a brisk breeze to flow through and carry off the worst of the smells and the dank heat. She set the basket on a milking pail and listened for sounds of her husband working. The animals were all out in the sunshine, but she could hear footsteps above her and see hay tumbling out of the loft. She headed for the ladder, climbed up and halted at the sight that awaited her.

He was dressed as usual in khaki work trousers and boots, but he was bare to the waist. His back was to her, so he hadn't seen her yet, giving her time to admire him. She steadied herself and stood, transfixed at the tanned back and arms, his lean form showing off powerful muscles gliding under the skin as he worked. Something in her belly clenched as she watched him, moving in rhythm to the *whoosh, whoosh* of the hay being pushed out of the loft and into the stalls below.

She swallowed audibly. She had had glimpses of him without a shirt before, of course, but that was in their bedroom, and even that was rare. Now that she could see him in action, she was mesmerized with the beauty of his form. Her mind was agreeably engaged in remembering the nights in their room when those arms and hands worked on her instead of some farm implement. His back glowed with sweat from his labor, and he turned around to push hay from the other side of the opening in the stall's ceiling.

He saw her then, standing and staring at him, cheeks flushed and eyes round. His face broke into a broad smile, dimples flashing, his hair in compelling disarray. She swallowed again, trying to look away but unable to tear her eyes from the well-defined chest and shoulders.

"Elizabeth!" he called, his expression conveying that he was pleased to see her. "What are you doing up here? I was just thinking of you, and here you are."

She climbed the rest of the way into the loft and picked her way over to him through the straw.

He wondered why she wouldn't answer or look at him, then he remembered his attire, or lack of it.

"Oh, sorry," he reached over for his shirt and put his arms through the sleeves, but before he could button it, she stayed his hand.

"Elizabeth?" he questioned.

Her hand touched the damp, soft hair on his chest and ran down his rib cage in a meandering path that ended at his abdomen, right above the buckle of his belt. Her other hand reached up around his neck and she brought him down to her for a slow, deep kiss. When they stopped for air, she leaned her forehead against him and tugged on his belt buckle, breathing in the clean sweet smell of alfalfa hay mingled with his sweat.

"Here?" he said hoarsely. "Now?"

She nodded.

"Are you sure?"

She nodded again.

In a flash, his mouth was on hers, not the gentle delicate kisses, or the confident, smooth ones, but raw hungry ones that mashed her lips and nose, his stubbly face scraping her skin as he devoured her. He lifted her off her feet and carried her over to a mound of hay in the corner. She started to pull him down on her, but he stopped and pulled away in a haze and shook his head. "No … scratchy hay." He pulled her down on top of him and resumed kissing her while he ran his hands all over her.

Elizabeth was in a frenzy. She had no idea what had taken over her body, what made her straddle him in a most un-ladylike manner, or what made her grind her hips against the burgeoning erection she could feel through his trousers. She sat up, unbuckled his pants, and opened his boxers to free him, while he pushed her dress up around her hips and ripped her panties in an effort to get them off. They hung in two pieces around her waist, but his objective had been achieved. She was open to him now.

He aimed and pulled her down onto him. One, two, three pushes and he was fully encased in the soft, hot darkness, almost touching her womb. She leaned down, her elbows on either side of his head, her eyes closed, and began to move against him. No knowledge other than instinct guided her, and he watched her in fascination, her lips parted and full, completely absorbed in her own gratification. It was the most exciting thing he had ever seen. He had learned quickly the grasping and clenching that signaled the advent of her pleasure, and she was doing it now, squeezing him and driving him toward his own release. He grasped her hips, trying to slow her down before he lost all control of himself, but she whimpered and still tried to move on him in an intoxicating rhythm, and he succumbed. It was as if he had struck his head on a rock and slid under water. He could see, but he couldn't breathe, couldn't think, and then he gasped and her name burst from his mouth.

"Lizzy!"

She fell over on him, her hair landing in his mouth and eyes, and he brushed it away, panting as if he had run ten miles. He heard mumbling against his neck. "What?" he asked breathlessly.

She lifted her head, her hair hiding her face. "I said, I'm mortified."

He began to laugh then, a deep well of joy springing up from some place carefully hidden from the rest of the world. "Oh, Lizzy," was all he could manage to choke out, but he stroked her face and her hair, and gathered the damp curls in his hand, holding them off her neck.

"Don't be embarrassed. I'm glad to see you too," he rumbled in a deep, warm voice.

She got up and averted her eyes as he did up his trousers. She could barely look at him. "I came to get you for lunch, I mean, dinner — or at least bring you something. It's… it's downstairs if you want it."

He turned her chin up to him and kissed her tenderly on the mouth, hoping his smiles and his caresses would take away her embarrassment. He could not bring himself to feel the least bit regretful though.

"Thank you," he said meaningfully. He kissed her again. "I was starving," he said, grinning at her, a trace of mischief in his eyes.

She gave him another shy smile and turned to descend the ladder.

They walked hand in hand up toward the maple tree that stood on a hill in the front yard of the house, stopping at the outside water pump to wash up.

"Oh, I almost forgot. The sheriff came by to see you this morning."

Darcy looked surprised. "Did he say what he wanted?"

"No, he didn't. He just wanted you to come by and see him today; he needed to talk to you."

"Hmm." He lifted her hand to his lips for a quick kiss. When they reached the tree, he sat down heavily, hands on his knees, and then he leaned over and opened the basket. "Let's see what we have here."

Elizabeth knelt down beside him and leaned over to pick some straw out of his dark hair. Then she too sat down, and peered in the basket.

From the front window, Mrs. Reynolds watched with a smile before turning away to give the newlyweds their privacy.

June 19, 1933

"MRS. REYNOLDS? COULD I SEE you in my study for a moment?"

"Of course, Mr. William."

"Shut the door please."

"Yes? What can I do for you?"

"Has Mrs. Darcy had anything shipped to the house recently?"

"No, I don't believe so, sir."

"No clothing? Books? Drugstore items? Toys for the little girls?"

"No, nothing that I've seen. Something may have come in, and I didn't notice…"

William smiled dryly. "I doubt if anything enters this house without you noticing, ma'am."

She laughed. "I s'pose not. No, sir, Mrs. Darcy is very frugal about her expenses."

"Quite."

"Is something the matter sir?"

"No, no thank you."

She looked at him inquiringly, but then she exited the study, closing the door behind her.

I notice every stitch of clothing you wear, Elizabeth, observe every book you read. You haven't bought a thing for yourself with the money in your household account, except for seeds and fertilizer.

He looked down at the bank ledger, a feeling of suspicion and dread creeping over him.

So, if you aren't spending the money on yourself, my wife, what are all these withdrawals for?

Chapter 21

A Stranger Comes to Town

June 22, 1933

Elizabeth ducked into Netherfield's to buy some flour. Mrs. Reynolds was going to teach her to make popovers tomorrow, and the flour bin was almost empty. Generally, Elizabeth avoided going into Netherfield's when she could. Now that Mr. Bingley was gone, there was no friendly face in there, and she grew tired of fending off Miss Caroline's verbal barbs and thinly veiled looks of disdain. *Jealous old shrew.* Thank goodness, William did not listen to her as her nephew apparently did. Mr. Bingley had been gone for five months now. Between his departure and Elizabeth's marriage, Jane had had a difficult winter and spring. Elizabeth felt sorry for her, but there was nothing she could do. The one time they had broached the subject only seemed to upset Jane.

"I did believe at one time that he cared for me, but I must have been wrong. Miss Caroline told me last week he might soon be engaged to a young lady from Glasgow. He has known her since he was young, and their mothers were friends."

"I don't believe that for a second, Jane. Miss Bingley saw that her nephew was enamored with you, sent him off to Glasgow, and now tries to convince you that he cares for someone else. She looks down on us, but she doesn't want to lose you as an employee. It pains me to see her use you that way."

"We need the money I earn, Lizzy. Besides, I think Miss Caroline was just try-

ing to protect me...so my feelings wouldn't be hurt."

Elizabeth was still unconvinced, but she was unable to persuade her sister. How she wished Jane did not have to work for that awful...

"Good afternoon, Miss Bennet," Caroline sniffed. "Can I help you find something?"

Elizabeth paused, counting to ten. *That woman is so irritating!* A slow, wicked grin spread across Elizabeth's face before she turned around, feigning surprise. "Oh, were you speaking to me? I apologize, Miss Bingley; I guess I've just gotten used to being called Mrs. Darcy."

Caroline squinted at her and lifted her lips in a twisted version of a smile. "Yes, of course, Mrs. Darcy."

"I just need to pick up some flour — a 10-pound bag should do." Elizabeth was momentarily distracted by the young man over by the tobacco. He had whirled around at the mention of her name. She thought little of it; a lot of people were curious about who had become Mrs. Darcy, and now that spring had come, people were coming into town from the outlying areas more frequently. He did not look like a farmer though. He was dressed in a suit and seemed well kept, if a little threadbare. She took a second look. *He's handsome too. I wonder if he's just moved in. And if Jane has seen him.* He looked up at her with a devastatingly charming smile. She returned the smile tentatively, and turned to find Caroline's suspicious eyes raking over her.

"Miss Bingley, I hope your nephew is doing well. We don't see him around Meryton much these days."

"No, he's been quite busy opening the new store in Glasgow. I think his residence there may be permanent. Of course, Louisa and I will miss him, but there's much more opportunity for him to engage in good society. Perhaps, after all this time, he's even meeting some young women fitting to his station, like Louisa and I recommended. Even William advised him as much."

"William? As in Mr. Darcy? My husband?"

Caroline narrowed her eyes at Elizabeth as if studying her the way a spider might study a fly before snaring it in her web.

"Why yes. William, I mean Mr. Darcy, of course, thought it best for Charles to relocate. He was of the opinion that Charles needed to escape some 'unfortunate entanglements' here. It was good advice too, because the young lady in question works for Charles." She feigned an awkward pause. "Oh dear, how thoughtless of me to mention it; the young woman was your sister, actually. I just didn't want her to feel uncomfortable working for us. I'm sure you understand. There was really no way for any relationship to proceed, you see, her being an employee." Miss Bingley seemed almost gleeful as she went on. "William's advice is always so practical, so sound. It's no wonder Charles always heeds what he says." She gave Elizabeth a self-satisfied smile.

Elizabeth paid for her flour, trying desperately to hide her expression, and left the store. She could hardly breathe as she headed toward the post office before returning back home. *William told Mr. Bingley to leave? Discouraged him from pursuing Jane? In spite of their obvious feelings for each other?*

"Pardon me," a pleasant voice sounded behind her. "Ma'am?"

She turned and saw the young man who had watched her at Netherfield's. He was approaching her with a spring in his step and an anticipatory gleam in his eye. "Excuse me, ma'am, I couldn't help but overhear the shopkeeper call your name back at the dry goods. Are you Mrs. William Darcy, of Pemberley?"

"Yes," Elizabeth replied, "I am. Are you an acquaintance of my husband's?"

His lips twisted into a wry smile. "In some respects, yes. I'm familiar with the family. You see, I'm Georgiana's husband, and Maggie and Ruth's father." He held out his hand. "I'm George, George Wickham."

Elizabeth had to force herself not to gasp out loud, but her eyes still showed her shock.

"Yes," he murmured quietly, withdrawing his outstretched hand. "I can see you've heard of me."

"I've actually heard very little of you. I didn't even know your name."

Wickham's eyes brightened slightly at her. "I didn't know Darcy had married."

"We've only been married since February."

"Ah, I see. Are you from around these parts?"

"No, actually, I mean, my mother is from here, but I grew up in Chicago."

"An outsider, like me. I must say I'm surprised."

"Really? And why is that?"

"I've always thought maybe that was one reason he never cared for me being with Georgiana."

"Oh."

"I apologize; I shouldn't have brought up that old family squabble to Darcy's lovely new wife. Not very gentlemanly, is it?" His brown eyes sparkled when he smiled. "I can't believe my good fortune in running into you. I've come into town from over at Brighton, where I've been staying for the last few weeks. I've been lucky enough to find a job at a service station there, but I came here looking for some word of my girls. I haven't laid eyes on them or their mother in almost two years. Do you get to see them regularly?"

"Why yes, I do, they live just up the road from us. They're precious little girls; I'm quite fond of them."

He beamed with pride. "Yes, they are, aren't they? I've missed them so much. But times were hard when Georgiana and I were trying to start our family, and the struggle to make ends meet was very difficult for her. So different from the way she was brought up, you know."

"Yes," Elizabeth looked anxiously up the street.

"Oh, forgive me, I'm keeping you from your errands."

"Oh, well, it's just that I need to get to the post office before they close."

"Allow me to escort you then."

"I wouldn't want to inconvenience you."

"Not at all. I would love to talk with someone who can tell me of my daughters." He gave a forlorn look off into the distance. "And their mother."

Elizabeth looked at him quizzically.

"I don't know what you've been told about me, Mrs. Darcy, but I can imagine. You're surprised that I should inquire so fondly about a wife from whom I'm estranged. But the truth is, I love Georgiana very much and always have. And I believe she loved me too."

"Whatever happened?" Elizabeth heard a warning bell go off in the back of her mind, but her curiosity overrode it.

"Well, as I said, times were hard for us a couple of years ago, as they were for many people. It was a tough time to begin a life together, but we were in love, and we thought we could surmount any obstacle."

He looked at Elizabeth to gauge her reaction, and seeing her encouragement, he went on.

"I was educated in business, slated to manage a shoe mercantile in the town where we lived, but after a few short months, the shop closed due to the Depression."

"Oh, I'm sorry."

"Thank you. It was hard on Georgiana. She was pregnant by then with Maggie and frightened I'm sure, for our future. We went from place to place, me finding work in this town or that, but I could never find anything permanent." He looked earnestly at Elizabeth, as if reliving the frustration of that time.

"Anyway, about a month after Ruth was born, she said she'd had enough, she couldn't live like that anymore, and she was going home to live and taking the girls with her.

"I was devastated. Not that I blamed Georgiana, like I said, she was frightened for herself and the girls, so she retreated to her familiar surroundings. I imagine some women are simply not made for that kind of hardship.

"Well, no matter what I think of Darcy otherwise, he has always been a very good brother to her. He took her in without question, moved her and the girls in with him, and apparently has cared for them very well. For that, I am grateful to him, no matter what else passed between us."

Elizabeth held her breath. Was she about to finally find out what happened between her husband and his brother-in-law?

"I found another steady job in Indiana, and I came here to find Georgiana. I wrote her a note, begging her to come home. In reply, I had a visit at my motel room from Darcy, telling me in no uncertain terms that I was not to contact my wife or my daughters again. He also produced a document declaring our marriage null and void. He had apparently used his connections and his money to obtain some kind of annulment.

"I couldn't believe that this was truly what she wanted. I asked Darcy if there was any work at Pemberley that I might do. I was willing to relocate, to be near my wife and family, if Georgiana didn't want to leave home. He was more threatening this time, insisting that he spoke for Georgiana, and she had no wish to see or hear from me. To this day, I don't know if she was ever aware I had returned for her."

"That's terrible." Elizabeth was deeply shocked. *Is this possible? Could William have done this awful thing just because the man was down on his luck?* Mr. Wickham seemed so sincere; there was truth in his earnest good looks. She looked around; all too soon, they had reached the post office.

"Yes, well, I keep trying to better my circumstances, hoping someday I will be worthy in his eyes of providing for my own family. I took the position over in Brighton in hopes that I could show him and Georgiana that I can care for them adequately." He twisted his lips into half a smile. "Although perhaps not in the manner to which she has become accustomed.

"So you see why, given our history, I would ask that you not tell him of my presence here. Honestly, I do not want to cause any trouble; I just wanted to see how my daughters are and how they have grown." His eyes grew misty. Suddenly, he looked across the street and the color drained from his face. Elizabeth turned and saw her husband with a furious scowl on his face.

"I think I'd best bid you goodbye, Mrs. Darcy. Perhaps we shall see each other again soon." He tipped his hat and hurried up the street and into the diner on the corner.

Darcy strode across the street and took Elizabeth roughly by the arm, leading her at such a fast pace that she could barely keep up with him.

"What are you doing, Elizabeth?" he said through gritted teeth.

"I was having a conversation."

"And do you know who you were having a conversation with?"

"Yes, not that I would have ever known if I had waited on you to introduce me. It was Mr. Wickham, as you well know — Georgiana's former husband and the father of your nieces."

His cheeks flushed dark red with anger. "Mr. Wickham? Is that what he's calling himself now?" he muttered under his breath.

"William, will you stop? I can't keep up with you." He stopped and whirled around to face her. She shook her arm out of his grip and huffed indignantly. "He only wanted to know how Georgiana and the little girls are doing. He seemed quite concerned about them."

Darcy snorted.

"William, maybe if you just talked with him…" she reasoned.

"No! I will not 'just talk' with that scoundrel! I'm amazed at your lack of common sense, Elizabeth. I have told you he is not to be discussed at all in my house. What on earth made you think it was acceptable to have an actual conversation with him on the street? What if the girls had seen you? Or God forbid, Georgiana had come around the corner and had to face him." His voice started low and menacing and rose in volume until he was speaking quite loudly. He stood over her, glaring at her in fury.

Something in Elizabeth snapped. She drew herself up as tall as she could manage, and lifted her chin defiantly. Her eyes flashed with the pent-up frustration and anger of several months. She spoke in a low voice, but her tone was every bit as menacing as his. "I am your wife, William. You will not dress me down in public as if I were a misbehaving child. I will not tolerate that kind of blatant disrespect from you, no matter what my sex, or my age, or my 'financial condition' when I married you." She turned and headed back the way they had come.

"Where are you going?" he asked her back.

"I have to mail my letters," she said over her shoulder, holding them up to show him.

He snatched them out of her hand and walked around in front of her. His unreadable scowl was back in place, and his voice was soft and tightly controlled. "I will mail the letters. The car is parked across the street. Please go over there and wait for me." A sarcastic tone crept into his voice. "And try not to start any heartfelt conversations with hobos, confidence men, or any other kind of miscreant before I get there."

Elizabeth stared after him, furious, and then headed toward the car, deciding it was time they had it out once and for all.

Chapter 22

Hunsfordesque

The Darcys' trip home was filled with angst-ridden silence, both of them knowing that a reckoning was to be had at the end of the journey. When they reached Pemberley, Elizabeth marched up to the door and let herself in, storming into the house.

William slammed the car door and stomped after her. He found her in the kitchen, gulping down a glass full of water in a futile attempt to calm herself.

She turned to face him and tried to keep her voice level. "William," she began, "how could you treat your brother-in-law that way? He loves Gigi and the girls. He told me he only wants to prove to you he can take care of them. How could you be so cruel to a man, just because he is down on his luck and doesn't fit some ideal you had in mind for her?"

He ignored her questions. "I'm going to ask you something, Elizabeth, and I need you to tell me the truth. Have you been giving Wickham money?"

"What!" Her incredulity knew no bounds. "For heaven's sake, I only met the man today! How could I be giving him money?"

"Did he ask you for any when you saw him this afternoon?"

"No! Do you really think so little of me, to believe me capable of that? Knowing how you feel about him, why would I do such a thing behind your back?"

"I don't know, but for the life of me, I can't figure out where you've spent the money I put in your personal account."

Elizabeth's eyes widened. "You check up on me?"

"I do not check up on you. I reconcile the bank statement. The money is there for your use, but I see no evidence of what you've spent it on — no new clothes, no books, nothing for the house. So can you really blame me for wondering what you've done with it? Are you squirreling it away in another bank? Building a nest egg so you can move out on your own someday? I know you didn't love me when we married, but I thought you would at least keep a marriage vow you made before God and everybody."

"You...are...delusional." She sat down and put her head in her hands and laughed mirthlessly. "I am not planning to 'run away'. The money I withdrew wasn't for me, William."

He crossed his arms and looked at her expectantly.

"I gave it to my mother for groceries, necessities and a few discretionary items for my sisters."

His mouth gaped open. "Elizabeth! Why didn't you tell me your family was in need? I asked your father not one month ago how he was faring, and he told me he was getting along fine."

Elizabeth's voice rose in anger. She leapt to her feet, fists clenched at her side. "Well, of course, *he* would say so. He's too proud to take any 'charity' from his son-in-law. As far as he's concerned, if there's three squares a day on the table and nobody's naked, everything is just dandy. He doesn't care that Kitty hasn't had a new hair ribbon in over a year even though she loves them, or that Mary's Sunday dress is threadbare. Or that Jane has to wear flour sack dresses to work, and allow that awful Bingley woman to make snide comments within earshot of the customers on how charming she looks in a reused flour bag!"

Elizabeth shook with anger, and tears ran down her face. She swiped at them with the back of her hand. "You *stupid* men and your stupid pride! Too busy to even look around and see what's going on in front of your faces! And you! You're the worst. You think you know it all. You know what I'm good for — I should decorate your arm and your house, but not do anything too useful. And Georgiana — you know who she should love and where she should live. You know how much candy the girls should have and what kind of schooling they should get. You don't even see how Gigi is trying desperately to lead her own life, or care that she wants to raise her own children." Elizabeth's voice cranked up a notch; she was on a roll now. "You're better than everyone else, and you're always looking down, on me, on my family. I see how your lip curls when they're around. I know my mother can be silly, but she's my mother, for

God's sake, and she does the best she knows how with the limited faculties she has. And I can't believe what you've done to Jane!"

His mouth moved in silence several times before he managed to splutter out, "And what have I done to Jane?"

Elizabeth was almost beside herself by this point. "You told Mr. Bingley he should move away, even though you knew he was falling for Jane, and she had feelings for him. Don't look so surprised that I found out. Nasty old Miss Bingley made sure I knew it was you who suggested he leave town to avoid 'unfortunate entanglements' with my sister. Her heart is broken, William! And it's all your fault!"

"Damned meddling woman!" he muttered.

Elizabeth wasn't sure if he meant Jane, or Miss Bingley, or herself.

His usual haughty voice returned, low and controlled. "Yes, I admit I advised Charles to relocate. He had an opportunity to open another store, before there was any additional competition in Glasgow, and I encouraged him to pursue it. He wanted Jane to move there too, and manage the new store."

"He did? Then why..."

"But," he interrupted her, "I discouraged him from asking her."

"Why?" Elizabeth blurted out despairingly.

"Because." His voice was rising again. "Think how it would look. He hires this pretty young girl, shows some interest in her, and then whisks her off — without marrying her, I might add — to another town, away from her family, where she knows no one."

"But..." Elizabeth rubbed her forehead in confusion.

"And, put yourself in Jane's position. She can't turn the job down for fear of losing the one she already has. It's unacceptable for a man to foist his attentions on a female employee."

"Mr. Bingley would never..."

William strode back and forth across the kitchen. "Well, of course he would never! I know that! But he doesn't think," Darcy pointed to his temple, "when it comes to women. Once I enlightened him to the evils of putting Jane in that situation, naturally, he agreed. He had just never thought of what he was doing to her."

"But she really liked him," Elizabeth began.

"Well, that can't be helped. What's done is done, and done for the best — for everyone concerned. I watched Jane, you know, at church, at Netherfield Hall and at Bingley's holiday party. She was always gracious and polite, but I never saw any indication that she truly liked him. Even after he left, she didn't seem that upset he was gone." He went on, muttering half to himself. "She just goes about her business, always with that infernal smile on her face, no matter what's going on around her."

"Am I to understand that, in addition to everything else, the omnipotent Mr. Darcy also knows the inner workings of my sister's mind and heart?" She threw up her hands in exasperation. "Who do you think you are? You *barely* know her! She doesn't share her feelings with anyone but me."

Darcy started at this, but said nothing.

"Between what you've done to my beloved sister, and to your own sister's husband, I'm wondering exactly what kind of man I married. If you ever gave me any inkling of what you thought, or how you felt, I might be able to discern some gentlemanly qualities in you, but as it stands now...I see nothing of quality at all!"

A deadly silence fell over the room.

"So this is your opinion of me? According to you, my faults are grave character flaws indeed. So the fact that I chose you, that I wanted to marry you, means nothing? After I took you from the squalor you were living in, made you mistress of my home, treated you like a queen, gave you anything I thought you might desire — you have doubts about my moral fiber? You want to know my thoughts? You want to know how I feel about you?" He paused, running his fingers through his hair, and began pacing again. "*This* is how I feel about you!"

He strode toward her and seized her face between his hands, taking her mouth in a bruising kiss. Her traitorous body responded to him, but at this moment, her pride was stronger. She pulled away and stared at him, breathing hard. Quick as a wink, a loud crack echoed throughout the room as her hand came up and struck his cheek. He took a step toward her, and on instinct, she backed away. Her hand covered her mouth in an expression of horror at what she had just done.

He stopped, vaguely aware of the fear in her eyes. Could it be that she was afraid of him? The thought was unbearable. He turned away sharply, unable to look at her anymore.

"Get out," he croaked hoarsely.

Without another word, she turned and fled the room.

Chapter 23

A Letter

Darcy stood with both hands on the kitchen counter, trying to catch his breath and talk himself down. He could hear her footsteps running up the stairs, running away from him, because he frightened her, because…she despised him. He thought he was strangling on the bile rising from his stomach. In a blind daze, he opened the kitchen door and stalked out into the night.

The dusk had turned to dark since they had come home, and a waning gibbous moon cast an eerie silver glow on his familiar landmarks. He seemed to be walking in another world, a world that was so topsy-turvy he couldn't find his way — where up was down, and right was left…and love was anger.

He strode on, looking briefly up at the barn. It was his preferred place to go when he wanted to think, but his last memories of that place were filled with the sights of his wife's desire-flushed face, the sounds of her taking her pleasure, and the heady scent of her aroused body. He would never be able to enter the hayloft again without thinking of her. No, it was not a place where reasoned contemplation was possible, at least, not tonight.

He passed the barn and walked the perimeter of the nearby fields, hearing the rustle in the trees by the creek. At one point, he felt a drop on his hand that felt like rain, but the sky was clear and bright. He realized that the drop was a tear and rubbed his thumb and forefinger over his eyes. He could not remember the last time he shed tears, but it was probably when his mother died.

He continued over the hill and down around the pond, seating himself beside the black water. A gentle breeze barely disturbed the surface. He picked up a small rock and tossed it into the pond, listening to the resounding 'plunk' and watching the waves spread further and further out, until they covered the pond's visible surface. *Funny how one little rock can move all that water. Like one young woman could change my entire life.*

Could Elizabeth have been right about him? About him looking down on her family? About the way he treated her? About Jane? He squirmed uncomfortably. Not for the first time, he thought that maybe he had made a mistake. Or, not a mistake exactly, but perhaps there had been another solution, one that would have allowed Charles to pursue his business and his interest in Jane.

But Elizabeth was definitely wrong about George Wickham. It had been a grave mistake for him to keep that knowledge from her; he could see that now. *Of course, her natural empathy would rise to the surface under the spell of an experienced liar like Wickham.*

Richard had told him the man had been seen in Brighton a few days ago, but that was fifteen miles away. They thought he would be smart enough to stay away from Meryton, but perhaps not. Or possibly, Wickham thought there was something in Meryton or at Pemberley that was worth the risk of showing his face there. Darcy's blood grew cold with fear.

He would definitely have to warn Elizabeth about Wickham now and warn Georgiana too. She was safe enough at the cottage, but she would not be able to go into town unescorted until the scoundrel left the area. How he dreaded telling her the bad news! Even after two years of relative peace, it seemed he could no longer protect her from that man. Their reprieve was apparently over.

He stood up, pulling out his pocket watch and tilting it to see the hands in the moonlight. It was close to midnight; he had been out by the pond for a couple of hours. Elizabeth would probably be asleep by now. Images of her in peaceful slumber floated across his mind and made his heart ache. He considered going to her, but eventually decided he would not disturb her tonight. He would sleep in the guest room and figure out tomorrow how to mend the mess he had made.

WILLIAM WOKE TO BRIGHT SUNSHINE in his eyes and the smell of bacon drifting up from the kitchen. The sun was high; he rarely slept this late. Sitting up, he shook his head, disoriented, before remembering why he was sleeping in his guest room. Elizabeth would probably be out at her garden by now. He sighed, threw off the covers and climbed out of bed. He needed to get up and face the music.

Downstairs he encountered Mrs. Reynolds, brewing coffee and gathering eggs, grits and bacon for his breakfast.

"Well, good morning, sleepy head," she teased good-naturedly. "Can't remember the last time you came downstairs after seven o'clock."

He cleared his throat. "Yes, well, I was up late last night and overslept, I suppose."

"Mm-hmm."

"I guess Mrs. Darcy has already eaten."

"Haven't seen her yet this morning." She stopped and turned to him, concerned. "You mean you haven't seen her either?"

They stood staring at each other for a long minute.

"Will you excuse me, please? Just cover up my plate; I'll eat it later." He left the room and ascended the stairs, two at a time.

He threw open the door to their bedroom and stopped suddenly. The bed looked like it hadn't been slept in. He strode over to the window and peered out anxiously toward her garden, but no one was there. Turning back to the room, he opened the closet. Her travel bag was missing, as well as some of her clothes. His heart began to pound as he rummaged through their room, looking for any evidence of where she might have gone.

After looking around frantically, he glanced down at the bedside table. Lying atop her copy of *Persuasion* was a white envelope with his name on it. She had been reading the novel to him in the evenings before bed. He tore open the envelope and read her slanted script on the page. His heart dropped to his boots.

William,

Please don't be concerned. I have gone back to Longbourn. I didn't know what to do or where else to go. I'm very confused, and I need some time to think.

Elizabeth

He sat down on the bed, his head dropping into his hands. *Why on Earth would she leave me?* Then he remembered the last words he said to her.

"*Get out.*"

"Oh, Lizzy, no!" he whispered in anguish as her letter fluttered to the floor.

WILLIAM THREW HIMSELF INTO PHYSICAL labor that day, pushing to a level of exhaustion that would keep him from thinking about his predicament. When he returned late that evening, he ate the dinner Mrs. Reynolds had put back for him, sitting alone at the dining room table, while she worked in the kitchen before retiring to her quarters. The dear woman said not a word to him about the glaring absence of his wife. He wondered if she had heard them arguing the night before. Her only acknowledgment of his trouble was to look down into his eyes when she served him his meal, smile wistfully, and pat his cheek in a motherly fashion.

William mechanically went through the motions of bathing and dressing for bed, and fell mercifully asleep with the lamp on, only to be awakened in the dark hours before dawn. Unable to return to the blissful ignorance of his dreams, he reached for the book Elizabeth had left on the nightstand. He recalled the way her eyes sparkled when she told him why she loved this story so much.

"It's about second chances, and how it's never too late to find happiness. Isn't that uplifting? Anne Elliot loses her home at Kellynch and the life she was supposed to have, but she finds a future that's better than she ever dared to hope. Well... we haven't gotten to that part yet, but you'll see..."

Knowing her the way he did now, he could understand why the story appealed to her. The main character's predicament was so like her own, and like Anne Elliot, Elizabeth's calm, intelligent manner was the center in the storm of her family. She had always been the one on whom the others relied in one way or another. He shook his head in confused disbelief. Why had he been so suspicious of her 'missing' funds? After a moment's consideration, he knew why; it was because her departure was the event he now feared the most. But it was much more in character for her to take her resources and spend them on her family — as if she had to choose either them or herself. Headstrong, obstinate girl! Why hadn't she come to him with her concerns? Did she think he would have refused her anything? *Perhaps you wouldn't have outright refused, but would you have expressed disapproval?* Yes, maybe he would have, and that would have embarrassed her. Suddenly, her new interest in that huge garden and learning to preserve food made perfect sense. She was going to share the fruits of her labor, apparently behind her father's back. Was Dr. Bennet that unobservant? Or would he have simply let her take care of his problem — without even acknowledging her efforts? His heart gave a painful little twist. *But it was wrong of her to deceive me. I can't believe she accused her father and me of stupid pride, when in truth, she is as prideful as we are.* That thought, that she had some human foibles after all, was oddly comforting to him, and he found her all the more endearing for her flaws.

He glanced down at the page, the words there floating into his mind as they might have sounded in her sweet, lilting voice. This scene was very near the end of the story, the surreptitious delivery of Captain Wentworth's letter, followed by its contents.

> *. . . I must speak to you by such means as are within my reach. You pierce my soul . . .*

Suddenly, he sat straight up. He leapt out of bed and pulled on his trousers. It occurred to him that Captain Wentworth may have been on to something. Was there a way William could express his thoughts, without the overwhelming distraction of his wife's presence? Whenever she was before him, all well-rehearsed speeches and his best-laid plans flew out the window, and he did stupid things like try to force his tongue down her throat. He walked down the stairs to his study, struck by how empty the house seemed without her in it. He did not know how they would fix the mess in which they found themselves, but he knew he had to start by being honest with her — about Jane, about her family, and about Wickham. He pulled out paper and a pen, and began to write.

THOMAS BENNET STEPPED ON THE spade under his foot and turned over the red earth. He was putting in a few more tomato plants beside the fencerow near the barn. The sound of a truck interrupted the rhythm of his work and he turned to see who had driven in. It was the man he had been expecting since yesterday, but still he wondered what he could say to his enigmatic son-in-law.

"Mr. Darcy," he said slowly, returning to his work.

"Good morning, Dr. Bennet."

"I suppose you've come to fetch your wife."

"Ah . . . I . . ."

"I've a mind not to let you have her. Would you like to explain to me why my daughter shows up at my door evening before last, after dark, on foot, with a tear-stained face and an expensive-looking carpet bag full of clothes?"

"I thought perhaps she would have told…"

"She wouldn't tell me a thing. Mrs. Bennet is fit to be tied, insisting that I take her back to you — 'where she belongs,' but…" The older man leaned his spade against the fence and turned to narrow his eyes at his son-in-law. "Want to tell me what happened, son?"

No, I don't. "We had an argument, sir, and I'm afraid I said some things that upset Elizabeth."

"I'll say." Bennet leaned over, picked up a tomato plant and put it in the ground. "You know, my Lizzy is not given to histrionics, so I'm disinclined to think that this was some little marital spat about curtains, burnt dinner, or some other such nonsense."

"No sir."

Bennet moved the soil around the plant with his spade. "If she doesn't want to go, I will not let you take her with you."

"I would never force her to come home against her will, but I would like to…well, I'm not sure she wants to speak to me in person right now, but it is imperative that I explain some things." Darcy drew an envelope out of his shirt pocket. "Will you be so kind as to give her my letter?"

Bennet nodded toward the house. "You can give it to her yourself, if you like."

Darcy whirled around. Elizabeth was standing on the porch, leaning on the column that held up the porch roof, watching him with her doe-like brown eyes. Without another word to her father, he approached her slowly, as if approaching an edgy colt.

"Um, good morning." He tried unsuccessfully to smile and was sure it only came out as a frightful looking grimace.

"Hello."

"Would you do me the honor of reading this letter? I seem unable to express myself adequately in person."

She looked at the letter in his hand, and then at him. Tentatively, she reached out and took it.

"I don't suppose I can convince you to return home with me. This looks…"

She shook her head solemnly. "I don't care how it looks. Please don't…"

"I understand. Good-day then, Elizabeth." He tipped his hat formally and retreated to his truck. He had made a start; now he had to await her willingness to respond to it.

ELIZABETH TOOK HER LETTER AND walked out to a large shade tree behind the chicken house. Plopping down on the ground, she opened the envelope and devoured every word on the page:

Elizabeth,

Please don't be alarmed on receiving this letter; I have no desire to continue any part of the disagreement in which we found ourselves the other evening. I hesitate to say anything further to upset you, but I must be allowed to answer the charges you laid at my door.

The first accusation was that I separated my friend Charles from your sister, regardless of the feelings of either of them. The second was that I willfully and cruelly sent away the man who claimed to be my brother-in-law, and thus destroyed my sister's marriage. The second charge is more grievous than the first, but I think I must explain both. The explanations, particularly as regards your sister, may bring you additional pain. For that, I can only apologize.

It was not long after your sister began working at Netherfield's Dry Goods, that I became aware of Bingley's interest in her. He talked incessantly of her beauty, her good sense and her pleasant personality. But it was not until the holiday party at Netherfield Hall that I suspected any attachment beyond a typical flirtation. After you and I danced together, I happened to overhear two 'gentlemen' (I use the word loosely) gossiping like old women about Bingley's supposed escapades with your sister. I will not offend you further by telling you what was said; rest assured, I set them straight. I was concerned for my friend though, because in a small town like this, a scandal could hurt not only his reputation, but also his livelihood as a business owner. As I mentioned to you before, Bingley often fancies himself 'in love' with some woman, only to find that his feelings are either not returned or have cooled after a brief separation. After watching your sister's interactions with Bingley, I concluded that this time was no different. She demonstrated no feelings for Charles, not in her speech nor in her facial expressions. As you said though, your knowledge of her is undoubtedly superior to mine. Therefore, I may have been wrong about her, and if so, I am sorry for it. Still, their separation was most likely for the best.

Shortly after the holiday party, Charles asked my opinion about opening the new store in Glasgow. As it is his hometown, and the opportunity seemed to be a good one, I advised him to take advantage of it. He often turns to me for advice of this sort. His business decisions are usually quite sound, but he lacks the confidence in himself that comes with age and experience. I don't think living with his aunts helps that situation much. There is but one piece of the counsel I gave him that day that bothers me, and that is that I advised him not to hire your sister to manage the new store. That may have cost her an increase in income, and given what I so recently discovered regarding the financial struggles of your family, I may have done her and the rest of your family a disservice. Again, if so, I apologize, but there is nothing to be done about it now.

This brings me to another sensitive topic — my attitude toward your family. You and Jane have always conducted yourselves as ladies of quality, and for that you should both be respected. For some reason that I cannot fathom, you seem to have the idea that I do not have a very high opinion of you. Nothing could be further from the truth; I would not have married you if I did not value your mind and spirit. But I have at times been dismayed at the lack of decorum demonstrated by your younger sisters and your mother. It has the unfortunate effect of discomfiting most people who are subjected to it, me included. Your father, while well-spoken and mannerly on his own, refuses to check their speech and behavior, and I find this difficult to overlook. I'm sorry to offend you, but that is the situation as I see it.

Now, with respect to one George Wickham, I have considerably more to say. You have accused me of separating him from my sister and nieces, basically breaking up a family, simply because I didn't approve of the man's vocation, or lack of it. I know not what he has told you about the situation, so I can't speak to any specific accusation he has made. Therefore, the best way to proceed is probably to lay before you the entire story. This is most painful for me, and I would ask for your discretion in not relating these events to anyone else, as they concern my sister and her children.

Georgiana, as you know, is about seven years my junior. She was very young when our mother died, and relatively young when our father passed. At the tender age of twenty-one, I became, for all intents and purposes, a parent to her. It was an almost overwhelming responsibility, and if I am honest, one of the reasons I considered marrying Anne de Bourgh. I was concerned about raising

Georgiana properly on my own. After my father passed away, I scouted around the area and found a well-respected boarding school in the Nashville area called Ramsgate Academy. Georgiana did well after a brief adjustment period, although she did at times admit to being lonely. I encouraged her to persevere, and for a while, it seemed as though she had. When she was seventeen years old, her letters became more and more infrequent, and then one day, I got a phone call from the school saying that she had disappeared.

I was frantic. The police were contacted, and I immediately left for Nashville in order to try and discover what had happened to her. A search of her room revealed a letter addressed to me, stating that she had fallen in love and was going to elope with a young man named George Whitman. She insisted that I should not worry, that she was safe and happily married, and she would contact me as soon as they were settled. The police investigation basically ended at that point; a man who seduces young girls and convinces them to run off with him is apparently not as compelling a threat to society as bank robbers and such.

I continued searching for her on my own, but weeks and months went by, and I never heard from Georgiana, except for a card at Christmas time. When I tried to find her at the return address on the card, she was no longer living there. I felt like I had failed Gi, and my mother and father too. It was almost more than I could bear. Richard was a stalwart companion for me during this ordeal. His friendship probably kept me from losing my sanity, actually. Then, about four years after she had disappeared, Georgiana suddenly returned home with the girls. Ruth was about six weeks old at the time. I was overjoyed to see her, but the three of them were in sad shape. They were shabbily dressed and malnourished. Georgiana was frightfully thin, and anemic, as it turned out. Maggie had begun to talk a few months earlier, Gi said, but now she refused to say a word. The poor little thing was absolutely terrified of me. After seeing to their basic needs, I finally succeeded in getting Georgiana to tell me what had happened to her.

After she and that man left Nashville, they went to Batesville, Indiana. He told her he had obtained work in a shoe retail shop, but once they arrived, the job was no longer available. According to Georgiana, he did try to find work and take care of her for a few months, but after a while, she realized that he would never be able to hold any kind of steady job. Being trusting and naïve, she had been unable to discern before they were married that he was a drunk — a drunk who also had a gambling problem. Additionally, over time, he developed a tendency to strike her when he was inebriated. Because he was continually out of work, they moved from place to place. How they lived, I know not. But somehow they ended up in Springfield, Illinois where she delivered Ruth. When the baby was about a month old, Georgiana said the police came to the door one afternoon, looking for her husband. They said they had a warrant for his arrest: charges of violation of the Volstead Act, theft by deception, and — to her horror — bigamy. Apparently, George Whitman was actually George Wickham of Valparaiso, Indiana. Mr. Wickham had left a wife and four children fending for themselves in another state.

Several days later, when Wickham returned, Georgiana confronted him, and an argument ensued. His tendency toward violence had been escalating, but up until that point, his abuse had always been confined to Georgiana. She confided to me that, in her misery, she mistakenly believed she deserved that fate, because of her rebelliousness in running away from school. But on this particular evening, when Maggie began to cry in response to the angry voices, the monster struck her too. That, combined with the shame that she was, in essence, an unmarried mother of two, living with another woman's husband, finally convinced Gi she had to get out. After he left the house, she gathered the barest necessities and ran to a neighbor's, a kindly older couple who had befriended her. I shall be eternally thankful to them, because they gave her the money to take the train back home to safety.

When the scoundrel tried to contact her several weeks later, you can imagine what I said and how I felt. I did threaten him and send him away, and I asked for Richard's help to sort out the legal matters with the girls' birth certificates and to dissolve the bogus marriage. Richard still keeps tabs on the man through his law enforcement connections. In fact, that's why he came to see me the other morning. He had reason to believe that Wickham was in the area and wanted to warn me.

In retrospect, I now believe I should have warned you too, but I honestly didn't think you would ever have to lay eyes on the man. I had no idea he would have the nerve to show up in Meryton again. He must be desperate indeed, and desperate men are often dangerous. I beg you Elizabeth, stay away from him.

I know what he is capable of, and if he hurt you, I would never forgive myself. That day I saw you standing with him on the street, I was genuinely frightened. As it is with many people, my fear often expresses itself as anger, and I had little control over myself the night we had our argument. I'm so sorry for assaulting your person when I kissed you. It was unforgivable, and I want to reassure you that it will never happen again.

I will try to find a way of putting this letter in your hands this morning. Perhaps there is some way we can move past this and restore our marriage, such as it is. But if not, at some point I suppose we will need to decide what your living arrangements will be.

I will only add, God bless you.

Your husband,
William Darcy

Chapter 24

Things to think about

Elizabeth read her husband's letter three times in a row, not trusting herself to absorb it all accurately the first time through. She seethed with anger at his brusque dismissal of Jane and her family's concerns; how dare he take so much upon himself where Mr. Bingley was concerned! And for that matter, how dare Mr. Bingley be so weak-willed as to listen?

But what truly disturbed her was the information about George Wickham. How could she have been so completely duped by the man? She had always thought herself a good judge of character. As she considered further though, she realized Wickham had seduced her mind, as surely as he had seduced Georgiana's heart. He was a criminal, a prolific liar and a very effective one too, all wrapped up in a handsome and charming package. It had not escaped her notice that Wickham had included just enough truth to make his lies of omission seem believable. His words of supposed affection for Georgiana now seemed malevolent and twisted. Elizabeth's heart ached for her sweet, shy sister-in-law. To have her heart so completely broken, her trust so violated! Elizabeth's hatred for Wickham began to swell in her breast. And Maggie! To strike that beautiful child, to terrify her so that she would not speak to anyone and was deathly afraid of all men! Elizabeth felt almost sick with outrage.

What a different light this cast on her husband as well. Although he should have told her about Wickham, she had jumped to hasty conclusions about his silence. What had seemed to her to be pride and a desire to protect his reputation in the community was really a desire to protect his sister — both physically and emotionally — from the effects of abuse. It explained some of his guarded nature around people he didn't know well, although she suspected that reserve was an ingrained part of his personality even before the situation with Georgiana occurred.

With chagrin, she remembered how suspicious she was of his solicitous treatment of her when they first married. She assumed he had some ulterior motive for treating her so kindly and wondered if that treatment would continue. She should have taken her cues about his kindness from his niece. Remembering how Maggie's eyes lit up whenever she greeted him with a delighted "Unca!" Elizabeth marveled at the kindness and patience William must have shown with the little one. Through the force of his love for her, and the security he gave her, he had counteracted the effects of Wickham's abuse and neglect. He had basically adopted Georgiana's children, as Miss Bingley had said, and taken a father's responsibility for them. No wonder he thought he knew what was best for them. No wonder either that Georgiana gave him so much leeway. He had saved her and her children from despair, and she was grateful. Elizabeth had a newfound respect for her sister-in-law; to leave the security of her brother's house and move to the cottage must have taken a great deal of courage after what she had endured. It also spoke highly of her independent spirit and her love for her brother; she wanted to give him room to start his own family.

Elizabeth felt a myriad of emotions for her husband: anger for his bull-headedness about Jane, pity for the loss of his parents' love and guidance, and pride in his loyalty to his sister and her daughters. Elizabeth felt sorrow for the loneliness he had endured after Anne's death and Georgiana's disappearance, contempt for his haughtiness towards her family, gratitude for his kindness to herself, and most of all, an undeniable fascination in the complexity of his personality. To have had the possibility of attaining the affection of a man like that, and then to have thrown it away due to her own prejudices against him, made Elizabeth feel miserable and ashamed. How she regretted her hurtful words! She had accused him of being too quick to judge others based on outward appearances, but was she not just as guilty of that as he was? Until this moment, she had never truly known herself, and the knowledge she had gained was troubling.

What was she to do? Should she go home and beg him to take her back? Did he really want her to come back, or did he no longer think her worth the trouble she had caused him? Would he want to divorce her? Should she simply await her fate at his hands?

His hands. She wriggled uncomfortably as memories of his hands came, unbidden, into her mind. His hands firmly and gently holding a terrified horse, his hand covering hers in a protective gesture while they walked up the aisle after their wedding ceremony, his hands pouring bourbon whiskey into a glass, holding her as they danced to "Night and Day." His hands summoning an ecstatic delirium from her body she had never imagined could exist. She began to ache for him, physically, certainly, but emotionally too. It was simply right to be with him; she could not explain it, but neither could she deny it. He was her husband; she was his wife, and they should be together. She needed his quiet strength; he needed her liveliness and spirit.

She began to tremble as she realized what was happening to her. Somehow, in this sleepy little backwater town, she had stumbled into a marriage of convenience — to her soul mate. She had fallen in love with her husband, a man who did not love her in return and who was possibly reconsidering his decision to marry her. Down deep, he might not want anything else to do with her ever again. Had he not mentioned separate living arrangements in his letter? Her heart shattered. She leaned back against the tree and began to cry.

Chapter 25

Mother's Lament

June 24, 1933

Mrs. Bennet stood at the sink, washing up the rest of the breakfast dishes as Elizabeth tried to sneak down the stairs and out the front door. It was late on Saturday morning, and she had lain awake in bed for over an hour too exhausted to face the day.

"It's about time you got yourself out of that bed. Your sisters have already had their breakfast and left to do their work for the day. Your father and I have been up since dawn."

Elizabeth cringed with annoyance and guilt. "I'm sorry, Mama."

"I suppose you're used to lying about all morning long up at Pemberley, now that you've got a houseful of servants."

"No, I still get up early. And there's not a houseful of servants, only Mrs. Reynolds."

"Hmmph, no Mrs. Reynolds around here — that's for sure."

"No, ma'am."

"If you lollygag about in bed all day, no wonder he sent you back."

"He didn't send me back," she sighed. "I said I'm sorry. I'm just not feeling too well this morning."

Mrs. Bennet dried her hands on a dishtowel and felt her daughter's forehead. "No fever, you must not be too sick. Heartsick maybe, over what you've done."

Elizabeth said nothing but picked up the damp towel and began to dry the dishes in the sink. They each continued working in silence, lost in their own thoughts. After she finished drying the iron skillet and hung it on the peg next to the stove, Elizabeth folded the towel neatly and laid it on the counter to dry. Her mother was right about one thing; if she was going to stay here, she needed to contribute somehow.

"Can I help you with something, Mama?"

Mrs. Bennet narrowed her eyes at her and pursed her lips. She thought for a second, and then she shrugged. "You can help me shell that bushel of peas, I guess. The girls picked them before they left this morning, and I was going to can them this afternoon."

Elizabeth retrieved the bushel basket sitting by the door and got out a can for the pods and a bowl for the peas. "Where are the girls anyway?" The unusual quiet in the house was one of the reasons she had slept so late.

"They went to the farmers' market over in Brighton, to sell eggs. Mary's gone to work at your Uncle Ed's office, and Jane's working at Netherfield's. Your father is out doing something, cutting hay, I think."

"The girls go all the way to Brighton? I thought they sold eggs in Meryton."

"They get a better price over in Brighton, so they've been riding over with John Lucas on Saturdays. He goes over there and sells those cedar chests and rocking chairs he makes." Mrs. Bennet sat down across the corner of the table from Elizabeth, moving the bowl and shell can between them, and began to work. "Nice boy, John. I think he might be sweet on Kitty, though I can't imagine why he would choose her over Lydia, who is prettier and has more personality. But to each his own, I suppose."

Elizabeth felt indignant on Kitty's behalf, but she had no will left to quarrel with her mother over favoritism toward Lydia. That was unlikely ever to change. She wondered if John Lucas knew what he was getting into. That thought led her to remember William's opinions about the Bennets, and she searched frantically for a conversation topic to take her mind off him.

"Is it safe over in Brighton? I heard there are some rough people over that way."

Mrs. Bennet waved her off. "They'll be fine. John's with them anyway. What could happen?"

Elizabeth could think of a couple of unpleasant things that could happen, especially given Lydia's indiscreet speech and flirtatious ways, but she said nothing.

Another period of silence ensued, with Mrs. Bennet getting more agitated as the minutes went on. Elizabeth kept working, although she was starting to feel a little queasy. *Perhaps I should eat something.*

"You know, I do not understand you, Lizzy."

"What do you mean?" Elizabeth asked in a resigned tone. *Sometimes I don't understand myself either.*

"Why can't you ever be satisfied with what you have? You marry this rich, tall and handsome man, live in that beautiful house with every possible convenience — and you pick a fight with your husband and come back home. How are we supposed to support you now? You gave Mary your job. Is it too late to ask William to take you back?"

Elizabeth felt tears sting her eyes, but she managed to keep her composure. "I'll find another job to help out more."

"Hmmph." Mrs. Bennet snorted. "You know we won't let you starve, but... I just don't understand why."

"I really don't want to discuss it. We quarreled. I left. I don't know what will happen now."

Mrs. Bennet looked at her shrewdly. "Did he hit you, Lizzy?"

"Mama! No! He would never do that!" Elizabeth was aghast.

Her mother shrugged. "I didn't think so. I didn't see any marks on you, and he seems too gentlemanly to hit a woman, but you never know. I told your father as much, but he still wasn't sure."

"Why didn't he just ask me himself?"

"You know your father," was all she said. It was all she needed to say.

An irritable look crossed Mrs. Bennet's face. "You're just like him, you know."

"Who? Papa?"

"Yes, always with your nose in a book and never thinking about the real world. Always looking for that something better somewhere else, and never happy with what you've got." She looked at her pointedly. "And yet, good things just seem to happen to you — and to him. But still you're so... ungrateful!"

Elizabeth thought this was an unfair assessment of her character and told her mother so, citing her job at Uncle Ed's and her garden at Pemberley as examples of her ability to deal with the real world.

"I know," her mother returned in an exasperated voice. "I thought there was finally hope for you, but then..." She picked up another pea and jerked on it roughly. "You go and pull a stunt like this."

"I *am* grateful — for everything, Mama. Truly." She reached over and squeezed her mother's work-worn hand, and went back to shelling peas. Several minutes of silence ensued, but then Elizabeth interrupted the rhythm of their task with a question.

"Does Papa confide in you?"

"About what?"

"Oh, about anything…his thoughts, worries, plans, what to do about the farm or us?"

"No, why should he?"

"Would you want him to?"

Her mother sounded perplexed. "He doesn't, so I never thought about it."

"Does it bother you that he doesn't share his thoughts with you?"

"Men don't talk like that with their wives."

"Uncle Ed talks about the vet office with Aunt Maddie."

"He does? I haven't noticed."

"I want my husband to talk to me, share his life with me. I want to be his friend *and* his wife."

"Is that what you argued about with William?"

"It was one of the things we argued about."

"Silly," Mrs. Bennet muttered under her breath.

Elizabeth smiled sadly at her mother. "Probably so."

Chapter 26

A Drunken Lout

July 1, 1933

lizabeth was sterilizing jars for canning. It was about the only thing she could do without feeling as if she were about to throw up. This past week she had been miserable, and not just because she missed William. She was starting to think something was seriously wrong with her. She had been so fatigued, she could hardly even think about her problems, much less address them. She knew, however, that eventually, she would have to make some decisions.

She heard a truck door bang closed and a cadre of loud, angry voices outside. *That must be Kitty and Lydia.* She frowned, looking up at the clock. *My goodness, they're home late; I wonder what...*

She walked to the front room and was almost trampled by Lydia bursting through the door in tears. The distraught girl took one look at her sister and rushed up the stairs, slamming the bedroom door after her. Elizabeth looked out the front window and spied Kitty and her Uncle Ed approaching the house. Kitty looked miserable, and Ed looked furious.

Elizabeth opened the door and exclaimed, "Whatever happened?"

"I need to see your father Lizzy. Is he in the house?"

"No, I think he's at the barn. Uncle Ed, *what* is going on?"

Kitty interrupted Elizabeth. "I'll tell her. You can go and find Papa, Uncle Ed."

Ed looked indecisive for a moment, as if perhaps he thought he should tell

Elizabeth what had happened, but then he let out a resigned sigh. "Fine."

Kitty sat down on the couch and put her face in her hands. Elizabeth took the chair across from her, now more worried than ever.

"What is it? Are you hurt? Is Lydia? Do I need to go check on her?"

Kitty raised her head, scowling. "No, she doesn't need you to check on her. She's fine. *I'm* the one who was humiliated, as usual." She leaned back on the couch and crossed her arms with a huff. "Well, you know we've been going into Brighton to sell eggs on Saturdays."

Elizabeth nodded.

"Last Saturday, we were down at the market and I look over and Lydia is off talking to some fella. Well, that's not so strange, and this fella *is* handsome, but he looks older than her — and kind of a drugstore cowboy. I mean what's he doing all dressed up to go to the farmers' market? Sheesh! So when she comes back, I tell her she shouldn't be talking to men she doesn't know, and she gets all in a snit and tells me to lay off. She says he's the bee's knees, and I'm just jealous because he looks better than John Lucas and doesn't smell like sawdust and wood varnish."

Elizabeth couldn't stifle the chuckle that came out of her mouth. *Lydia is immature and annoying, but she does have a way with words!*

"Lizzy! I'm trying to tell you what happened!"

Elizabeth waved her on. "I know, I know. I'm sorry. Please, go on."

"So I say, 'You don't even know him', and she says 'His name is George Wilson, and he just moved to Brighton from Chicago. And I told him I was from Chicago too, and we started talking about the theaters and the White Sox, and all the fun things to do there that they don't have around here.' So I figure she'll forget about him in a day or two, and I don't think another thing about it."

"And what happened today?"

"Well, today we get there and set up our stand and sell the eggs as usual. We had a good day, sold 'em all, and some raspberries too. And John sold two rockers and four cedar chests, and he got orders for three more rockers!"

Elizabeth looked at Kitty, exasperated, and waved her arm in a gesture that said 'hurry up'.

Kitty cleared her throat. "Right. So we're packing up our stuff to go home; this was about four o'clock. I turn around and Lydia is gone. She's over by the entrance talking to that George guy again. I hear her big loud mouth just a yammerin' away. She gets all excited and comes back to where I am *working*, and says George has invited her to go over to this joint called The Bank to go dancing. She begs me to take care of the egg money, and she'll be back in an hour. That way we can still get home way before dark.'"

"Oh, dear."

"So after she leaves, John asks me where they were going, and when I tell him, he says 'The Bank? Talk around town is that place is kind of a speakeasy, and the crowd supposed to be pretty rough.'

Now, I don't know what to do. So John and I just wait around for her. We go over and get some ice cream, and John talks to some of the other woodworkers, and I saw the prettiest quilt. One of the ladies in Brighton makes them and sells them at the market and different places around. The pattern I saw was 'Drunkard's Path'. Isn't that a funny name?" Kitty paused, musing about quilt patterns. Elizabeth cleared her throat.

"Oh, right. Well, after an hour and a half, Lydia's still not back, and the market is getting ready to close. So we're talking about whether to go get her, and guess who comes up to the stand? You'll never guess."

"Who?"

"Never in a million years. Come on, guess…"

"Good Lord, Kitty, I don't want to guess! Who was it?"

"William Darcy."

Elizabeth's heart stopped, and then started pounding against her ribs.

"My husband?"

Kitty nodded. "I didn't say anything about you coming home last week, 'cause you told us not to."

"Thank you for remembering that."

"Oh, I'm not as dim as everybody thinks."

"Of course not."

"William doesn't say anything about you coming home either. Just says he came over to speak to John about a rocker for his sister's new cottage. He asks about everyone at Longbourn — and he did that staring thing of his and emphasizes 'everyone' — just like that, 'How is *everyone* at Longbourn, Catherine?'"

Elizabeth's lips twitched. Kitty had done a fair job of imitating William's deep, imperious baritone.

"Did you ever notice he did that staring thing?"

"Yes, Kitty," Elizabeth said, exasperated, "I noticed. Now, please go on with your story."

"Right. So he asks if Lydia's with me, and John blurts out 'she's over at The Bank with some fella name of George Wilson.'"

"Well, William gets all in a lather and says 'with who?' like he can't believe it. I say, 'George Wilson'. And he turns all serious, and tells me that George Wilson isn't his real name; his name is really George Wickham. He's just been using that name around Brighton, and he's not on the level, so if I see him anywhere near us or near Longbourn, I need to get up to Uncle Ed's and call the sheriff. You all right, Lizzy?"

Elizabeth was white with fear. *What, if anything, has Lydia told Wickham about Georgiana?* "Oh no," she whispered.

"Does William know George?"

"Yes…well, no, not really. He knows about him though. What happened next?"

"William takes John with him to go get her, and they come back with Lydia about a half-hour later. She's all sulky, and John's looking all wild-eyed and scared."

"And William?"

"William's just scowling like he always does. Jeepers, Lizzy, how do you stand it?"

"Never you mind. Did Lydia believe the truth about George?"

Kitty shrugged. "I don't know. William told John to take us straight to Uncle Ed's house. He was going to go and telephone Uncle Ed, so he could tell him to be on the lookout for us and make sure we got home safely.

"John said when they went in The Bank, there was liquor all around; he could smell it. They went over to the booth in the corner, and Lydia was almost sitting in George's lap, necking. William tapped her on the shoulder and told her it was time to go home, her friends were waiting for her. And he was sure her father would not approve of her spending time in a place like that, or in that man's company. Then John said George stood up and smirked at William, kind of bumping his chest against him, you know, like men do when they're about to fight."

Elizabeth's eyes were round. "They didn't fight, did they?"

"No. They had a couple words; John couldn't hear what they said because the music was so loud, but I bet William could have taken him. John told me George was a little sozzled, and you know William's kind of a big six."

"A what?" Elizabeth wasn't sure whether to be offended or not. Kitty's propensity for slang was getting worse every week.

"A big six, a big, strong fella."

"Oh."

"But they didn't throw any punches or anything, and John was glad of that, because he would have had to have Darcy's back he said, and some of those fellas looked pretty rough."

"I'm sure."

"And then they left George just standing there and walked out."

"What did Lydia say?"

"Nothing. She cried all the way home, I think because she knows she's gonna be in trouble. If William hadn't been there, I don't know what would have happened."

"I have a pretty good idea," Elizabeth muttered.

Kitty looked at her, puzzled.

"Never mind." Elizabeth was relieved that William had left with John and Lydia instead of brawling with Wickham in a dance hall. She hoped he made it home all right.

Elizabeth heard the screen door slam, and she turned to see her father storming in through the kitchen. She could hear her mother sobbing in the background, and Mary trying unsuccessfully to calm her.

When her father spoke, his voice was like ice. "Where's Lydia?"

Both girls looked toward the stairs, and he went up them slowly. A minute later, they could hear his yelling and her crying coming from above them. Ed came into the parlor and sighed.

"Well, this is a sad business, Lizzy." He cast a look toward the stairs. "I must say, your young man certainly came through for our family today. Apparently, this Wickham character is a real piece of work. I spoke with the sheriff after I got off the phone with Darcy; there's a warrant for his arrest in Indiana, Illinois and Missouri. Mob connections too. I think Lydia may have had a narrow escape today. It was strange, though; Darcy didn't want you to know that he was the one who found her and made her come home. He wanted me to keep that from you, but I can't for the life of me figure out why. I told him my brother-in-law would certainly like to show his gratitude or at least thank him in person, but Darcy said it was for the best that everyone think I had found her. Have you any idea why he would say that?"

"None."

"Well, when you go home tonight, give him an extra kiss or two." Ed winked at her, teasing. "Tell him I hope he's not upset with me for telling you, but I couldn't take the credit for his chivalrous deed."

Elizabeth faltered. "Yes...I will."

"I'm heading up to the house now." Ed winced as a fresh round of parental yelling floated down from above. "Good-night, Lizzy, Kitty."

"Good night, Uncle Ed."

Elizabeth closed the door behind her uncle. The sounds of consternation were still coming from upstairs, and she knew it was going to be worse once her mother joined in. "I'm going for a walk."

Kitty sat back down heavily on the couch. "I don't know why Lydia has to act like she does. Now everyone's going to think she's some kind of vamp. What will John Lucas think of me now?"

Elizabeth just shook her head, and headed out into the early evening air.

Chapter 27

Going home to Chaos

July 3, 1933

Elizabeth groaned, her stomach turning fitfully before she even opened her eyes.

"Lizzy?"

She opened her eyes slowly. The fuzzy outlines of Jane's concerned face gradually became sharper. Her sister was leaning over her, eyebrows drawn up into a worried frown.

"Hand me the wash basin. Hurry!" Elizabeth's voice was urgent; she closed her eyes again, her hand covering her mouth.

Jane disappeared and Elizabeth felt the cool porcelain bowl in her hand. She sat up quickly and emptied the contents of her stomach, which was precious little, into the basin sitting in her lap.

"Oh, Lord," she whimpered, setting the bowl on the floor away from her. "I feel awful."

"I'm getting Mama. You're sick."

Elizabeth put out a hand to stay Jane's departure. "No, please! Don't get Mama. I...I think I know what might be wrong."

"Did you have something bad to eat?"

"No, I don't think so."

"An influenza?"

"No, it's nothing like that."

"Are you homesick, Lizzy? Do you miss William?"

Tears pricked Elizabeth's eyes. "I was so wrong about him Jane, so terribly awfully wrong, about everything, well, most everything." She remembered his unwanted interference with Bingley, but she couldn't very well relate that story to her sister.

"Then tell him. He cares about you; he'll want you to go back to Pemberley."

Elizabeth set the bowl down and pushed it away from her. "I should, but I don't know what to say to him. I can't...I can't seem to think straight. I've been so hurtful. I've ruined everything! If he truly loved me, like a husband loves a wife, he might be able to forgive me. But you know and I know he doesn't love me like that." Her voice began to quiver. "I've been so foolish, and now I'm..." she sobbed quietly. Jane retrieved a handkerchief out of the bureau, and put it in her sister's hand.

"Oh, Jane, you have to promise not to tell anyone this. Not Mama or Papa or William."

Jane's voice became stern and her face was solemn. "What is wrong?"

Elizabeth lowered her voice to a whisper. "I think I might be pregnant."

Jane's eyes opened wide. "How do you know?"

"That's the thing; I don't know. I know that your monthly cycle stops when you're going to have a baby, but mine has never been regular anyway, so I didn't think anything about not having one. Then a few days ago, I started feeling so terrible in the mornings, but I don't have a fever or anything, and I'm fine by lunchtime. I need to ask someone, someone who knows."

"Mama..." Jane began.

"NOT Mama," Elizabeth insisted stubbornly. "She'd send me back to Pemberley before I could say 'baby booties'. And William will feel obligated to take me back because of the baby."

"So?"

Elizabeth balled up her fists in grim determination. "I don't want him to take me back out of pity or obligation. I didn't mind it when we first married; I thought then that I could live that way, knowing that all we would ever have was a distant, respectful friendship. Because at the time, friendship was all I felt for him. But now." Two fat tears rolled down her face, and she swiped at them viciously. "I want more, God help me. I love him, and I want him to love me back."

"Oh, Lizzy." Jane sat beside her and enclosed her in a comforting embrace.

Elizabeth said nothing, just sniffed and wiped her nose.

"And what do you think he'll do when he finds out you're pregnant? That's his child, Lizzy."

"He's wanted a child so much. He was looking forward to starting a family." She let out a dejected sigh. "I know it's probably too much to hope for, but I want him to ask me to come home before he finds out about the baby — because he loves me, not just because I'm carrying the heir to Pemberley. I don't think I could bear to live in the same house with him and know that he only tolerates me."

"What will you do?"

Elizabeth hugged her knees to her chest and sighed. "I don't know." After a long minute, she set her chin on her knees; a determined expression grew in her eyes, and she set her jaw firmly. "First thing I have to do, is find out what I'm dealing with. I need to find out if I'm pregnant. I can't ask Mama, that's for sure, but…" she raised her head, eyes wide. "I could ask Georgiana."

"Won't she tell William?"

"If I don't, she eventually will, but, Lord, Jane, this is a small town. I couldn't hide it from him anyway, at least not for long. Besides, Mama would never keep a secret like that, and I certainly won't be able to hide it from her much longer."

Jane's lips twitched. "That's true."

"And if anyone knows how to handle William, it's Gi. Maybe she can give me some advice. I'll get some breakfast in me; by lunchtime, I should feel well enough to walk over to the cottage. And then, I'll just have to see. I can't think ahead any farther than that, or I'll go crazy."

Jane reached over and stroked her sister's hair. "Come on, sweetie. Let's get you cleaned up a little."

ELIZABETH TRUDGED UP THE DRIVEWAY to the cottage; the hot summer sun was beating down on her, slowing her pace considerably. She stopped and sent a wistful look toward the big house on the hill. It felt like her home now, not because her clothes and her garden and her other things were there, but because it was where William was. A soft breeze blew across her face, bringing some strands of hair with it. She resumed walking toward the cottage but stopped short when she saw an unfamiliar car parked behind a grove of trees.

A strange sense of foreboding stole across her mind. She continued up the drive, listening intently, and broke into a run when she heard crying and raised voices. It was not Ruth's toddler screaming that urged her to hurry, but the unheard-of sound of Maggie's tears. Maggie never cried; something must be very wrong.

What Elizabeth heard right before she reached for the door made her halt abruptly and her blood ran cold. A man's loud voice could be heard through the open window. She flattened herself against the side of the house and peeked through the lace curtain, careful to conceal her presence.

"Just come with me; we'll make a new start somewhere. It'll be different this time, I promise. We'll have your money to live on."

"Get out of here, George, now!" Georgiana's voice was quivering slightly, but her tone was firm.

Elizabeth gasped. *Wickham! Oh God, what is he doing here?* Her heart pounded in her chest. *What do I do? What do I do?* Her panicked inner voice repeated that refrain over and over. She stopped and shut her eyes tight. *I've got to think!* Her eyes popped open. *William!* But should she leave the girls and Georgiana alone with Wickham? *I can't help them by myself, but William can help, and I can call the sheriff from the big house.* She looked up; the house was almost a half a mile away. She could be up there in ten minutes, even less time if she ran. She eased off the porch without a sound. Once she was far enough away that she couldn't be heard, she broke into a sprint. She only prayed he was in or near the house when she got there.

As she rounded the last bend in the drive, she saw him walking up from her garden. She nearly cried with relief.

"Williiaamm!" Elizabeth felt like she was screaming, but given that she was out of breath from running, her voice was barely louder than normal. She began waving frantically and tried again. "William!" He stopped and stood, staring at her in disbelief. She put the last of her effort into running and fell into his arms. He grabbed her elbows and pushed her back to look at her.

"Elizabeth? What are you doing here?"

She was too out of breath to speak at first.

"Why are you running in this heat?" Suddenly, he processed the panic on her face. "What is it? What's wrong?"

She pointed behind her. "Georgiana...Wickham...He's at the cottage....He's trying to make her go with him. The girls are crying; we have to call the sheriff!"

He stood for a second as if deciding what would be best. He looked toward the cottage.

"Is he armed?" he asked her.

She looked up at him, horrified.

"Elizabeth!" He shook her slightly. "Tell me! Is he armed?"

"I…I don't know. I didn't see…Oh William!" She began to cry.

He took off toward the big house, shouting directions to her as he ran. "I'll get my rifle." She followed him as fast as she was able. "You go in and call Richard. His number is by the phone. Then you stay at the house until he gets here. Do you hear me?"

"I hear you." *But I'm not letting you go down there by yourself.* They split up at the foyer. She ran into the parlor to dial the phone; he retrieved his gun from his study. She heard the front screen door slam behind him barely seconds later as he dashed down the porch stairs and made for the cottage.

Mrs. Reynolds hurried from the kitchen, wiping her hands on her apron. "Mrs. Darcy! What…?"

"Mrs. Reynolds!" She grabbed the older lady's arm and relayed William's directions.

"Of course," the housekeeper was already reaching for the phone. "But where are you going?"

"I'm going with him!" Elizabeth shouted over her shoulder.

By the time Elizabeth reached the cottage drive, William was nowhere to be seen. She hid behind a tree, searching, and realized that Richard's truck was parked down on the road, away from the house.

Thank God! He must have been coming out here anyway. Suddenly a large hand came around her from behind and covered her mouth, preventing her scream from escaping.

A low voice sounded in her ear. "I told you to stay at the house." He let her go, and she turned around, returning William's fierce glare with one of her own.

"No."

"No?"

"No."

He was loading his rifle. "Please, Lizzy. I don't know what we're dealing with here. I can't protect you and the girls too."

"You may need me," she whispered urgently, "to help with the girls, or…or go get more help."

He considered. "All right. But stay way behind me until I tell you, and don't do anything foolish. Promise?"

"I promise."

"Richard is around here somewhere. We need to find him so we don't shoot each other by mistake."

Elizabeth shuddered. A sudden movement caught her eye. Richard had just silently vaulted over the porch railing and was running toward them, crouched low. There was a pistol in his hand.

"What's going on?" Darcy whispered.

"The bastard's in there all right. I been having one of the deputies check on her, 'cause I was afraid something like this might happen. Mercer's gone for more help."

Richard spat on the ground and looked seriously at Darcy. "He's got a pistol tucked in the back of his belt; I don't know if it's loaded or not. He's drunk too — which may be to our advantage, or it may make him do something stupid. Georgiana is doing a good job of keeping him calm; she's had a lot of practice doin' that." His face darkened momentarily, but then the cold, hard calm returned. "But she's refusing to go with him, and the little ones is screamin' and cryin', and I'm 'fraid that might set him off."

Tears were running unchecked down Elizabeth's face, but she kept repeating her mantra and her prayer: *I've got to think! I've got to listen! I've got to think! Please, God, help us!*

"They're in the front room and he's got his back to the door. I think I can sneak up on him. Darcy, you cover me by the steps there. I'll signal before I go in, and you follow me. Mrs. Darcy…" he turned to look at her as if seeing her for the first time. "Good Lord, woman, what are you doing here?" He shook his head.

"I can't leave them," she said simply.

He smiled at her kindly. "No, I s'pose not." He turned and surveyed the front of the house. "You hide behind that hydrangea bush for now. I expect Miss Darcy's gonna need some help with the babies once I get him in custody. If you see the deputy pull up, you head him off and tell him what's going on. "

He turned, and as quick and silent as lightning, he crept back up to the front door. He stood beside it, listening, and Elizabeth took her place behind the hydrangea at the corner of the steps. She could hear Wickham's voice, louder and angrier than before.

"You're my wife, and these are my children, and you're all coming with me!"

"I am not your wife," Georgiana's voice was raised too, but she was still in control of it. "My daughters and I are staying here!"

"Why didn't you tell me about that nice little trust fund of yours before? Oh, yes, I know it all. Some old coot who works at the bank told me the whole story over a game of cards last week. Did you think you could slink out in the middle of the night and come crawling back to your mansion on the hill to spend all your money and me not find out about it?"

"You must not have missed us too much. It took you almost two years to darken my door." Her voice rose again. "What happened, George? Did you run out of money? Did Mary Wickham find out what you did to her and throw you out? Are the police after you again? Or maybe it's the mob that's come for you this time?"

"How dare you hide that money from me! I'm your husband! I need that money." He paced back and forth, and stopped with his back to the door. Georgiana was hidden from view.

"But I don't need you. Maybe I don't even need you to get your money." He reached down and grabbed Ruth, hoisting her up into his arms. "You want to come with Daddy, little lady? I bet Darcy would pay through the nose to get you back. You can be Daddy's little insurance policy." Ruth let out a terrified scream and reached her arms toward her mother. Maggie hid her face in her mother's skirts, crying uncontrollably. Georgiana finally lost her composure.

"No! Please! Give her to me, please! Please, George! I'll give you anything you want."

"Yes, I know you will — you sneaky, conniving little bitch!" Wickham shifted Ruth to one arm, and as he said the last word, he punctuated it by back-handing Georgiana across the face. Elizabeth heard the sickening thud, which almost made her vomit, and then everything happened all of a sudden: Fitzwilliam nodded and silently opened the screen door. He put his pistol to Wickham's head and cocked the trigger with a click. His other hand lifted Wickham's gun from the back of the man's trousers and handed it back to Darcy who had followed him in. William checked it, stuck it in his own belt, and resumed his aim on Wickham.

"Now," Fitzwilliam said evenly. "How about you give the baby back to her mama, real nice and slow?"

Wickham eased Ruth down to the floor. The moment her feet touched the ground, she was running. Her mother scooped her up and held her tight, stroking her hair and murmuring to her. Georgiana reached down briefly and put a protective hand around Maggie's shaking shoulders.

"I wouldn't have hurt her," Wickham slurred, "She's my daughter after all."

"She's not your daughter; a man like you don't deserve a sweet child like that," Richard returned in a cold, grim voice. He fished a pair of handcuffs off his belt, and slapped them on Wickham's wrists. "Now, I'm gonna let the nice deputy that's coming out here take you back to the cell at the sheriff's office. Then we're calling the Bowling Green police. I do believe there's a warrant for your arrest in about three different states on various charges." He leaned in toward Wickham's ear and said in a low, menacing voice, "And I don't want to see you no more, Wickham. You understand me? 'Cause if you come around these parts and scare this good woman and make her babies cry ever again, I will personally hunt you down and kill you with my bare hands."

Elizabeth had heard the entire interchange from her hiding place. She stepped out and walked to the door just in time to hear the sheriff say, "You can stand down, Darcy." Then, with a hint of unease, he repeated, "Darcy? I said stand down." She looked at William, his gun still trained on Wickham's head, and her fear rushed back with a vengeance. William didn't move; his eyes held a wild, crazed look she had never seen before. It was terrifying. She tried to speak, but her voice was caught in her throat.

William's tone was quiet and deadly. "I should kill him."

Richard spoke with a forced calm, although his voice was filled with trepidation. "You listen to me real careful now. You don't want to do this in front of the little girls or in front of your sister. You don't."

There was still no movement.

"William, stand down. Look at the babies; look at Maggie. She's watching you. She needs you here, not rottin' inside the pen at Eddyville. Don't do this." Richard's voice was low and insistent.

William's eyes flitted to his niece. She was looking at him with those dark brown eyes, so like his own. He shook his head a little and blinked, and then he lowered his rifle.

A deputy rushed past Elizabeth from behind.

"Mercer!" Richard barked. "Get Darcy's rifle and the pistol and put them outside in my truck. Then you and Hendricks get this criminal down to the jail."

When they were gone, Elizabeth hurried inside, putting her arms around Georgiana and the girls, and clutching them to her. She took Ruth from her mother's arms and coaxed Maggie to come sit down with her on the couch. Georgiana's cheekbone was already starting to bruise and swell. Elizabeth was thinking that she needed to put some ice on it, when she noticed Georgiana hadn't moved. Her sister-in-law stood, transfixed, staring at Richard Fitzwilliam.

Suddenly, Georgiana rushed toward him. His arms opened and enfolded her, as she sobbed, "Richard" over and over again. He held her as her knees gave way, and stroked her hair, murmuring comforting phrases. "It's over; he's gone.

He won't hurt you anymore. You're safe now. You were so brave. My darling, my precious girl." Georgiana lifted her head from his shoulder and without another word, she planted a kiss on him that left no doubt in anyone's mind about her feelings for the good sheriff.

Darcy fell back against the door frame, his mouth actually hanging open in shock. Elizabeth could not stop staring at them.

"They hug like that all the time."

Elizabeth looked down at Maggie, who was standing beside her. Her cheeks were tear-stained, but her voice was back to normal and as precocious as ever. "They think I don't know about it, but I can see them out my window. They stand beside Sheriff's truck, and say good night about seventy-hundred times and hug about seventy-hundred more. Sometimes I just give up waiting for her and go back to bed."

Elizabeth looked back up at William, who was listening to Maggie's revelation in total disbelief. Elizabeth began to giggle. The sound grew louder until it was near hysterical proportions. Maggie, not quite sure what was so funny, started to laugh too. William looked at them all without speaking, and then turned and slowly headed out the door.

I better make sure he doesn't turn his rifle on Richard. She told Maggie to hold Ruth and followed him out to the porch. He was heading off toward the house, not toward his gun, so Elizabeth went back in and got Georgiana some ice. She told Maggie to stay and help her mother, squeezed Richard's arm affectionately, and made her own way toward the big house at Pemberley.

Chapter 28

The Poet Who Didn't Know It

Elizabeth slowly ascended the stairs to the large front porch of the Pemberley house. The painted grey floorboards were shiny and clean; a large welcome mat graced the door stoop. She had always loved the porch; it wrapped around one side of the house to the kitchen door. A porch swing graced the front, and a couple sets of rocking chairs and low tables were scattered about. Baskets of ferns and impatiens hung from hooks in the ceiling. The house was situated facing south, so the westerly winds blew a near constant breeze, bolstered by the massive ceiling fan. Elizabeth felt a warm tug on her heart for Mrs. Reynolds, who quietly kept the entire house running like clockwork and beautiful on top of it all, no matter what was going on inside or out, or how badly its occupants behaved.

As if thinking of Mrs. Reynolds had summoned her, the older lady appeared at the front door.

"Mrs. Darcy? Is everything all right down at the cottage? The deputy said they were on their way."

"Sheriff Fitzwilliam was there when I got back. The man is in custody."

"Thank the Lord!" Mrs. Reynolds exclaimed, her hand over her heart.

"Yes." Elizabeth cleared her throat and tried to make her voice sound casual, "Has Mr. Darcy come back to the house? He was heading this way."

Mrs. Reynolds looked at her shrewdly. "No."

Elizabeth shuffled her feet. "I need to talk to him. I need to apologize. Do you know where I might find him?"

"Does this mean you will be coming back home, Mrs. Darcy?"

"Yes, if he will have me." The words came out of her mouth effortlessly. Apparently, she had made her decision sometime between approaching Georgiana's cottage and ascending Pemberley's front porch steps. No matter how William felt about her, she didn't want to be without him, ever. She was coming home to take care of him, body and soul.

The housekeeper smiled and gently patted Elizabeth's shoulder. "Good. He needs you, my dear — and he doesn't need anyone. Try the hayloft in the barn. Since he was a little boy, he's gone there when he wants to think or be alone."

Elizabeth impulsively embraced Mrs. Reynolds and kissed her soft, wrinkled cheek. "Thank you!" she replied and hurried down the porch steps.

She made her way over the rise behind the house. There was a little rolling path and then the barn sat on another rise behind that. She entered the barn and climbed the ladder. Her head rose above the hayloft floor.

"William?" she called softly.

"Over here."

She saw him, sitting on the loft floor, leaning back against the side of the doorway, which was open to the rolling hills below. His arm was propped up on one knee, and he held a blade of hay between his teeth. He was so beautiful; it made her heart ache with longing.

"May I come up?" she asked.

"Of course," he sat up straighter, turning so his legs hung over the loft window edge. He pitched his hay blade to the ground outside. "I saw you coming. I was hoping you were coming to see me. Whoa, be careful there." He steadied her with a hand on her arm as she approached and sat beside him.

She reached over and took his hand. "You left Georgiana and the girls at the cottage."

He smiled ruefully. "I don't think she needs me all that much, do you? Richard seems to be doing a fine job of taking care of her."

"Don't sell yourself short. She does need you, and the girls do too. Maggie adores her 'Unca.'"

"I'm ashamed of what I almost did today. Would Maggie still adore me if I gunned down her father in front of her? Or would it scar her for life?" His shoulders slumped. "I thought I had everything under control. Until today I never knew myself, or what I might be capable of; I'm not sure I like what I learned."

"You didn't do it, William."

"But would I have done it if Richard hadn't been there to stop me?"

"But he was there. You mustn't blame yourself for wanting to protect the ones you love."

"Fitzwilliam loves them too — as I also discovered today. He kept control of himself."

"You don't have Richard's experience with criminals or violent situations. Why would you know exactly what to do?"

"You won't even let me wallow in my self-pity for a moment?" He gave her a smirk.

She squeezed his hand. "No." She went on, in a more serious tone. "You're wrong, you know. They do need you and always will, but perhaps not in the same way they used to."

He gazed at her intently. "So young, yet so wise."

"Not so wise." She looked away, embarrassed. "I'm so sorry about what I said to you, about Wickham, about my family, about everything. And for slapping you." Her eyes welled up with tears. "I am so very sorry for that; I've never hit anyone before in my life. And then you saved Lydia from that horrible man! How can I ever thank you adequately for what you've done for her?"

"Please...don't..."

Her heart sank. Was this when he would finally turn her out, if she worked up the courage to ask him if she could come back home?

He spoke in an agitated voice. "How could I have been so wrong? About all of it: you, your family, Charles and Jane. I should have explained to you about Wickham instead of just ordering you never to speak of him. He almost stole your sister the way he stole mine — all because I wouldn't warn you." He shook his head. "And Richard and Georgiana. You saw what was developing between them, but I refused to believe you."

She started to reply, but he went on. "I know what happened there. I didn't want to see it. I wanted the girls to stay at Pemberley. I thought that was what I was supposed to want, what I was supposed to do."

He gazed off over the tops of the trees, deep in thought for a moment. "I wondered, all those years ago when Anne died, I wondered why that happened to her and to me. I tried to make some sense of it. Both my parents were gone, and I had to come home to assume my responsibilities here. I decided maybe I was supposed to take care of Pemberley and Georgiana, so I threw myself into doing those things. And then those years when Gi was gone and I had no one, nothing to care for, no one to love — except Mrs. Reynolds and Pemberley — I was so lonely then; it was almost unbearable. Thank goodness for Richard; he was a good friend to me during that time. He knew about loneliness and loss, and his wisdom helped me endure it. And then suddenly, Gigi was back and she needed me, and the girls — they were such a precious surprise, a godsend really. They gave me so much joy. Finally, I thought, *this* was the reason I was here, to care for them. There would be someone to carry on our name, someone to pass Pemberley to when I was gone. They were my reward for persevering, even though I would never have a wife and children of my own. And I gave up the idea of having a family."

He stopped and gave her one of his intense, dark looks. "And then I met you. Somewhere in my soul, I must have known that you were what I needed, because I couldn't stop thinking about you. But then I tried to force you into the family I had made for myself. Gi knew it wouldn't work that way. She was going to make her own life; she knew what she wanted and what I needed."

He shook his head and chuckled humorlessly. "I thought I had so much to offer you. I never realized that what you offered me was so much more important."

"What?" she whispered.

"A reason . . . a reason to do all this." He gestured around to the house, the fields. "And someone to help me do it, someone to share it with."

Elizabeth felt warmth begin to spread from her heart to the rest of body. She felt out of breath as she had when she was running earlier.

William kept his eyes on her. "When my father was dying, he told me that in a crisis the things that really matter become crystal clear, and the path one must take is plainly marked. I didn't understand that for a long time. The first time I understood was when Gigi came home with Maggie and Ruth. I knew, without a doubt, what I had to do, and I did it. Nothing mattered but her and the little ones. Do you know what I mean?"

Elizabeth nodded, tears in her eyes.

Realization dawned on him. "You do know, don't you? It was when you lost your home last year, and when things were so bad for your family last winter." He looked at her incredulously as he put the pieces together. "That's why you said yes when I asked to marry you, isn't it? It was all clear to you. You knew what you had to do."

Her lip quivered. "I overheard my father talking to Uncle Ed. He was thinking about sending Mary or Kitty away to his aunt so he could feed the rest of us. He didn't think he would make it through the winter. That was about three weeks before you asked me to marry you." She shook her head. "It was wrong of me, William. I shouldn't have done it."

He looked stricken and paused a long moment. "Well it's done now, isn't it?" he said in a soft, resigned voice. "We thought we knew what we were about, and it all spun out of our control. Damnation, what has my selfishness cost you, Lizzy? A chance for real happiness? A full life with a man you love? I never even considered what you might have wanted for yourself." He withdrew his hand.

Elizabeth looked at him in confusion. *What happened? What did I say?* She reviewed their conversation and gasped.

"No! No, William, you don't understand what I mean. It was wrong to accept you for the reasons I did, but…it wasn't wrong to marry you."

"It wasn't?"

"I don't think so. I…I hope not." She looked down at her hands in her lap. She saw his large hand reach over and cover hers. He picked one up and brought it to his lips for a kiss. Fire ignited at her hand and raced up her arm like he had lit a torch.

He held her hand to his chest. "Do you know the second time everything became crystal clear for me?"

She shook her head.

"It was today. After Georgiana and the girls were safe, I knew exactly what I must do next. Now, I just have to work up the courage to do it. It's more important than anything else."

"What is it?"

He took a deep breath. "I have to convince you to come home, Elizabeth. I love you and I miss you so much."

She smiled through her tears. "You do?"

He gave her a ghost of a smile, a sign that his equilibrium was returning. "How can I convince you? Get down on one knee? Show up at your door with flowers? Recite you poetry perhaps? Let's see…" He paused.

"Come live with me and be my love,
And we will all the pleasures prove…"

She stared at him, all astonishment. *Mr. Serious can recite love poetry?*

He saw her expression and muttered under his breath, "Well, in for a dime, in for a dollar…"

He went on:

"… The shepherds' swains shall dance and sing
For thy delight each May morning:
If these delights thy mind may move,
Then live with me and be my love.

"Now I've convinced you, surely…" A slightly anxious smile twitched his lips.

She recovered a little from her surprise and tried unsuccessfully to suppress a giggle.

Encouraged by her smile, he went on teasing her gently. "You laugh? But I had always considered poetry to be the food of love."

She took a deep breath and arched her eyebrow at him in a mischievous manner. "It might be, for a stout, healthy love. Everything nourishes what is strong already. But if it is only a slight infatuation, I am convinced that one good sonnet will destroy it for good." She brought their hands to her lips and kissed his knuckles, each in turn. "How fortunate for you, then," her expression turned soft and affectionate, "that I love you so much already."

His eyes darkened. "Or maybe, I should just write you a letter. Oh, I did that." His expression turned serious. "Did my letter make you think any better of me? I'm afraid that when I wrote it I was still angry. I might have sounded a little bitter."

"Perhaps a little at the beginning, but it did make me see you in a different light, and appreciate you more." She held his hand against her cheek.

"Lizzy," he whispered. He leaned over and kissed her tenderly on the mouth. "Can it be so easy?"

"You call all of this easy?" She shook her head in amazement.

"No, I guess not." He stood up and held out his hand to her. "Come with me."

She took the offered hand willingly, realizing that he would probably always express himself in words that sounded like commands. He was after all, 'his own man', the master of all he surveyed.

"Where are we going?" she asked.

"Home."

Elizabeth's face lit up in a jubilant smile. They climbed down from the hayloft and ambled, hand in hand, toward the house.

"There's one thing I meant to ask you though."

She nodded at him in encouragement. "Yes?"

"What brought you to Georgiana's today? I mean, I'm forever grateful to whatever power took you there, but…"

She faltered; in all the excitement, she had temporarily forgotten why she had come to see her sister-in-law in the first place. "I needed her advice."

"About what?"

Elizabeth felt the blood drain from her face. A strange dizziness crept over her, whether from the heat, or the intensity of the last few hours, or uncertainty about how he would receive her news, she wasn't sure. "I'll tell you, but do you think we could get something cold to drink first? I'm not feeling too well all of a sudden."

"Of course. That was thoughtless of me; you've been through quite an ordeal today." He put an arm around her, and she leaned into him, grateful for the assistance. She took a deep breath, relaxation diffusing over her entire body. She stumbled.

"Lizzy, are you all right?"

She looked up at him; his dark eyes were filled with concern. She tried to smile and reassure him, but nothing came out. The edges of her vision grew dark and he seemed to recede from view before blackness overtook her. She heard him shouting something unintelligible and felt herself being swept up, and then all light and sound went out and she felt nothing at all.

Chapter 29

What Matters Most

Elizabeth came to slowly, a whispered cadence calling to her across the blackness in her mind. Her eyes fluttered open and slowly began to process what lay beyond the dark. It was dusk actually, and she could barely see enough to tell that she was in the master bedroom at Pemberley. She looked toward the whisper, soft and sure like the sound of a rushing creek. A lump formed in her throat when she heard the soft rumbled, "Amen," followed by the sting of tears as she saw her husband's dark head rise. He was praying over her. Slowly, he straightened up and reached over to take her hand. He looked up at her, overjoyed when he felt her stir.

Giving her a brilliant smile, he brushed a lock of her hair to the side. "You're awake," he murmured and leaned over to kiss her cheek. "How are you feeling?"

"I'm fine." She lay still, her eyes wandering over the features of the man before her — his hair tousled as if he'd been running his hands through it, a straight Roman nose, and shadowed, stubbly cheeks. His collar was open; she could see his pulse beating in the notch between his collarbones. His onyx-like eyes shone with a new spark, as if he was lit from within. She sighed happily. "It's good to be home."

He looked almost absurdly pleased. "Yes, very good indeed." He picked up a glass of water from the nightstand. "Are you thirsty at all? The doctor said you should drink when you awoke; he thought you might be dehydrated."

"The doctor was here?" Elizabeth rose up on her elbows, looking at him in surprise. "Whatever made you call the doctor?"

"You were unconscious, Elizabeth. I thought something was terribly wrong."

She lay back, looking out the window at the stars just beginning to wink in the violet blue sky. "What did he say?"

"Not much, to be honest. Just that you had probably fainted, from exhaustion or mild dehydration, or both. He said he couldn't determine that anything else was wrong, but that you must be extremely tired to be in that deep a sleep. He asked me if you had been sleeping well." William looked down. "But of course, I had to say I wasn't sure."

"Oh." She pulled herself up to a sitting position. "I'll take that water now." He handed her the glass and she took a sip, smiling at him over the rim of the glass.

He grinned at her. "What?"

"Nothing." She couldn't stop smiling though. "I missed you."

He looked down sheepishly. "I missed you too." Standing up, he reached over and kissed the top of her head. "I'll let you rest some more; I just wanted to make sure you were all right."

Elizabeth scooted over and patted the bed beside her. "No, stay. I..." She wanted to tell him about her suspicions, but she wasn't quite sure how to begin.

He sat down on the side of the bed and turned on the bedside lamp. "What is it?"

She took a deep breath. "You asked me earlier why I came to see Georgiana today."

"Yes, I remember. You said you needed her advice." There was a question in his eyes.

"I needed to ask her about...hmm, what the signs were..."

He was looking at her with a puzzled frown.

She met his gaze directly and held it, his eyes giving her the courage to finish what she had to say. "I think I might be expecting."

"Expecting what?"

Elizabeth rolled her eyes. "A baby."

He was stock still, staring at her as if she had just sprouted two heads. "A baby," he whispered.

"Yes," she began, "I've been sick in the mornings, and so tired I could hardly move."

"How long have you suspected?" he asked softly.

"Just a few days. At first, I thought I was sick or maybe only very upset…" she trailed off.

"I had wondered." His eyes traveled down to her belly. "I mean, you only had your…" he gestured toward her abdomen, "monthly…you know…once since we married. And I know we've had plenty of opportunities to…make one."

She gave him an amused look. "I've never been particularly regular. But this was different — I felt different — and I wanted to ask someone who might know."

"Georgiana."

"Yes."

He was staring at her intently. For the first time in a long time, she found it unnerving and looked down. "I had hoped you would be pleased, but perhaps…"

He looked startled. "Pleased? I'm…" he laughed softly. "I'm over the moon about it, but, Lord, Lizzy," he shook his head. "If I get another shock today, I think my head will burst."

"You poor darling, it has been quite a day, hasn't it?" She brought his palm to her lips and kissed it, laying it gently against her cheek.

His hand slid down to her belly and stopped, as if trying to discern if life might be growing there. "You should have told me. I would have taken care of you; I would have insisted you come back home where I could make sure you got the best care possible."

"I know you would." She bit her lip, wondering how much else she should say, but decided honesty was probably the best policy. "Maybe it was selfish, but I wanted you to want me too, not just the baby." Her expression hardened a little. "And I was angry at you at first, and you told me to get out…"

He put his forehead against her hand in supplication. "I'm so sorry I said that. I didn't mean it." He lifted his head. "Surely now you believe that I want you with me, baby or no."

"That means so much to me, but, William, it hurt when you didn't trust me enough to tell me the truth about Georgiana."

"You didn't tell me the truth," he said softly.

Elizabeth gave him a questioning look.

"About your money, about your family."

There was a long silence. Elizabeth sighed suddenly and brought her head up, wiping away the tears that were there. "You're right, William. I was wrong to keep that from you. I should have come to you, but…"

He was rubbing those blasted circles on the back of her hand again, melting her bones with the gentle pressure of his fingers. His piercing gaze cut through to the innermost corners of her heart, where she was not rational, where she simply was…herself.

"I am a selfish creature; I've been told so all my life by my mother. My father indulged me with his time and his interest, and I studied very hard to please him. I was his 'Princess.' He treated me like an adult for almost as long as I can remember, and it made me feel like I was unique."

She smiled wistfully. "I've always thought that was what drew me to Maggie. She's so much like I was at that age."

William looked in her eyes, waiting.

"Anyway," she went on abruptly, "when we lost our home, and my father lost his position, my individual qualities were no longer useful. I was one of the many poor now. Tired and disheartened, my father barely noticed me anymore. He became a shell of the man he was when he could not work at what he loved, and it grieved me to see that, but what could I do?" A tear rolled unheeded down her cheek. "There was nothing I could do. But I could accept my situation and make the best of it. I chose only to remember the past as it gave me pleasure and not look back with regret."

"I've always admired your bravery."

"I'm not brave. I simply had no other choice. But after you and I married, I began to feel sort of distinctive again. I was Mrs. Darcy of Pemberley, but even more than that, *you* made me feel unique and interesting. I think that's why I began to fall in love with you."

He smiled at her, dimples breaking through like the sun bursting through a cloud. She traced one with the forefinger of her free hand, and dropped it back into her lap.

"I needed to help my family, but I guess I was embarrassed, not only by their situation, but also by their behavior. I knew how you felt about them because I was anticipating it. It certainly wasn't the first time my mother embarrassed me, and it probably won't be the last. I didn't want you to regret marrying me. So I convinced myself that I could help them without your knowing if I went without some luxuries and raised some extra vegetables. And then you wouldn't think any less of me. It was my pride that kept me from telling you." She looked at him sheepishly. "As my mother would tell me…silly."

"I don't know what to say. I would have assisted your family if I had known, but perhaps I wouldn't have been particularly gracious about it. Not for the reasons you think…but because I would have wished I could inspire that kind of love in you. You're precious to me. Although," he admitted, "I haven't been very good about saying it."

"If my keeping secrets from you hurt half as much as you keeping yours from me, I'm dreadfully sorry for it. If I had one wish now, it would be that you would let me share your joys and help you carry your burdens. A wife is supposed to be a helpmeet, after all. How can I be one if I don't know what needs helping?" She thought about Mrs. Reynolds' words, *'He needs you, my dear, and he doesn't need anyone.'* "You can trust me with your heart, William, and I will try to trust you with mine."

"Can we start over, Lizzy? If we're honest with each other, trust will come in time. And with a new life possibly beginning," he carefully touched her belly, "It seems we have a very good reason to try."

She nodded wordlessly. It seemed speech had suddenly deserted her, and now she only wanted to be as close to him as she could get. She held up the covers and tugged on his hand in invitation.

"You need to rest, my love."

"I need you."

She didn't have to ask again; he took off his shoes and slid in beside her, determined not to make demands, but only to hold her until she went back to sleep.

Elizabeth, however, had other ideas. She accepted his cuddling for a few minutes, but then she had an overwhelming desire to feel his skin against hers. She opened the buttons on his shirt and pressed him to her. She drew back and pressed kisses across his neck and shoulders, then began to move toward his abdomen. His muscles clenched in response to the pressure of her lips.

"Lizzy," he breathed, "stop."

"No." Her hand brushed the front of his trousers. "You want me; I can feel that you do." She sat up, unbuttoned her dress and peeled it off, tossing it to the floor.

He lay on his back, his shirt open, and watched her in fascination. "Yes, I do, but..."

Reaching behind her back, she undid her bra, catching it in her hands as it fell from her breasts. Her hands disappeared under the covers and reappeared a few seconds later with her panties in them. Both items joined her dress on the floor. She reached over and began to ease his shirt off his shoulders. When she couldn't remove it, she tugged on it and he leaned up and let her pull it the rest of the way off. His eyes were fastened on her breasts, round, full...*fuller?* He reached up to cup one in his hand. She winced, and he drew back.

She smiled at him. "They're tender; I think it's from the baby."

"They're bigger too," he replied before he thought, and then, unexpectedly, he blushed.

She looked at him with an impish grin. "You noticed?"

He looked in her eyes. "I notice everything about you, my love."

"Oh, really?" She smirked, as she began to unbuckle his belt.

"Yes. You like coffee in the morning, but iced tea with your dinner. You have a decided preference for caramels, and lemon icebox pie." She laid him back and unzipped his trousers. He groaned helplessly. "You twirl a lock of your hair while you read, and you tap your lips with the end of your pen while you're deciding what to write." He helped her remove the rest of his clothes, and pushed them to the foot of the bed with his now bare feet. "You hum while you're puttering around the house or in your garden," he paused, "and when you sleep, you look like an angel." She took him in her hand, and he let a low moan escape him. "Damnation, Lizzy, I can't think when you do that," he rasped.

"Don't think," she whispered urgently. "Come into me. Comfort me, William," she put her arms around him and pushed the length of her body against him. "Comfort me, and let me comfort you." She kissed him tenderly on the mouth, and he rolled her beneath him.

Drawing back to gaze at her, his eyes darkened with anticipation. Her hair was spread across the pillow, her eyes filled with love, her red lips parted and full. It was so close to his fantasies of her from the early days of their marriage that he felt a ghost of the insecurity he suffered at that time. Those were the days when he was beginning to love her and was uncertain of her feelings toward him. A deep, agonizing possessiveness tore through him. He spread her legs and poised himself to enter her. "Tell me you love me."

"I love you, William."

He entered her swiftly, watching her eyes slide shut in ecstasy. She let out a low, plaintive moan. She felt full and ripe around him, as if she might burst. "Tell me again," he demanded, punctuating the last syllable with a strong thrust into her.

"I love you," she gasped.

"You're mine."

"Yes."

"Mine, and I'll never let you go." He thrust in a seductive cadence with his words.

"Oh, God!" she cried. "William, please!"

"Yes, my love. Beg me."

She cried out, and began to come all around him. White light began to obscure her from his sight and he felt as if he were drowning in her. He gasped for air, shuddered violently, and called for her in a desperate, rough voice.

When he was spent, he slid down her body and laid his head between her breasts, listening to the pounding of her heart as it slowly returned to normal. He dimly realized that her arms and legs were wrapped around him. He sighed and closed his eyes. Her erotic embrace induced a shiver of echoed pleasure to ripple through him. "Beg me, Lizzy," he said softly, "and I will beg you. I love you so. Please, be kind to me." He felt her hand travel up to her face and he knew she was wiping tears from her eyes. Her hand came down on his head in benediction. He mumbled again, "I love you," and drifted into a deep, peaceful sleep.

WILLIAM AWOKE TO THE SOUND of gentle knocking on the door. He lifted his head from Lizzy's breast and looked around, slightly disoriented. She was sleeping soundly, and it was dark outside. The lamp beside the bed illuminated the clock's face; it was ten-thirty. Another knock and the sound of Mrs. Reynolds' concerned voice came from the hall outside the door.

"Mr. William? Is Miss Lizzy doin' all right?"

"Umm," he rubbed his hand over his face, and guiltily removed himself from his position half on top of his wife. She rolled to her side without waking. "Yes ma'am, she's sleeping now."

"Oh, that's good." There was a pause. "I fixed y'all a cold supper; it's in the fridge. I can bring it up if you like."

William sat up, reaching hurriedly under the covers for his clothes. "No, no, that's all right. I'll go get it."

"You all right, Mr. William?"

He felt his face get hot. *What is wrong with me? This is my house, and this is my wife, for Pete's sake!* He smiled. *My wife. My wife is home, and maybe with our child inside her.*

"Yes, I'm just a little unsettled, ma'am. I fell asleep too." His voice became stronger with each word.

"Oh." There was a pause. "Well, I'm going to retire then."

"Yes, that will be fine."

"You come get me if she gets sick again, or you need anything, you hear?"

"Yes, ma'am. Thank you."

"Good night, my boy."

He smiled; she would probably call him her boy until her dying day. "Good night."

He leaned over and brushed Elizabeth's lips with a kiss. She gave him a little smile, but otherwise didn't stir. "I'm starving, Lizzy. I'm going to go bring up our supper. I'll be right back, darling." He got up, and quietly as he could, he opened the door and slipped through it into the hall.

Chapter 30

The Wedding of the Year — again

October 14, 1933

William stood in the corner of the dining hall at Pemberley, sipping from a white china cup. He needed some coffee to strengthen him after that tortuous forty-five minute receiving line. He should be glad that people thought so well of his sister and his new brother-in-law. But spending all afternoon in the company of people he barely knew was exhausting. It had never occurred to William, but because of the sheriff's job, Richard knew almost everyone within a twenty-mile radius of Meryton. Apparently, he was on good terms with them all too, judging from the number of people who attended today.

He cast a look at the long table at the end of the room. His new brother-in-law was standing there, looking a little out of place in a formal double-breasted suit and tie. He was smiling though, his usual engaging grin. He laughed at something spoken by a wedding guest and picked up a knife to cut the wedding cake. It was a buttery, frosted, three-tiered monstrosity with edible silver beads and piped ivory flowers for decoration. The cake top sported an Art Deco-attired bride and groom, with sprays of pearls and spun silver strands arching gracefully over them. Richard took his bride's arm to gain her attention — she was turned away from him, chatting — and he was rewarded with a luminous smile. William felt his heart tug with a strange, wistful kind of joy; his sister was a radiant, blushing bride. Earlier, when he was escorting her down the aisle of the church in her candlelight satin gown and fly-away layered veil, he wondered when the thin, gangly girl had turned into the elegant woman beside him. In fact, he had never seen her as glowing and resplendent as she looked today. All due to Richard. *Richard.*

"Mmpph," he growled, remembering the visit he had had the week before.

"Richard, this is a surprise." William extended his hand. "If you're looking for Georgiana, she's not here. I think she went with Elizabeth into town for something or other."

"Actually, it was you I came to see, Darcy. Can I have a few moments of your time?"

William looked at his future brother-in-law questioningly. "Of course." He gestured to a chair and turned toward the sideboard. "Can I interest you in a glass of iced tea, or maybe a bourbon?"

"Yes, I believe I will have a little glass of the fire-water, thank ye."

William poured two glasses and gave Richard one before sitting down in one of the overstuffed leather chairs in front of the hearth. Richard took the other.

"Here's to a long and happy marriage. Slainte." They clinked glasses and each man took a drink. "So, what's on your mind?"

Richard crossed one ankle over the other leg and held the glass on his knee. He stared down into the amber liquid before picking it up and swirling it in the glass. He took another sip. "I need to tell you something, now, before the wedding. I don't want there to be any bad feelings between us, well, afterward."

William was astounded. He had known Richard Fitzwilliam for years; what could the man possibly have to tell him? A sense of foreboding invaded the room. "Go on."

"It's about Georgiana." He cleared his throat. "Your sister and I are expecting our first child in about seven and a half months."

Darcy gave his old friend a look that would have frozen Hell itself. "I see."

There was a full minute of stone cold silence.

"Can you give me one good reason why I shouldn't come over there and beat you to a pulp, Fitzwilliam?"

Richard smiled his easy-going smile, and sat up straight in his chair, setting his glass on the table beside him. "Well, I don't think you want to wheel me up to the altar next week — that's one. We got a friendship that's lasted more'n ten years — that's another. Georgiana will be none too pleased with you if you do — there's a third. And…" He leveled a piercing look at William. "There is the fact that I love her more than life itself, which is the best reason of all."

William continued to stare at him, but finally, he looked away, dejected. "How could you let this happen, Richard? After what she's been through?"

"Now Darcy, the timing is unfortunate, perhaps, but the event itself is a blessing." Richard's blue eyes grew misty. "I never thought I would feel this kind of joy again. Georgiana and the little ones ... well, I'm fortunate that after all this time, the Lord saw fit to give me a wife and a family to care for. That would have been enough for me, but this is a miracle beyond anything I ever hoped."

Another period of awkward silence ensued. Darcy leaned forward to rest his elbows on his knees and stared into the empty fireplace.

Richard went on quietly. "I'm gonna need you, William, as her time draws near. I'm gonna be pretty skittery, given my experience with the whole business."

William gave him a solemn look, not yet forgiving, but at least a look with empathy behind it. "I imagine you would be."

Richard stood, walked over and put his empty glass on the sideboard. "Well, that's all I came for. I wanted to let you know beforehand. Own up to my responsibility, and tell you that, in my heart, she's already my wife. I've made my vow, to her and to God."

"Mr. Darcy, it is your sister's wedding day." He shook himself from his reverie and looked over to see his lovely wife approaching. She stepped up beside him and brushed a crumb of petit fours icing off his lapel. "Wipe that frightening scowl off your face right now," she teased, "or people will think you're not happy about the marriage that took place today."

"Mmpph," he repeated. "In truth, I'm more than a little relieved that the marriage took place today."

"What? Oh..." She put her arm around him and gave his back a loving caress. "So, if you're relieved, then why are you scowling?"

His face relaxed a little into a wry smile. "I can't seem to help myself." He leaned over and spoke in her ear. "Have you forgotten who gave me advice about my wedding night?"

"Ohhh," she replied, "yes, that's right. It was Richard."

"Mm-hmm."

"Can't stand the idea of your little sister being a wife? Good Lord, William, she's got two children, and..."

"Yes, but I can't seem to forget that he was the one who told me what to do and how to do it. And I when I think about that conversation and what he's going to do — hell, what he's already done ... Oh, just forget it," he mumbled and blew out an exasperated breath.

Elizabeth laughed softly, and he felt his clenched jaw loosen a little more. How he loved to hear her laugh!

"Darling, look at them. Do you think you could ask for a better husband for her? If you searched the whole world over, you couldn't find a man who adores her any more than he does, and she's glowing with happiness."

"And I know why she's glowing," he said crossly. "I still can't decide if I want to congratulate him, or take him out back and thrash him." He looked around glumly. "I'm just glad they're actually married now."

"Poor dear, I know your gentlemanly sensibilities are offended, but, really William, all's well that ends well."

"Hmm."

"There isn't too much you can do about it now."

"Mmm."

"And they're very happy."

"Hmm."

"And so are we."

He twisted one side of his mouth into a lopsided smile. "You won't let me wallow in my self-pity for a moment, will you?"

"No, I won't." She brought his hand to discreetly touch the new little bulge in her stomach. "We have too much to be thankful for."

The rest of his tension floated away on her encouraging words. "You are right, as usual, Mrs. Darcy." He set his cup down. "I believe I'm supposed to have this dance with the bride. You'll save me the next one won't you?"

"Of course."

LATER, AS THE HAPPY COUPLE was leaving the house for their honeymoon, Elizabeth saw her husband pull the good sheriff aside. They spoke in low tones with their heads together, looking at the ground. She saw William straighten up and extend his hand to his friend. Richard grinned widely, and took the peace offering. William clapped his new brother on the shoulder with his free hand, and Elizabeth watched as her Mr. Serious smiled a genuine, dimpled smile that lit up the hall.

"Thank goodness," said a relieved voice beside her. She turned to see her sister-in-law, looking over her shoulder at the two men. "I didn't think William would ever come around."

"He loves you very much. It's hard for him to let you go into the care of another man."

Georgiana smiled. "Yes, he's very old-fashioned that way, isn't he?" She looked at her sister-in-law thoughtfully. "You know, if anyone's to blame for this situation, it's me."

"Gi, if I remember right, it takes two to create that situation."

"Oh, I mean the whole situation, not just this one," she glanced down at her still flat abdomen.

Elizabeth lifted her eyebrow inquiringly.

"When I was coming home from Illinois on the train, running away from George, I decided life was too short to live in fear, and I wasn't going to live that way ever again. But then, I was back in my old house, letting my brother and Mrs. Reynolds care for me, and I started slipping back into my old ways. It's very easy to do when you're in familiar surroundings. A few months after I came back, I realized I was falling in love with Richard, but I was afraid — afraid to trust that love, afraid he wouldn't want me because of my past, afraid of what William would say, and on and on. After a while, I thought Richard might feel something for me too, but I knew he would never pursue me." She chuckled. "He thought he was too old for me; he told me that once." Georgiana straightened her shoulders and held her head up high. "So I thought long and hard about it, and I decided I must at least *try* to obtain my happiness, no matter what the outcome. So I pursued *him*. Oh, not in a demanding way but just over time, and I discovered that he loved me too." She turned and looked at Elizabeth earnestly. "Tell William he shouldn't worry about letting me go. Richard and I will take care of each other and the girls." Her eyes fluttered downward, "and anyone else who comes along." She embraced Elizabeth tightly and whispered in her ear, "I'm so excited that our babies will be born close together. I'm glad we have you, Elizabeth. I always wanted a sister."

Richard came up behind her and touched her elbow. "Are you ready, my dear?"

Georgiana took his arm, and looked up at him, eyes shining. "Yes, I'm ready. Let's go say goodbye to Maggie and Ruth, and we'll be off. Take good care of my girls, Elizabeth. I know it's only for two days, but I've never been away from them overnight."

"We'll keep them safe and sound," Elizabeth replied. "William will spoil them terribly, and it will take you a week to sort them out."

Georgiana laughed. "I'm sure he will. Good-bye and thank you again!"

Elizabeth watched her husband's face as his eyes followed the newlyweds, walking out to the car under a shower of birdseed. He scanned the room for his wife, and when his eyes found her, he gave her a sad smile. Then he held his hand out to her, and his action drew her to him from across the room as surely as if he had a rope tied around her waist. When she reached him, she took his hand, and they turned back to the dining hall and the rest of their guests.

"Miss Bennet?"

Jane Bennet turned at the sound of her name, and found herself looking directly into the face of Charles Bingley. She startled slightly and lowered her punch cup to her saucer with a clink of china. In typical Jane Bennet fashion, however, her unreadable expression moved quickly into place.

"Good afternoon, Mr. Bingley."

There was a pause while Charles simply looked at her. He cleared his throat nervously. "How are you?"

"I'm doing well."

"You look well."

"Thank you." Jane fished around for a topic of conversation. "How is the new store in Glasgow coming along?"

"Quite...well," he replied inanely. He took a deep breath. "Actually, it could use your touch. The displays in the Meryton store are much more appealing, and I'm at a loss about what to order."

Jane gave him a look of cool appraisal. "I'm not sure what I can do about that from here, sir, but I will advise you as best I can."

"Oh, no, I wasn't suggesting...I...was just making conversation, I guess."

"Oh."

"Lovely wedding, wasn't it?"

"Yes, they look very happy." Jane, on the other hand, looked a little miserable.

"Darcy told me your sister is expecting in a few months."

"Yes, we are all looking forward to it."

"Darcy is about as happy as I've ever seen him." Charles chuckled. "He smiles and seems almost giddy, at least for him."

Jane smiled graciously at his observation, but said nothing.

Charles looked across the room wistfully at his friend, who was standing with Elizabeth and holding her hand. "My friend is certainly a lucky man."

"Yes," Jane replied. "My sister is good for him, I think."

"Of that, I am quite sure."

Another silence.

"Miss Bennet, uh...Jane...may I call you Jane?"

Jane looked at him, surprised. "I suppose."

"Jane, I would like to call on you tomorrow at your family's home, but I don't want you to feel obligated to see me."

"Call on me?" Jane said softly. She could feel herself losing control of her emotions and her expression.

"Yes, I . . . I wanted to before, but I was concerned. I didn't want you to think you were being asked to spend time with your employer outside of work. I figure if I call on you at home and talk to your father right away, it will make my intentions very clear and not feed the gossip mill."

"Your intentions? Surely, your young lady in Glasgow would not be pleased if you courted someone else while you were out of town."

Charles looked confused. "Young lady in Glasgow?"

Jane simply looked at him with an impassive expression and cold blue eyes.

He shook his head. "I'm sorry, but I don't have any idea who you mean."

Jane's composure began to crack. "But, Miss Caroline said . . ."

Charles' face turned stern. "You mean my Aunt Caroline?"

Jane nodded.

He set his lips in a grim line. "What did she say to you, Jane? I think I need to know."

Jane lifted her chin. "She said many things, but the gist of the message as it regarded you, was that you were shortly to be engaged to the daughter of an old family friend in Glasgow."

His mouth dropped open, then shut, then opened again as if to speak. Then he shut it again. "I see the situation quite clearly now. May I be perfectly honest with you?"

"I would like that, for a change."

He took a deep breath. He couldn't blame her for being suspicious of his motives, given what she had been told. "Would you be willing to have a seat out on the porch? I think this might take a while."

Jane tried to look around circumspectly. She definitely didn't want her mother to witness her leaving with Mr. Bingley. She would never hear the end of it. Instead of her mother though, she caught the eye of her brother-in-law. William was looking intently at her and Charles. When he noticed Jane's questioning gaze, he smiled at her and looked around before putting his finger to his lips in a gesture of hush, suggesting that her secret was safe with him. She returned the smile and nodded to Charles. "Yes, I think that would be all right, Mr. Bingley."

He offered her his arm. "I would like it very much if you would call me Charles."

"Charles then." She looked up at him with a hesitant smile and blue eyes that barely hinted at a sparkle or two.

"You really are the most angelic creature," he murmured, almost to himself.

Jane let a soft laugh escape her lips, and he blushed, embarrassed. They headed toward the corner of Pemberley's wrap-around porch, and its waiting swing. Charles took a deep breath and began. "I suppose it all started the day I hired you to work at Netherfield's..."

Chapter 31

In which a crack opens in the heavens

March 26, 1934

William paced up and down the hall at Pemberley, nervous as a cat. Richard appeared in the doorway. He smiled, but he also looked a little unsettled. "Darcy, stop that infernal pacing and come sit down. Wearing a hole in the floor will not make this go any faster."

William glared at his brother-in-law, with an intensity that spoke volumes.

"Come have a bourbon," Richard cajoled.

He shook his head. "No, I want a clear head in case . . . in case she needs me."

"She's got her mother and your sister, and the doctor's coming. What does she need you for?"

William jabbed a thumb at his own chest. "It's *my* child!" he barked.

Richard sighed and turned around to go back into the parlor.

"We should have gone to the hospital in Glasgow. I should have rented a house there, so we would be close enough." William was muttering to himself and running his hand through his hair as he walked back and forth.

A shrill voice called from above him. "Mr. Darcy, you are going to wear yourself out. Just go on about your business; Lizzy will be just fine, and we'll call you when the baby gets here."

He looked up and saw Mrs. Bennet descending the stairs. A wisp of her graying hair had come out of its clasp, and she was wiping her hands on a towel. "It will probably be a while; first babies usually are. It took me fourteen hours to have Jane."

Fourteen hours! He didn't think he could take fourteen hours of this boundless anxiety. He stared despondently at Mrs. Bennet.

She returned the stare, and then her expression softened and grew thoughtful. She got to the bottom of the stairs and sat down on the bench in the hallway. "Come here and sit for a minute." She patted the seat beside her.

He considered that he would rather do almost anything than sit and try to make polite conversation with his mother-in-law, but his worry had overridden every other emotion at this point. He plunked down on the bench and leaned over, resting his elbows on his knees and his chin in his hand.

"My goodness, you certainly are a tall fellow," Mrs. Bennet remarked. "Look at you; when you sit down, your knees are almost up around your ears."

He smiled in spite of himself.

"You shouldn't worry you know. Lizzy is doing fine; she's healthy as an ox — always has been. And just as stubborn too."

William gave her a withering look, which she missed entirely.

"I know you must want a boy, but you should prepare yourself in case it's not."

"I couldn't care less if it's a boy or a girl, as long as I have a healthy wife and child at the end of this ordeal."

"That's probably a good attitude," she mused. "Then you're not disappointed either way."

He rolled his eyes.

A cry was heard from upstairs and he leapt to his feet. Mrs. Bennet sighed.

"Well, the noise has started. I suppose I'd best get up there; she'll scare your poor sister to death."

William sat back down, his head in his hands.

The voice was louder this time, and he could make out his name. She was calling for him! He looked at Mrs. Bennet pleadingly. "She wants me."

His mother-in-law looked at him in surprise. "Why would you want to go in there?"

"She wants me," he repeated. "She's calling my name."

They looked at each other as if in a stand-off, and he was shocked when he saw a motherly smile cross her face. She leaned over and patted his hand. "I guess it won't hurt for a little while. But be warned, the doctor will probably chase you away when he gets here."

William stood up abruptly and raced for the stairs.

"And don't listen to anything she says," Mrs. Bennet called after him. "She will let you touch her again someday, and she doesn't really hate you." She rose and slowly followed him up the stairs. "She loves you," she continued softly to herself, "almost as much as you love her."

As it turned out, the doctor didn't chase William out of Elizabeth's birthing room. By the time Dr. Nelson arrived, the entire event was over. He ran upstairs just in time to see Mrs. Bennet laying the baby on Elizabeth's stomach. She was matter-of-factly discussing with Mrs. Reynolds whether they should cut the umbilical cord and with what. William was at his wife's head, sitting on the bed with her leaning against his chest, arms and legs on either side of her in a protective gesture. His face was pale, and he had a harried look in his eyes, but he also had a huge smile on his face. The baby's fists were clenched, eyes shut tight and he was wailing like a stuck pig.

Mrs. Bennet whirled around when the door opened. "It's about time you got here."

"I thought we had time," he returned. "This is her first one."

"Well, her first one decided he was coming without you." She stepped back and let the doctor examine the scene. He called over the noise. "Mrs. Darcy? Can you hear me?"

She looked up at him, exhaustion written all over her face, and gave him a weak little smile. William brushed a sweat-soaked lock of hair out of her face and kissed her temple.

"He's got a good set of lungs," the doctor continued. Then he spoke loudly again. "Mr. Darcy, I need to cut the cord, deliver the afterbirth and clean them both up a little. Everything looks just as it should be. Why don't you go down and tell the rest of your family you have a son." The doctor smiled at him indulgently.

"Will you be all right?" he spoke in her ear.

She barely nodded, and he slipped carefully out from under her, laying her back gently on the stack of pillows. He kissed her softly. "You are my brave, strong darling. I'll be right back."

He walked down the stairs, his shirt damp with her sweat — and his own. Georgiana, Richard, Maggie and Ruth instantly appeared in the doorway. William looked at them, his expression tired but ecstatic. "She's doing fine. It's a boy." The four of them whooped and hollered for joy. Maggie was jumping up and down, and Ruth was insisting, "Wanna see baby! Wanna see baby!"

"Soon, Ruth darling," Georgiana assured her. She hurried over to her brother and threw her arms around his neck. "Oh, William, I'm so happy for you!

Congratulations!"

Richard stepped up, shook his hand and clapped him on the back. "Congratulations, Brother!"

"Thank you. I'm going to go call the Gardiners so they can tell Dr. Bennet and the girls. They said they would drive over once the baby arrived, and I'm sure Elizabeth would like to see them after she's rested up a little. Think I'll go clean up too, while the doctor finishes tending her." His brilliant, dimpled smile spread across his face, and drew big grins from the rest of his family. He thought his heart might explode with joy.

SOMETIME LATER, AFTER THE COMPANY had gone, William approached the bedroom door again. He peeked in and saw Elizabeth, sleeping soundly. Beside the window, his mother-in-law sat in a rocking chair, looking down at the little bundle in her arms. She was smiling at him, and cooing softly. She looked up at the sound of the door opening.

"He's awake and just staring at me like he was trying to figure me out. Reminds me of you." She rose from the chair. "Here. Would you like to hold him for a while? When he squawks again, she should probably try to feed him; it will help her milk come in."

She directed William to sit in the rocker, placed the baby in his arms, and stood back to look at them. He looked up at her in wonder. "I still can't believe he's here." His voice cracked with emotion. "He's..." he paused, looking for the right adjective, "he's amazing."

"Well of course he is," she replied. "He's yours." She patted his cheek. "I'm going back home. My poor nerves are shot."

William grinned.

Mrs. Bennet stepped over to the bed and brushed a lock of Elizabeth's hair off her cheek. William watched in disbelief as she leaned over and kissed her daughter's forehead. "You did well, little Lizzy. Mama loves you." She turned to go.

"Mother Bennet?" William called softly.

She stopped and turned, the doorknob in her hand. "Yes?"

"Thank you."

"You're welcome, William. Good night."

The door clicked behind her. William knew Mrs. Bennet would continue to try Elizabeth's patience and his, for that matter, but he could not help but notice she had stayed when the going got rough today. He supposed his mother-in-law could be … tolerable.

The moon was rising outside the window and cast an ethereal light across the room. William moved the baby around until he held him on his lap, large hands cradling the round head, tiny feet up against his stomach. The baby continued to stare at him with a dark, penetrating gaze.

"Well, little man," he crooned, "What should Mother and I name you?"

The little one responded by screwing his face up into a wrinkled grimace and letting out a squall that shattered the peaceful quiet. Elizabeth woke and turned toward the pair sitting by the window, bathed in moonlight.

She rose up on her elbows. "I should try to feed him. Mama and Georgiana say he needs to drink the newborn's milk often." She eased herself gingerly up against the head of the bed, wincing as she tried to sit up. She gave up about half way there and opened her arms for her son. William got up and laid the baby in her embrace. She put him to her breast like her sister-in-law had shown her, and the squalling ceased as he sucked greedily. William sat down on the edge of the bed and put his hand on the baby's head. Then he leaned over slowly and bestowed a reverent kiss on the soft, fuzz-covered warmth. He could feel the little jaws working. He whispered, a smooth, sure rush of unintelligible words. After several seconds, William raised his head and looked adoringly into his wife's face.

"What did you tell him?"

"I wasn't talking to him, Lizzy. I was thanking God for him … and for you."

Her eyes filled with tears. She smiled through them. "I suppose we need to finally decide on a name for him."

"He and I were just discussing that," William grinned.

"Oh? And what was his opinion on the matter?"

"He didn't seem too interested. He just squawked at me, so I did what any good father would do."

"Really?"

"Yes," he said, feigning complete seriousness, "I gave him to his mother."

She laughed. It was amazing to her that Mr. Serious managed to make her laugh so often.

Her laugh faded to a tender smile as she gazed down at her son: body tense, fists clenched, eyes shut, deep in concentration on his task. After a few minutes, he relaxed into a limp slumbering creature, jaw slack. She disengaged him, and winced.

"This is going to take some getting used to," she stated, grimacing. "So, what are your thoughts on the name?" She yawned.

"Lizzy," he admonished, "you're exhausted. We can talk about this later."

"No, I think I want to decide now. At one time, you were thinking about Richard."

"Hmm, but that was before I knew he and Gi were expecting. If their baby is a boy, they may want to name him Richard."

"That's true. I hadn't considered that. Would you want to name him William?"

He shook his head. "Too confusing, and I don't like the nicknames for William. What about Thomas, after your father?"

"Perhaps. What was your father's name?"

"George Joseph."

Elizabeth closed her eyes in thought. She was quiet for so long, he thought she might have dropped off to sleep again. Rising to leave her in peace, he felt her stir and saw her tired eyes open.

"I like the name Joseph, and I was thinking, perhaps his middle name could be Edward, after my uncle. If he hadn't suggested my family come and live at Longbourn, you and I wouldn't have met, you see."

William smiled broadly. "Joseph Edward Darcy — I think it's perfect." He leaned over and kissed the little head again. "Sweet dreams, little Joseph."

He lifted his head and looked intently at his wife. "It's extraordinary, isn't it? As if the heavens opened and he fell right into our lives."

"It was a little more involved than that," she said wryly.

He kissed her softly. "I do love you, my wife." He trailed a finger over her brow and cupped her cheek in his hand. "Now," he reached to take Joseph out of her arms. "He's sleeping, at least for a while, and so should you be." He gently swaddled the baby and laid him in the bassinet beside the bed.

"William?"

"Yes?"

"I would like it very much if you slept here tonight."

"If you wish," he said, pleased at her invitation.

"I do wish."

"Then I will be back shortly."

"William?" she ventured, as he opened the door.

"Hmm?"

"I love you too."

William smiled, dimples flashing. "Sleep, darling."

She leaned back against the pillows and closed her eyes. Very quietly, he shut the door behind him.

Epilogue

May 31, 1970

"William? May I come up?" Elizabeth stopped and looked at the figure sitting at the window of the hayloft, leaning back against the frame, a blade of hay in his teeth.

"Of course," he sat up, flinging the hay blade to the ground below. "I saw you coming. I was hoping you were coming to see me." He reached out his hand, and Elizabeth picked her way over to him through the hay. She took his hand and sat down beside him, each of them dangling their legs over the edge of the hayloft window.

"Aren't you coming in? The children and their families will be here soon."

"I know. I just wanted to come up here and think for a while, before the crowd descends on us."

"I'm glad the weather's good and we can have the celebration outside. It will keep the grandbabies occupied while we get the lunch, I mean, the dinner ready."

"It's hard to believe," he said softly, "that they're all truly out of the nest now." He looked at her intently, dark eyes heavy with veiled emotion. "David is the last one to finish college, and they're all grown."

"It's a new phase of life for us, but we've been making our way toward it for some time, since Joseph left home, what was it, eighteen years ago? Goodness, it doesn't seem that long."

David Darcy was the latest in a long line of Darcy college graduations.

Joseph, of course, was the first. He was a pediatrician now, living in St. Louis with his wife and daughters. Thomas became the heir apparent to Pemberley. After finishing his agriculture degree at the University of Kentucky, he had returned home to help his father run the ever-expanding Pemberley Farms, now a commercial farm for grains, soybeans and tobacco. Thomas lived with his wife, Margie and their brood of five just up the road in a large farmhouse. Richard had tried his hand at many things, and now was back in school, studying to be an architect. Susan, the only Darcy daughter, was studying to be an archeologist, currently pursuing her Ph.D. And now David was heading off to Vanderbilt's Medical School in the fall, still undecided about his specialty. He insisted he wanted to return home and practice family medicine in the community where he grew up, but William and Elizabeth knew he might change his mind, especially if he met some Tennessee beauty who wanted to live somewhere else.

Elizabeth, Mrs. Reynolds and Georgiana had spent the years after the War developing their line of Pemberley Preserves. Mrs. Reynolds' Raspberry, Elizabeth's Elderberry, Pemberley Peach, and other cleverly-named varieties now adorned the shelves of little specialty food shops all over the Southeast. Gigi and her family now ran the business almost exclusively; precocious Maggie had turned into a marketing genius. Unwilling to return to her teaching position in the Meryton Elementary school after she had her children, Maggie began helping with the accounts, and soon the business expanded three-fold. Her sister, Ruth, was happily married and living in Nashville.

There had been a few sad moments along the way: The passing of Mrs. Reynolds in 1959, and Dr. Bennet in 1962. William had had to say good-bye to his best friend and brother-in-law Richard the winter before last. Sheriff Fitzwilliam's heart had begun to fail about two years before. This necessitated retirement from the Sheriff's office (he had been re-elected every term) at the ripe old age of seventy-three. The third heart attack was too much for the man with 'the biggest heart in three counties', as he was eulogized. William was comforted by their last conversation, in which Richard was able to reflect on his good fortune to have had Gigi, the four daughters they shared, and a friend who was as close as any brother could be.

The temporary safety net for the Bennets back in 1932 had become permanent. Dr. Bennet never returned to academia. By the time faculty positions began opening again, he was really too old for the stress of a tenure track position. Jane and Charles, who had married in June 1934, settled permanently in

Glasgow. Mary had married paunchy Mr. Collins, and then replaced him as librarian when he passed away. Kitty and John Lucas had a farm and wood-working shop outside of Franklin, and six children to help them work it. Lydia tried her hand as a country back-up singer in Nashville, making ends meet as a diner waitress in between singing gigs. Ed and Madeline had welcomed Madeline's nephew, a handsome young vet named Peter McGaughey, so Ed could eventually ease into retirement. Peter found himself completely smitten by the vivacious youngest Miss Bennet, and he stole 'Nashville's brightest jewel' (as Mr. Lucas declared) to be Mrs. McGaughey.

"Are you going to take a slew of pictures today, Mrs. Darcy?" He looked serious, but she knew him well enough to catch the fleeting spark of amusement in his eyes.

"Of course," she replied, feigning haughtiness. "And I plan to get several of the graduate's papa, so don't you be hiding from the camera." She put her hands up in front of her face, and imitated clicking the camera shutter. Lizzy had developed an avid interest in photography, and the last twenty years of their lives had been chronicled on film and in her dark room.

He rolled his eyes. "Lizzy, I hate having my picture taken."

She batted her eyelashes at him. "But the camera loves you; you're *so* handsome."

"You best be careful with your flirting, Mrs. Darcy. I know we conceived at least two children in this hayloft."

She sputtered a laugh. "You are incorrigible! I can't believe I ever called you Mr. Serious."

He rubbed his fingers over his lips in an attempt to hide the grin that was threatening to escape them. His rough, work-worn hand reached for her wrinkled one. They sat hand in hand for a long time, until the sound of a station wagon could be heard in the driveway. He released her and stood up slowly. He held a hand down to her in invitation. "Come with me."

"Where are we going?"

"Home."

She put her hand in his, and they made their way down the hayloft stairs (the ladder had been replaced years ago) and up toward the house. A little girl with brown braids and sparkling eyes was racing toward them, a tow-headed toddler hot on her heels.

"Papaw!" She threw herself at him, and he scooped her up in his arms, kissing her on the cheek. "Hello, Katie Kat," he rumbled in a deep voice. The toddler ran up and hugged his leg before turning and reaching her arms up to Elizabeth.

William Darcy looked behind him at the barn, ahead of him to the house and its waiting company, and to his side at the woman who had shared his life and, God willing, would for many years yet. He took a deep breath and filled his lungs with the sweet-smelling, thick Kentucky air. There was a time, long ago, when he didn't think he would ever be a happy man. Every day, he thanked the Lord that he had been wrong.

The End

Breinigsville, PA USA
18 January 2011
253575BV00001B/98/P